Dashanan: Adi

by

Kranti Gopaluni

Cover design and illustration by
Sri Nilayaa Rentala

notionpress.com

INDIA · SINGAPORE · MALAYSIA

ISBN

Hardcase 979-8-90319-718-7
Paperback 979-8-90207-322-2

To my grandparents—
who told hundreds—perhaps thousands—of stories
to a curious child who never stopped asking,
"Just one more?"
This book lives because their stories lived first.

TABLE OF CONTENTS

AUTHOR'S NOTE

This story began with a single verse. When I first encountered the Shiva Tandava Stotram—composed by Dashanan, the Rakshasa-king, in praise of Mahadev—I was struck not by the villainy often told of him, but by the depth of his devotion, the sheer poetic ferocity of his surrender to Mahadev. That moment stayed with me. I didn't know it then, but my inspiration had already found me.

Dashanan is a tribute to the mind behind the legendary piece of art. The seeker. The scholar. The poet.

This is a work of mythological science fantasy. It draws from Indian itihasa, from fragments of history, and from the boundless terrain of speculative thought. Some liberties have been taken with chronology, cosmology, and character.

I am deeply grateful to my family and friends for their constant support. My parents and brother believed in me from the start, and my wife motivated me when I faltered, reminded me why I began, and made the front cover design possible through her tireless work.

To you, dear reader: Dashanan is not a retelling and should not be confused with our itihasa. It is a resurrection—one that takes creative liberties to bring Dashanan back to life. The story begins in Ādi, the origin, but where it leads is yours to uncover.

– Kranti Gopaluni

CHAPTER 01

“Jai Sri Ram! Jai Sri Ram! Jai Sri Ram!”

The chant rose like a tide from the sanctum of the ancient temple, washing over the sounds of the streets beyond. Honking rickshaws, clanging carts, and shouting vendors dulled beneath the thundering devotion that poured from within. The final hymns of the evening echoed through the stone corridors, blending with the scents of marigolds, sandalwood, and incense that filled the thick, warm air.

Inside, oil lamps flickered against carved granite pillars, casting dancing shadows across walls blackened by centuries of faith and prayer. The rhythmic cadence of Vedic hymns layered beneath the priest’s voice, which rose and fell like waves over the gathered faithful. Seated cross-legged on straw mats, devotees faced the sanctum, where an ornately adorned idol of Lord Ram stood radiant in the golden glow of oil lamps. Many were elderly, wrapped in cotton shawls. Some clutched palm-sized books, their lips moving in murmured synchrony, fingers tracing the script as they followed the story.

In their midst sat a young boy, no more than ten, still and wide-eyed. His gaze remained fixed on the priest, but his attention drifted from time to time to the man beside him—his grandfather—who sat with eyes closed, perfectly still, as though listening not with ears, but with his very soul.

As the priest's tale neared its end, his voice carried the weight of divine finality.

"And that is how Lord Ram eradicated evil in Treta Yuga—through Dashananvadh! Even after many millennia, we still bow before Ram as the perfect man and eternal God."

The boy blinked. His brows furrowed, lips parting slightly—not in awe, but in the silent birth of a question too large to shape into words. Slowly, he leaned towards his grandfather and tugged at his sleeve.

"Thatha... what happened?"

His grandfather remained unmoved. With a soft shake of the head and a raised palm, he gestured for silence. The boy nodded, but his eyes continued to search the face of his elder, the question still restless inside him.

As the final hymn swelled, they joined the crowd in chanting, the boy's voice hesitant but sincere. The aarti flame circled the idol, temple bells rang out in a chorus of metal and prayer, and the great doors creaked open to release the devotees into the dusk.

Prasad in hand, the boy and his grandfather stepped out into the thickening night, their silhouettes swallowed by the crowd as it streamed back into the living chaos of the city.

As they walked together through the lamp-lit streets, the warmth of temple bells and fading chants still lingered in the air. But the boy's mind was already elsewhere, whirring with questions too big for his small frame to hold.

He looked up at his grandfather, eyes gleaming with innocent urgency.

"Thatha, what happened to Dashanan after his death? Everyone knows Lord Ram was born again as Lord Krishna... was Dashanan born again too?"

The question hung in the night like an arrow loosed from a silent bow.

His grandfather—silver-haired, wrapped in a crisp white kurta and a traditional dhoti—stopped mid-step. There was a brief, almost reflexive chuckle, low and uneasy, as he looked down at the dust-covered path beneath their feet.

"Ahh... that's a good question," he said, laughing again, this time nervously. His eyes searched the road, as if hoping some grain of forgotten truth might rise to meet him. He could feel the boy's excitement—pure, reverent, hungry.

After a pause that stretched just long enough, he placed a hand gently on the boy's shoulder. His voice, when it returned, was steadier—marked by something deeper. A memory, perhaps. Or a story buried too long in silence.

"Listen, kanna..." he began softly. "Everyone knows how Dashanan died. But very few ask what happened after."

The boy's eyes widened. His steps slowed.

"The death of Dashanan was not just fate—it was prophecy. It was written into the very threads of time. The Devas, the Rishis, the Naras, the Vanaras—all beings waited for it, holding their breath."

Now his voice shifted, taking on a slow, reverent rhythm—part sermon, part sacred storytelling.

"On the tenth day of the Yuddha, Dashanan finally fell to Lord Ram's arrow. The skies themselves responded—celestial flowers rained down from above. Rishis chanted praises. The Vanara Sena cried out in joy: 'Jai Sri Ram!' And perhaps... that was the last thing Dashanan saw—his enemies rejoicing, dharma triumphing, and his great empire slipping into silence."

The boy said nothing. His lips parted slightly, caught between awe and a deeper yearning.

"Lord Ram, in his boundless righteousness, ensured Dashanan's last rites were performed with full honour. His body was returned to his followers. His brother, Vibhishan, was crowned king of Lanka. And Lord Ram returned to Ayodhya, victorious, Ma Sita beside him. That is the story the world knows."

He paused again, eyes narrowing, voice softening to a whisper.

"But..." he said, leaning in with a glint of mystery, "...there is more to Dashanan than the Sita-haran, or his battle with Lord Ram. A truth hidden in the folds of time. A truth that was buried... not burned."

✦

Dashanan, master of the Artha Shastra, Ayurveda, Jyotishya, Sahitya, Vedas, and Yantra Nirmaana, understood one truth above all: knowledge unpassed is knowledge lost. He had studied at the feet of celestial beings, learned from Rishis whose wisdom echoed across yugas, and uncovered truths inscribed in the very pulse of the universe. But even he knew that war was inevitable—and with it, the risk that everything he had discovered could vanish in a breath of ash and blood.

Anticipating a day such as this, Dashanan had formed a secret order to preserve his knowledge. He did not choose princes or bloodline heirs, but minds that burned with brilliance and hearts tempered by unwavering conviction. He took ten disciples under his wing and passed on all his knowledge, everything he learned. Among his disciples, four stood unmatched: Kanaka, Veerabaahu, Pashupati, and Dharmapaala.

Pashupati, the healer, had nearly mastered the unmasterable—the art of rebirth through flesh. His Ayurvedic experiments bordered on the miraculous: severed limbs regrown, ruptured organs revived, the breath of life coaxed from the brink of death.

Veerabaahu, master of Yantra Nirmaana, was the forge behind Dashanan's vision. He birthed machines that pulsed with cosmic energies—devices that stitched wounds without contact, machines that shot energy pulses through the air, summoned fire without a spark.

Kanaka, the alchemist, could breathe soul into metal. Through secret alloys and ancient transmutations, he forged blades that sang, chariots that levitated, and armour that regenerated faster than living flesh. His hands shaped the very skeleton of Lanka's military might.

Dharmapaala, the sage, was scripture made flesh. His command over Jyotishya allowed him to see through the veils of time. He read omens in the wind's curl, in birdsong, in the shimmer of firelight. It was Dharmapaala who cried out before Hanuman's fire burned Lanka, who saved hundreds by urging them to flee to the water canals.

But even prophecy could not halt the inevitable.

On the tenth day of the Yuddha, Dashanan fell, struck down by Lord Ram's arrow. The skies rejoiced. Rishis sang. The Vanara Sena roared, "Jai Sri Ram!" And perhaps, in that final breath, that was all Dashanan heard—not silence, but the sound of his end written in joy. The war was over, and Dashanan died.

But for one of his disciples, a greater battle had only just begun.

Pashupati could not accept it. Not this. Not like this. His master—the fiercest mind, the brightest flame, the scholar of ages—could not simply vanish into dust. Not while his knowledge still pulsed through scrolls and yantras left behind.

He summoned the others.

He proposed the unthinkable.

He would find the wound. Rebuild the torn tissues. Restore the organs. And with the device he and Dashanan had designed together—the Vaayu Yantra, a machine that could circulate life essence—he would bring him back.

After nights of grief and debate, Veerabaahu and Kanaka joined him.

Together, they placed Dashanan's body on a chariot forged from rare metals. Its frame gleamed under the sun, etched with protective yantras of silver and copper. Four white horses, draped in garlands and bound with prayer thread, were yoked to the cart.

As twilight bled red across the city, the disciples pulled their master's body through the grieving streets, towards the heart of Lanka.

There, before a stunned crowd, Pashupati stood—his robes torn, his eyes ablaze not with madness, but with conviction.

And he declared:

"Our master shall not be burned.

He shall not be buried.

We will not mourn him as dead—because he is not done.

He shall rise again... not as memory, but as Dashanan himself."

The crowd froze.

Then, it ignited.

Grief turned to rage. The people, who had gathered to bid farewell with fire and prayer, cried sacrilege. Denying final rites was blasphemy. It was unnatural. It was unforgivable.

Stones flew. Pots shattered. Curses filled the air.

Blood streamed from Pashupati's brow. Kanaka shielded him; Veerabaahu seized the reins. The golden chariot turned, wheels thundering over temple stone, the mob at its heels.

And then—silence.

A new voice cut through the storm.

"Enough."

Vibhishan, cloaked in white and gold, stepped forward as dharma incarnate. His guards fanned behind him, unmoving, like statues of justice. He raised a single hand.

The crowd stopped.

Their fury, their grief, their cries—held still by one man's stillness.

Only the wind dared whisper.

And then, Vibhishan spoke.

"I understand your anger," Vibhishan said, his voice calm but unyielding. "He was my brother. I worshipped him no less than you worshipped him as your king. But under no circumstance will I allow his disciples to take his mortal remains."

He stood beneath the darkening sky, his silhouette edged by torchlight. Grief shimmered in his eyes—but so did something colder. Resolve.

"An ordinary warrior did not defeat Dashanan. Lord Narayana himself slew him. He lived a life of sin—and of greatness. And now... he deserves rest, not return. All I want—for him, for this land—is peace. The kind that only his final rites can bring. The kind that only moksha offers."

✦

The sun had already slipped beneath the horizon. In the purple hush of twilight, the stars blinked to life above the city, bearing silent witness to the pronouncement that followed.

"At the break of dawn," Vibhishan declared, "his last rites will be performed."

Then, turning to the disciples, his voice turned iron.

"If any of you disobey your king's command, you will be captured. You will be beheaded."

Stillness fell over the gathering, sharp as a blade drawn in a temple.

Pashupati turned slightly, locking eyes with Veerabaahu and Kanaka. In unspoken accord, all three lowered their gazes, nodding in false submission. The crowd exhaled, their faith in order restored.

But in the hearts of the disciples, no vow of obedience had been sworn. Only a deeper promise remained—one not to their king, but to their Guru.

The people of Lanka broke into chants, hailing their new monarch with cries of "Jai Vibhishan!" even as they mourned the fallen Dashanan. The golden chariot was seized by royal guards and drawn towards the palace, its wheels grinding across stone as it carried the body of the Rakshasa-king away. A stream of citizens followed, praising the dead and honouring the living, offering flowers, chants, and tears in equal measure.

Gradually, the tumult faded, leaving the three disciples behind in the hush of approaching night.

Lanka's lamps began to flicker to life. Workers moved through the avenues, placing oil wicks into carved lanterns. Courtyards gleamed in pools of gold. Some towers still glittered with the grandeur of Dashanan's age; others bore dark scars—the charred remnants of Hanuman's fire, when his flaming tail had scorched pride into ruin.

✦

Far from the palace, in a secluded ashram nestled at the southern base of Trikuta Parvata, Pashupati summoned his brothers-in-dharma. The chamber was aglow with oil lamps.

Scrolls of palm leaf lined the walls, alongside hanging herbs and stone tablets etched with ancient formulas.

Upon a table, he unfurled a rough map of the palace grounds and the hills beyond.

"We will burn Shayana Sundari," he said. "A rare mix of sleep-herbs. Its fumes will send even the sharpest guards into a dreamless stupor."

He looked to his companions.

"Once the palace slumbers, we enter the crypts and retrieve our Guru's body. We take him to a cave north of Trikuta—abandoned, forgotten, hidden by an ancient forest. There, the restoration begins."

Veerabaahu stepped back, his face stricken. "You said we would revive our Guru, not steal him away like grave robbers. If this is your path, I can't follow it."

Pashupati placed a steady hand on his friend's shoulder—gentle, but firm.

"I understand. But we are not robbing the dead—we are protecting the living by preserving his knowledge. And if we wait until dawn, there will be nothing left but ash."

He paused, voice softening.

"Trust me, Veerabaahu. I do not want to possess him. I want to preserve him. I want to bring him back—not as a tale, but as Dashanan himself."

The fire in the chamber crackled softly. Kanaka and Veerabaahu exchanged looks. Doubt clouded their eyes—but beneath it, something else lingered: faith.

Pashupati was no ordinary healer. He had learned from Dashanan himself. If there was even the slimmest thread of possibility, he was the one who could pull it.

There was no third choice.

The fire of antyeshti… or the spark of resurrection...

And so they agreed.

The funeral pyre would not take their Guru.

Not yet.

Pashupati moved with deliberate reverence. Every vial, scroll, and herb he packed was handled with care—like an offering, not a tool. He gathered tinctures distilled from ancient roots, oils steeped in moon petals, powders of rare minerals, and surgical instruments forged in Veerabaahu's workshop. These were not mere medicines. They were relics of ancient science and sacred lore, entrusted now to a singular, desperate mission.

He turned to his companions.

"Prepare two wagons," he said. "One for the equipment... the other for our Guru."

Veerabaahu and Kanaka nodded silently and vanished into the night's silence. The first wagon, weighed with crates of sealed jars, scrolls, heating stones, and obsidian blades, was stationed outside the barracks, its contents hidden beneath coarse canvas. Lanka's once-mighty army was now broken—many warriors dead, others wounded beyond return. The barracks were quiet, but not from sleep. It was the silence of absence.

Within those hollow walls, the disciples changed into the armour of the royal guard: deep-blue breastplates edged with gold, crested helms, and crimson sashes. Only the royal guard and Vibhishan himself were permitted entry to the Ananta Garbha—the inner sanctum where Dashanan's body lay in state.

Before departing, each of them took a glass ampoule from Pashupati. The liquid shimmered under the moonlight like molten pearl.

"Drink this," he said. "It will shield us from the Shayana Sundari's spell."

The mixture burned their throats, but it chilled their blood and cleared their minds. Their limbs felt sharper. Their will, firmer.

The walk from the barracks to the palace was short—but each step thudded like a war drum. The wind carried with it the scent of sandalwood and distant ash. Shadows stretched along ruined courtyards as if even the city held its breath.

They entered through a side corridor, skirting the sea-facing windows, and climbed to the palace's highest floor. There, Pashupati unpacked sachets of Shayana Sundari—a potent blend of dreamroot, datura, and powdered lotus mist. He burned them in bronze censers, placing them beside windows that opened to the inland breeze, where the air was steady and fresh.

And then they waited.

Five breaths. Ten. Twenty.

Then it began.

Thud. Clank. Clatter.

Weapons fell from limp hands. Armour clattered as bodies collapsed. One by one, the palace guards surrendered to slumber.

Shayana Sundari did its job as always.

Now, the real task began.

✦

Descending quickly, they reached the Ananta Garbha. The chamber's entrance loomed like the maw of a sleeping god—an enormous doorway plated in hammered gold, carved with cosmic mandalas and encrusted with Navaratna gems, each stone aligned to tantric precision.

The door was nearly immovable. All three had to press together, muscles straining, as groaning metal echoed down the marble halls.

Inside, the guards lay in perfect rows—fallen like temple statues shattered by time. The silence within was sacred.

And in the centre, bathed in the glow of oil torches, lay the one they had come for.

Dashanan.

Pashupati broke. He rushed forward, falling to his knees. Tears streaked down his face as he clutched his Guru's feet, trembling. He bowed low, his forehead pressed against the warrior's flesh.

"Bless us," he whispered. "Be with us... guide our hands."

Kanaka and Veerabaahu moved to his side, each placing a hand on his shoulders.

"Pashupati," one said softly, "I understand your heart. But now is not the time for emotion. We must hold fast to the mission."

Pashupati rose slowly, his expression hardening, and turned to examine the bier that held Dashanan. It was a traditional, cooling board—crafted of polished teak, bound with bamboo cord, and supported by four long carrying shafts. The base rested upon a platform of inlaid diamonds, glowing faintly in reverence and wealth.

Dashanan was majestic even in death. His body was wrapped in silken funeral robes, his chest adorned with garlands of fresh flowers. The scent of sandalwood still lingered around him, untouched by decay.

But then the moment of reckoning came.

Dashanan, towering at over fifteen feet, broad and battle-scarred, was a titan in every sense. His bier was too heavy for three men to lift. It had been built for at least four carriers—six, ideally.

They exchanged a glance.

The perfect plan had one fatal flaw.

They tried lifting the board—but it didn't budge. The weight of Dashanan's colossal form was simply too immense.

Pashupati rushed to a window. A thin band of orange crept across the eastern sky. Dawn was near. Time, like sand from a shattered hourglass, was bleeding out.

"We don't have long," he said, turning back to the others, voice taut with urgency.

Panic flashed across Veerabaahu's face. "If we're caught now—if we fail here—Vibhishan won't hesitate. We'll be executed. And Dashanan... truly lost."

From the pouch tied at his waist, Pashupati pulled a red-glass ampoule, its contents glowing like molten fire. The liquid pulsed in rhythm with his breath.

"This is Prabhanjan," he said. "A formula I developed. It'll give me strength beyond mortal limits—but only for a few minutes. After that, I'll collapse."

Kanaka's eyes widened. "This is madness."

But before either of them could protest, Pashupati bit into the ampoule—glass and all—and swallowed it.

His body shuddered violently. Breath came in rapid gasps. His chest rose and fell like a war drum. His heartbeat grew thunderous—echoing unnaturally, like gongs in a sanctum.

Veins bulged across his arms. Muscles swelled like storm clouds.

He stepped to the bier, grasped the front shafts of the board, and heaved.

The polished wood groaned beneath Dashanan's immense weight, rising an inch—then sagging again.

Still—not enough.

Then Kanaka and Veerabaahu rushed forward. Without a word, they grabbed the rear shafts and lifted him.

With a shared roar, the three disciples raised their master—not in resurrection, but in rebellion.

Together, they bore him across the chamber, down long halls heavy with incense and silence. Their sandals slapped against the marble floors, each step echoing like ghosts fleeing fate.

They burst into the night.

The wagon waited near the barracks, its horses stamping anxiously. With care, they laid Dashanan onto the platform, securing the silk over his form. Kanaka and Veerabaahu took the reins, snapping them hard.

The wagon lurched forward.

Inside, Pashupati collapsed beside his master, drenched in sweat, limbs trembling from exertion. He looked up at the others, a faint, satisfied smile flickering across his lips.

"Brothers," he whispered.

Then he fell unconscious.

The wagons tore through the forest roads, swallowed by jungle and night.

✦

At dawn, the drums began.

Booming alarms thundered from Lanka's palace towers. Guards scrambled, bells rang. The city had awoken to the unthinkable: Dashanan's body was gone.

In the wagon, bathed in golden morning light, Pashupati stirred. He opened his eyes slowly, sat upright, and looked towards the shadow of the cave ahead—hidden beyond Trikuta Parvata.

He turned back once more. The city of Lanka, distant now, shimmered on the horizon. It looked like a memory.

He sighed. "He knows. Vibhishan knows."

His voice was barely a breath.

"The body is gone. We're the suspects. We have no time left."

He turned again to his Guru.

Dashanan's face, still and mighty, stared towards the cave. The beard thick. The scars deep. It was the face of a king carved by war, by devotion, by time itself.

And then, once more, Pashupati fainted.

The wagons reached the mouth of the cave.

Veerabaahu and Kanaka leapt down without hesitation. They unloaded crates, arranged herbs, unrolled scrolls, connected valves, and lit the burners—transforming the cave into a makeshift medical chamber. Every motion was precise, executed from memory, following Pashupati's instructions to the letter.

Then they approached the wagon, where Pashupati still lay motionless.

They looked at each other.

"He called us brothers," one said.

The other nodded. "We are brothers."

Together, they placed their hands on Pashupati's shoulder.

And waited.

Pashupati stirred.

Golden light filtered through the cave mouth, casting a warm glow over the stone. The soft rustle of leaves and distant bird calls greeted his return to consciousness. His body still ached from the strain of Prabhanjan, but within him, a flicker of hope endured.

He looked around.

The equipment had been unpacked and arranged with precision. Pipes, scrolls, tinctures—all set in place exactly as he would have done himself. Kanaka and Veerabaahu lay nearby, asleep on the cold floor, their forms curled beside flickering lanterns and open crates.

Pashupati smiled—humbled by their faith.

He reached out and gently woke them.

They stirred, eyes heavy with exhaustion.

"You did well," he whispered. "Thank you... for believing in me."

They offered quiet nods. Without a word, they rose and unlatched the wooden canopy that shaded the wagon, exposing the body of their fallen master to the light.

Pashupati stepped forward, heart tight in his chest, and gazed upon Dashanan.

He was ready to face the wound—the mythic gash carved by Lord Ram's divine arrow. A deathblow that had felled a titan.

But as his eyes traced Dashanan's massive torso... there was nothing.

No wound. Not even a scar.

His brows drew together. He leaned in closer, hands trembling, scanning every inch—from abdomen to chest, legs to throat. Nothing.

Veerabaahu watched him closely. "Is something wrong?"

Pashupati didn't answer. His eyes widened in silent panic as he re-examined the body—again and again—desperate for some sign, any mark, of the fatal blow. But there was none.

"This... this cannot be," he whispered.

Kanaka stepped closer, peering down at the body of the warrior they had once called indestructible. Even without formal training, they could see it. This wasn't normal. This wasn't natural.

"An arrow must leave a mark," Kanaka said. "And there's none."

Pashupati pressed trembling fingers to Dashanan's wrist. Then his neck. Then his heart.

No pulse.

No warmth.

Only silence.

Something was deeply, horribly wrong. And for the first time since their escape, Pashupati felt fear—not of Vibhishan, nor of the law, but of his own brothers. He had promised them a miracle. Revival. A second life. But now, standing before the untouched body, he realised he may have promised the impossible.

✦

His mouth went dry. Sweat clung to his brow. His hands shook.

One of the brothers asked, gently, hopefully: "Can you revive him? There's no damage—that's a good sign, isn't it?"

Pashupati said nothing. His lips parted. No words came.

Two paths opened before him:

He could speak the truth—that he didn't know what had happened, that there was no explanation, no plan.

Or he could lie.

And if he lied... he would need to kill them.

His thoughts spiralled. "Would they forgive me? Would they turn me over to Vibhishan? Would they kill me themselves?"

Every path ended in blood.

And so, he reached into his waist pouch.

His fingers touched the cool glass of a teardrop-shaped ampoule—Neela Sarpa, a neurotoxin refined from the fangs of shadow serpents. Silence in seconds. Death in minutes.

He formed the lie in his mind.

He would say he needed a final ingredient—one that had been left behind in his lab outside the city. He'd send one of them. While the other stayed behind, he'd use the poison.

One lie. Two deaths.

But before he could speak, the two stepped forward. Suspicion darkened their faces.

"Pashupati," Veerabaahu said, voice firm. "Tell us. Can you revive Dashanan?"

He turned towards them. Sweat glistened on his skin. His breath hitched. The lie perched at the tip of his tongue—

—and then, it struck him.

A memory.

Dashanan was no ordinary mortal.

The sages had whispered it. The scrolls had hinted at it.

The king possessed the power to restore his own body—not with herbs or science, but by sheer will.

Pashupati gasped.

Could it be?

Had Dashanan healed himself in the instant of death?

Is that why there was no wound?

His knees buckled—not in fear, but in awe.

And in that moment of stunned realisation, a shadow swept over them.

An eagle—massive, golden-feathered, and silent—descended from the sky, its wings slicing the air with divine grace. It landed gently upon Dashanan's chest.

The three men froze.

Tied to the eagle's leg was a silken scroll, sealed in crimson wax.

A sign.

A warning.

Or perhaps... a divine command.

Pashupati stepped forward.

With hands of reverent caution, he reached for the eagle. The creature remained still, golden feathers glowing in the filtered cave light. Tied to its leg was a silken scroll—worn by wind, yet still firm and crisp.

He untied it gently and unfolded the message.

Kanaka and Veerabaahu approached, their eyes narrowing in disbelief.

"How is this possible?" Kanaka whispered. "We never told anyone where we were going..."

Pashupati offered no reply. He inhaled deeply and began to read aloud.

"I know that you are planning to revive Dashanan.

I want the same. But it is not that simple.

You can only bring someone back to life if they have suffered mortal wounds.

Dashanan was not slain by an ordinary man—he was killed by Lord Ram, the perfect man, born to uphold dharma.

His death was not just an event; it was a turning point etched into the very fabric of time.

It has happened before. It will happen again.

And so, his body now lies outside the natural order. It can no longer sustain life. It has lost the ability to respond to his Jeeva Tatva.

Your medicines will not work. Your methods will fail.

But all is not lost.

There is still a path.

Extract his Jeeva Tatva from this vessel,

and find—or forge—a mortal form that is capable of receiving it.

When Jeeva Tatva finds a worthy host, Dashanan will live again.

Not as he was, but as he must become."

✦

The torchlight flickered over the parchment as silence settled in. The message rang like prophecy.

Pashupati's voice remained steady, but tension buzzed between the brothers. Their minds whirled with implications.

"I came to the same conclusion," Pashupati said quickly, seizing the moment. "After examining the body, I knew revival in this form was impossible. His Jeeva Tatva must be rejoined with a vessel it can inhabit. That is our path. And we'll need technology capable of guiding that transition."

Before another word could be spoken, the eagle spread its wings and leapt—alighting softly on Pashupati's shoulder.

Beneath one wing was a second scroll—tighter, harder to spot.

He retrieved it.

Another message.

"Vibhishan's army is looking for you.

Save your lives.

Dashanan must live again."

Pashupati's jaw tightened.

"They're coming. We have no time."

Who had sent the messages remained unknown—but their urgency rang with unmistakable truth.

The brothers said nothing.

They simply nodded.

Pashupati sprang into action. His healer's mind reawakened, sharp and commanding.

"Kanaka—attach a fine steel needle to the end of the collection tube. Veerabaahu—connect the other end to the regulator on the Pranic Extractor. Now."

They moved swiftly, without hesitation.

Pashupati crushed herbs and rare minerals, blending them with oils to create a blue, shimmering elixir. He turned to them.

"This will preserve his body for decades—centuries, if needed. Apply it thoroughly on every inch."

The two men worked in silence, coating Dashanan's immense form with the mixture until his skin glistened like wet stone beneath the moonlight.

Then came the most delicate step.

Pashupati knelt beside Dashanan and gently slid the needle into the spinal cord—the deepest anchor of the Jeeva Tatva.

The extractor came alive with a low hum. The crystal container began to glow faintly—then darkened—as a viscous, black-gold substance spiralled into its heart.

Dashanan's Jeeva Tatva.

Pashupati did not blink. His hands moved with sacred precision, eyes gleaming with awe.

Following the scroll's instructions, he added powdered minerals, concentrated elixirs, and purified oils to the container. Once it was sealed and Dashanan's body fully preserved, they stood in solemn silence.

It was time to hide them.

They journeyed deeper into the cavern, carrying the crystal first. Through winding corridors and narrow stone paths, they discovered a crevasse—tight, perfect, as if nature itself had been waiting for this offering.

They placed the crystal inside and rolled a boulder over the gap, sealing it from view.

Then they returned, steering the wagon through the cave's deeper veins. Through winding passageways and stifling darkness, they advanced more than one-tenth of a yojana.

At last, they reached a chamber—circular, domed, silent.

There, at the heart of stone and shadow, they unhitched the horses, closed the wagon, and left Dashanan's body behind. Draped in silk, preserved in stillness.

A tomb.

Or perhaps... a cradle.

They walked away from Dashanan's resting place in silence.

No words. No glances. Only footsteps echoing through the cave's winding stone halls, slow and solemn, like the toll of unseen mourning bells.

When they returned to the main chamber—where scrolls lay curled, and instruments waited in quiet anticipation—it was Pashupati who finally broke the silence.

"Who do you think sent the message?" he asked.

One of the brothers replied without hesitation.

"There's only one person who ever wanted Dashanan to live more than we did."

They all fell still.

The name was not spoken, but it didn't need to be. They had always known. They had never forgotten.

Before doubt could take root, Pashupati stepped forward and spoke again—his voice stripped of pride, softened by remorse.

"We have two problems. First, neither our Guru nor I ever discovered how to reunite Jeeva Tatva with a mortal body. And second—perhaps the greater challenge—is finding a body capable of containing Dashanan's Jeeva Tatva. I'm sorry. For what I've done. For leading you into danger. For giving you false hope."

His words were low and sincere. There was no performance this time, only truth.

For a moment, the brothers said nothing. Then, as if moved by a single, silent impulse, they stepped forward and placed their hands on his back—firm and forgiving.

Veerabaahu met his eyes.

"Then tell us, Pashupati… what must we do to bring him back? You are the greatest healer in Lanka. However difficult it may be—trust us—we'll do it."

Pashupati looked away.

The truth was: he didn't know. The instructions in the scroll—the fusion of technology it hinted at—were far beyond his understanding. Beyond Lanka.

And yet… he wouldn't give up.

Not now.

Pashupati had travelled far in pursuit of knowledge. In his travels, he had witnessed many revival techniques—some ancient, some scientific, and some that could only be described as miracles.

He was familiar with every method known in Lanka, and none could bring their master back. What was lacking was not knowledge, but the will to defy finality.

But now, he had an idea.

A possibility. A hope.

He placed a hand on each of their shoulders.

"There are other kingdoms beyond our shores," he said. "Some lost to time. Some ruled by wisdom instead of war. Somewhere—perhaps in Bharatakhanda, perhaps across the oceans—someone has discovered how to reunite Jeeva Tatva with a living form."

His voice strengthened as he spoke. Conviction followed like a rising tide.

"Let us search for them. Let us journey across the world. And if we do not find the answer in this lifetime, then let our descendants carry the torch. Let this be our legacy—generation after generation, devoted to one purpose: to bring our Guru back."

✦

"Let us swear it now." And they did.

Three brothers.

Bound not by blood, but by vow.

They swore beneath the silence of gods, the sound of the ocean, and forgotten stars that they would never rest until Dashanan lived again.

They packed their scrolls, their instruments, and the few remaining potions into the wagon and emerged from the cave. The forest light was soft, dappled with the sounds of birdsong.

They travelled to the northern shore of Lanka, where the port cities still clung to life—surviving through trade, barter, and prayer.

There, they sold everything. Every tincture, every blade, every scroll not vital to their quest. In return, they secured two ships and a loyal crew.

Pashupati, still burdened by guilt like a wound that would not close, made his decision.

"You two," he said to his brothers, "will sail to the faraway kingdoms—those beyond the oceans. Search their temples, their labs, their ruins. Learn everything you can."

"And you?" Veerabaahu asked.

"I will walk north," Pashupati said. "Across the Vanara bridge. Across Bharatakhanda. I will climb the Himalayas and seek the Rishis, the yogis, the ancient sages. If knowledge of the soul's return exists anywhere, it lives in the mountains."

They stood together at the water's edge.

The ships were ready. The sky, painted in bruised hues of sunset.

"Every five years," Pashupati said, "we meet in Ayodhya. Share what we've learned. Build what we can. And never abandon our oath."

They embraced—long and wordless.

Then came the parting.

Pashupati stood on the shore, watching as his brothers boarded the ships. He had never left Lanka before. The island was his whole world. His whole past.

The sails caught the wind. The ships glided towards the horizon—first ships, then specks, then grains of white against the setting sun. And then—nothing.

He turned north.

And began to walk.

Towards the bridge.

Towards Bharatakhanda.

Towards the mountains.

Towards the impossible.

Towards the vow that would outlive the **Anveshi**.

CHAPTER 02

Pashupati stood still at the gates of Ayodhya. The wind rustled the saffron banners above him, but his thoughts wandered far beyond the city's golden towers. It had been five years since he last saw his brothers—five long years since they had parted to fulfil a sacred vow. Much had changed since then.

When he first arrived in Ayodhya, he lived simply, offering Ayurvedic care to the sick without asking for coin. But the city, prosperous and grateful, had repaid him with honour and wealth. His healing touch had become legend, whispered from palace corridors to village streets. And yet, as he stood before those gates of sandstone and memory, none of it brought comfort. His heartbeat raced with questions he dared not speak aloud. Would they come? Were they still alive? Did they remember the pact?

As the sun dipped behind the domes, silence settled like a blanket of dust. He paced beneath the reddening sky. Ayodhya shimmered in gold—fountains caught fire, shadows lengthened beneath banyan trees, birds circled back to their nests. The city exhaled its evening breath. But in Pashupati's chest, something collapsed. They had forgotten. He turned away; his shoulders bowed beneath the weight of quiet betrayal. As he walked home, the ache of abandonment crept in like frost.

And yet, within that ache, something stirred. He looked again at the streets awash in amber light, at children laughing beside lotus basins, at the scent of jasmine carried on the wind. Beauty, he realised, belonged not to those who had much—but to those who still chose to see. He smiled—not from joy, but from survival. "Perhaps," he whispered to no one, "I am a little wiser today."

His house appeared at the end of the lane—a graceful structure nestled between trees. But something felt different. A man stood at his gate. Pashupati quickened his pace, then broke into a run. It was Veerabaahu. Before he could speak, another voice rang out behind him: "Pashupati!" He turned. Kanaka. His legs gave way, and he collapsed to his knees.

The brothers rushed to him from opposite directions and embraced without a word. They were here. They had come. And more than seeing each other again—it was the knowing. None of them had forgotten.

That night, the fire in Pashupati's home burned long and bright. They spoke of lost lands and stranger kingdoms—of alchemists in icy peaks, of scholars tracing starlight across golden deserts, of sunken ruins and libraries older than cities. They shared everything—except success. None had yet found a way to reunite Jeeva Tatva with a mortal vessel.

Still, they were no longer mere men. Their master's teachings had transformed them into sages and seers, inventors and healers. One had mastered frost-forged alloys in the snowy lands that would one day be called Norway. The other had uncovered rites of resurrection and light-based machines in the deserts of the east that would become Egypt. They had carried Dashanan's vision across continents—and returned with treasures of insight.

But tonight, their focus was not wealth, not fame, not even failure. It was each other. And the vow they had made.

By the time dawn touched Ayodhya's spires, their purpose had been renewed. Pashupati laid palm-leaf manuscripts before them—each inscribed with diagrams of the Jeeva Tatva, theories of soul-separation, and coded maps to the hidden cave where Dashanan's essence still waited. "Copy these," he told them. "Let this knowledge survive, even if we do not."

They spent days refining their maps, updating timelines, and engineering new ways to communicate across oceans. They agreed to return—every five years—to the city of Lord Ram. Not to seek protection. Not to beg for guidance. But to continue, in secret, the mission of the Anveshi.

And then, once again, they parted.

✦

Years passed. Centuries folded into millennia. Yugas turned like pages in a cosmic chronicle. The founding fathers of the Anveshi Saubhratra—Pashupati, Veerabaahu, and Kanaka—

never lived to see their Guru reborn. They faded into the dust of time. But their oath endured.

Their descendants carried it forward. Families became dynasties. Manuscripts became secret scriptures. Knowledge once whispered in jungle caves began to ripple through empires—encoded in laboratories, hospitals, machines, and minds. But the oath... the oath never changed.

The lineage of Pashupati blossomed into a powerhouse across Asia. Drawing on ancient palm-leaf wisdom, his heirs refined branches of Ayurveda and incorporated them into the modern medical field. The result was a pharmaceutical empire—research towers crowned with yantra symbols, hospitals engraved with sacred carvings, and beneath it all, in the heart of Varanasi: a sacred library whose scrolls had never been touched by public hands.

At the helm of this legacy stood Dr Tara Pashupati—a brilliant geneticist, a CEO, and the last active voice of her lineage in the brotherhood. She had only one child.

Ahindra Pashupati.

A name crafted to carry legacy. But the man who bore it had been forged by different fires. He earned his doctorate in genetic engineering at the age of fifteen. Built his first gene editor at sixteen. Declined a royal science award before he was eighteen. Yet the deeper he went into discovery, the more solitary he became.

His work was a private language. His lab—carved beneath the ancestral mansion—was his sanctuary. He dismissed the Anveshi Saubhratra as a sentimental relic, a myth tolerated only out of respect for his mother. He believed in sequences, not stories. In proteins, not prophecies.

Even his marriage had been arranged—a gesture of duty, not devotion. He barely spoke to his wife or to his parents. His experiments rarely failed. But when they did, Ahindra sought the garden, waiting for nature to whisper the answer his equations withheld.

Rain or sun, monsoon or midnight, he would sit—silent and still—as if waiting for nature to whisper a new equation into his soul. Occasionally, he would speak. To the maid. To the gardener. To his mother. To the squirrels and sparrows that no longer feared him. But his words were never emotional. Always searching. Always thinking. Always processing.

He wasn't cold. Just misplaced.

Then came the child.

His wife gave birth in the early hours of spring. Ahindra didn't visit the hospital. He said nothing. Offered nothing. She had long prepared herself to raise the child alone.

But two days later, as she sat in the garden cradling the newborn, something shifted.

Ahindra emerged from the basement—unshaven, sleepless, eyes like glass. He paused. Then stepped forward. He extended his arms—a silent request. Startled, she handed the child over with quiet caution, expecting indifference.

But when Ahindra held his son, the baby stirred... and smiled in his sleep.

Ahindra froze. Something ancient broke open in him—a breach in the walls he had so carefully built.

His wife looked up, almost afraid to hope. "Would you like to name him?" she asked softly.

Ahindra stared, lips parted. Words failed him. "I don't know," he stammered. "You should decide."

It wasn't the answer she expected. But in that moment, she saw something more—a father beginning to awaken.

Time passed.

Ahindra, once a ghost in his own house, began to orbit his son like a second sun. He carried the boy everywhere—even into the lab, especially into the lab.

There, he spoke more than he ever had before—explaining ideas, narrating failures, imagining futures. "This DNA is memory," he whispered once, pipette in hand, while his son blinked up at him from a padded chair. "We're just trying to help it repair." The boy cooed. Ahindra smiled.

To the rest of the family, it was madness—a newborn in a gene lab.

To Ahindra, it was clarity. He wasn't exposing the child to danger. He was exposing him to the truth.

No one else knew what he was working on. Not his wife. Not his parents. Not even the board of his mother's company. Only the boy.

Who wouldn't remember any of it.

But perhaps, somehow... would carry it.

✦

Years turned over like pages soaked in time. The world changed, but the Anveshi Saubhratra endured. Its founding fathers had long returned to dust, yet their cause remained—passed down, protected, preserved. Across borders. Across bloodlines. Across centuries of silence.

Their descendants had become powerful. Respected. Impossibly wealthy. But their legacy was not written in riches. It was etched in the oath.

Dr Ahindra Pashupati's son was nearly ten years old. And Ahindra—once the detached prodigy, the ghost in his own home—was now closer to his boy than he had ever been to any living soul. His research had slowed. But his time in the garden—laughing, playing, simply watching—had never felt more sacred.

Above them, the mansion stirred with purpose. It was time again—the five-year gathering of the Anveshi Saubhratra. As tradition dictated, this year's conclave would be hosted at the ancestral home in Ayodhya. The halls were swept. Security tightened. The gates were prepared to receive emissaries from Egypt and Norway.

Dr Tara Pashupati oversaw every detail with the precision of a general. She was, after all, the last active voice of Pashupati's lineage within the brotherhood. Her son had inherited the name—but not the fire.

That morning, she descended into the basement lab. The door opened into a low, humming silence. Test tubes shimmered under soft light. Ahindra barely looked up.

"The meeting begins in a few hours," she said. "I'd like you to attend."

He looked at her for a long moment. Then shook his head reluctantly.

She exhaled. Not relief. Just disbelief. She turned to leave, but before the door closed behind her, she muttered—just loud enough for the walls to hear, "This is why I wanted two children. At least one might have been... normal."

Ahindra smirked. He waited for her footsteps to fade. Then quietly resumed his notes.

Outside, the sun crept over the rooftops. The mansion awoke. Servants moved through the corridors with assignments. Security patrolled the perimeter in quiet loops. And one man—Lalit—watched it all.

Lalit was more than Dr Tara's security chief. He was her confidant. Her protector. Her archivist. A former soldier in his forties, Lalit had left the army after losing a leg in the field. His father—a revered explorer in the service of the Anveshi Saubhratra—had vanished on his final expedition into the jungles of Africa. That loss had brought Lalit to the brotherhood's doors. They had welcomed him like blood. And he had served the cause ever since.

He knew every archive, every passageway, every forgotten whisper of the mansion's hidden past. His instincts were sharp. His eyes missed little.

And he understood Ahindra better than most.

He saw in him not arrogance, but restraint. Not coldness, but distance. A man who had walled himself off from his own destiny.

But walls, Lalit knew, always crack.

By mid-morning, the members of the Anveshi Saubhratra had arrived. Twenty men and women—scientists, mystics, financiers, and explorers—gathered in the sprawling garden of the Ayodhya estate, seated in two concentric circles. In the inner ring sat Dr Tara Pashupati, poised as ever, and across from her sat two men who had arrived in silence: one cloaked in desert white, the other wrapped in a fur-lined grey coat that whispered of colder lands.

Ahindra stayed apart—as always—reclining in his favourite chair at the edge of the garden, eyes half-closed, pretending not to notice the ancient gathering unfolding before him. He watched the squirrels instead.

He heard laughter at first, then formality. Greetings softened into updates—progress reports, failed experiments, rare discoveries, and inevitable dead ends. He had heard the word 'Jeeva Tatva' more than once. He didn't react. But he was listening.

Then, the air shifted. The tone sharpened. The man from Egypt leaned forward, his voice laced with agitation. The Norse scholar gestured sharply in Tara's direction. Accusations. Blame. Frustration hung like heat above the grass.

Ahindra turned his head. He had never seen his mother take the blame before. She sat tall, her spine straight, her silence thunderous. She did not flinch. But she didn't defend herself either.

What was this oath she bore alone? What weight had she carried all these years—one even he, her only son, had never thought to ask about?

The voices rose once more, then abruptly fell. The men stood. Chairs scraped against stone. Engines growled. Within moments, they were gone.

Dr Tara remained seated—back straight, face unreadable. She spoke quietly to Lalit, who stood behind her like a sentinel.

From across the garden, Ahindra watched them. He couldn't hear it all—but fragments floated across the grass.

"More researchers..."

"Breakthrough is overdue..."

"We have the knowledge. We need the will..."

Then her eyes found his. Their gaze locked—hers sharp and aching, his distant and unreadable. She stood abruptly, stormed past Lalit, and vanished into the mansion.

Lalit lingered. He turned towards Ahindra, waiting—hoping he might rise, approach, ask what had happened.

But Ahindra said nothing. He only stared at a nearby tree where birds had begun to gather. Silent. Still. Thinking.

Lalit waited a moment longer. Then turned and walked away.

And in the garden, alone once more, Ahindra Pashupati closed his eyes.

He listened—not to arguments, not to expectations—but to the wind rustling through old leaves.

And to something older still, stirring behind his thoughts.

✦

The next morning, just after sunrise, Ahindra Pashupati did something he hadn't done in years. He walked down the long, teak-panelled corridor of the mansion and stopped at the doorway to Lalit's office—an austere room cluttered with blueprints, satellite images, ancient maps, and biometric scanners. Lalit looked up from a screen and blinked.

Ahindra stood awkwardly on the threshold, hands buried in the pockets of his coat, his gaze drifting across the shelves as if he'd stumbled into a museum of unfamiliar relics.

"Do you ever get a phantom itch?" he asked, without preamble.

Lalit raised an eyebrow. "On my leg?"

Ahindra gave a single nod, still not stepping in.

Lalit leaned back in his chair and smiled faintly. He understood. This wasn't about nerves. Or limbs. Or phantom sensations.

Ahindra wanted to talk about his mother.

He just didn't know how.

"Yes," Lalit said softly. "Sometimes. Usually after long days."

He let the silence settle between them before continuing, voice casual, as if discussing the weather. "She's leading the search to reunite Jeeva Tatva with Dashanan's body, you know. And despite the best minds, the best labs... we're no closer than we were the day it was extracted."

Ahindra's face barely moved. But Lalit saw it—the faint dilation of the pupils, the quiet shift in posture. A flicker of interest beneath the surface.

A smirk tugged at the corner of Ahindra's mouth. "What do you mean by 'no one'?"

"I mean no one," Lalit replied. "Not in more than five thousand years. Not across yugas, according to some. Not since the day Dashanan fell, according to others."

For a moment, there was nothing.

Then, with deliberate calm, Ahindra said, "Send everything to my lab. Every document. Every manuscript."

He turned to leave.

"For her," he added, almost offhand.

And he walked out, not waiting for acknowledgement.

Lalit watched him go, then allowed himself a quiet smile.

"As you wish, Ahindra."

That night, a stack of documents and some ancient manuscripts appeared in Ahindra's lab—some in files and some bound in silk cords, some had numbers and graphs and others were inscribed in flowing Sanskrit.

He started with the files. Hours turned into days. Days into months. He combed through every line of data, running numbers, cross-checking variables. But the truth remained out of reach. No matter how deeply he read, no matter how many simulations he ran, he couldn't grasp what Jeeva Tatva truly was.

One afternoon, his son was with him in the lab. The boy wandered to the manuscripts and began flipping the pages with innocent curiosity.

"Stop that!" Ahindra snapped, his voice sharper than he intended.

The boy froze, wide-eyed. Then, tears welling, he dropped the manuscript and ran out of the lab, his small footsteps echoing down the corridor.

The silence that followed cut deeper than his anger.

Ahindra bent to pick up the fallen manuscript. As he lifted it, a loose sheet slid free. Across the page was an ancient diagram—hand-drawn, faded by centuries of time.

Viruses. Budding from the membrane of a mammalian cell.

His breath caught. He stared, transfixed.

Slowly, he sat down, the manuscript heavy in his lap. He turned the pages one by one. Symbols and diagrams filled the parchment, dense with metaphysical notations—alchemy, mechanics, Vedic geometry, pulse medicine, soul theory, gene lore.

Ahindra wasn't searching for myths. He was hunting Jeeva Tatva.

But as he read, something began to shift. He couldn't stop.

One manuscript described a procedure by Pashupati, the ancestor whose name he bore. It spoke in poetry and metaphor of regenerating limbs with oils, saps, and a rare substance called *Punarautpatti Kana*.

Ahindra's eyes narrowed. The language was archaic, veiled in allegory. But beneath the verse was unmistakable science.

Stem cell therapy. Autologous regeneration. Documented... centuries ago.

His breath caught.

He tore through the next pages, searching for ingredients. But most were untraceable—extinct flora, vanished minerals, lost methods.

His shoulders slumped. Still, he read on. Manuscript after manuscript.

But the *Jeeva Tatva*—the essence itself—remained elusive.

Midnight came and went. Finally, with a frustrated slam, he shut the last book. The echo rang against the cold stone of the lab.

He stormed upstairs. Through silent corridors. To Lalit's quarters. He pounded the door—once, twice, again—until it creaked open.

Lalit stood before him, tired, shirt half-buttoned, balanced on crutches. His prosthetic leg rested against the far wall.

Ahindra blinked. He had never seen Lalit like this. Human. Vulnerable.

Before he could speak, Lalit raised a hand.

"They analysed it," he said quietly.

Ahindra froze.

"The *Jeeva Tatva* sample," Lalit continued. "Mass spectrometry."

Ahindra's eyes widened.

Lalit nodded, almost reverently. "It's made of some organic compounds."

The silence cracked.

Ahindra's entire expression shifted. The tension dissolved. The smirk returned. His eyes lit with something fierce—something focused.

He smiled—not politely. Not socially.

But purely.

The smile of a man who had just found a puzzle worth solving.

✦

Ahindra Pashupati was no stranger to complexity. Though absent from academia since his teens, he had never stopped pushing the boundaries of what could be known. While his peers chased recognition, Ahindra chased patterns—raw, unfiltered, unsupervised. He had mastered every known form of biological analysis: spectroscopy, sequencing, crystallography, and even methods most researchers hadn't yet heard of. Science, to him, was a private language.

So, when he requested the raw mass spectrometry data of the *Jeeva Tatva*, Lalit immediately understood: the puzzle had taken root.

Lalit was already halfway to his office, hobbling slowly on crutches. He wasn't used to them—he preferred his prosthetic—but he had taken it off to sleep. Most people, even the well-meaning, instinctively offered help.

Ahindra never did.

And Lalit appreciated that, not out of pride, but because with Ahindra, he didn't have to perform gratitude. He didn't have to be the soldier-turned-caretaker with a broken past. He could just be Lalit. And Ahindra, for his part, liked that Lalit treated his silence as a complete sentence.

They reached the office. Ahindra took the file without a word and rushed back to his lab, the pages flaring in his hands.

He examined the data once. Then again. And again.

Each pass confirmed the same finding: nucleic acids. Proteins. The very blueprint of biology. The unmistakable material signature of life.

Then he opened the report itself. Carefully. Slowly.

There was a signature at the bottom—but what caught his eye was the date: ten years ago.

Suddenly, Ahindra laughed. The sound echoed through the sterile lab, sharp and hollow, like a truth unearthed too late.

He tore down the staircase and sprinted to the house phone.

"Trunk call," he told the operator. "Stanford University. United States of America."

The line crackled. He paced the floor, rehearsing in his mind. A new microscopy technique—Electron Microscopy—had emerged shortly after the original report was filed. He remembered the journal article. Resolution down to the atomic scale. Exactly what he needed to see inside the *Jeeva Tatva*.

The call connected. His old colleague answered—not surprised, not hesitant. Just a warm, curious voice: "Ahindra? What do you have for me this time?"

The conversation was brief. The agreement, immediate.

Yes, they could run a sample.

Yes, no questions asked.

Yes, no one will look at these results.

Ahindra hung up before his friend could slip into small talk.

He sprinted again—this time to Lalit's quarters. The sky was still grey with dawn. He knocked hard. Then again. And again.

The door opened. Lalit stood there—bleary-eyed, crutches under both arms. His prosthetic rested against the far wall. Ahindra blinked. He had never seen Lalit like this. Human. Unarmoured.

Before Lalit could speak, Ahindra blurted, "I need a sample. Of *Jeeva Tatva*."

Lalit sighed, rubbing his forehead. "You don't trust the report?"

"I do," Ahindra said. "I analysed the chromatograms myself. The analyst was right. I want to run a different analysis—on an electron microscope."

Lalit blinked. That... was unexpected. But his reply came without hesitation.

"There's no sample left here," he said flatly. "You'll have to go to the source. Back to the cave in Sri Lanka."

Ahindra paused.

And then, like a storm giving way to sunlight, a slow smile cracked across his face.

Of course.

He turned and walked away without another word.

Lalit closed the door, shaking his head—but smiling.

✦

Back in the lab, Ahindra pulled one of the original manuscripts from the collection Lalit had sent. There it was—faded, but intact. A map. A path. A point marked along a mountain range of Sri Lanka.

He traced the route with a trembling finger—not from fear, but because, for the first time in years, the puzzle had just become real.

Ahindra was already halfway across the Palk Strait. The ferry from Rameswaram to Talaimannar carved a steady line through the waves, each crest cutting into the silence like a blade against steel. Salt spray clung to his coat. He stood by the railing, one hand gripping the cold iron, the other resting on a satchel—inside it, the most valuable thing he had ever carried: a map.

Not a new one. A copy of a copy. Its origins are buried beneath centuries of annotations, commentary, and secrecy.

He had not paused to plan. The moment he returned from Lalit's quarters, he had tossed a few essentials into a bag—torch, notebooks, gloves, sterile vials—and boarded the next train to Chennai. From there, he charted the rest of the journey by instinct just as he did with science.

Only once the train began its slow sway through the Tamil countryside did he unfurl the map. The parchment was dense with script—Sanskrit verses, coded diagrams, directional glyphs—but more revealing were the notes penned in the margins. Different hands. Different centuries. Some were nearly erased by time. Others were added only decades ago.

The latest trail, sketched in modern graphite, traced a route from Rameswaram to Talaimannar, then deep into the Rangala forest—a mountainous wilderness of steep ridges, serpentine rivers, and a canopy so thick it could strangle the sun. Beyond that lay the cave. And within it—the source.

By the time Ahindra reached Talaimannar, exhaustion had set in. The overnight ferry, the labyrinth of cross-border protocols—it had drained him. He boarded a local bus bound for the forest.

It was the first time he had ever left his son behind.

He stared out the window as palm trees blurred into the jungle. A memory rose—his son chasing butterflies in the garden, laughing at nothing, asking strange, brilliant questions no one could answer. Ahindra smiled. Then fell asleep.

The journey through Rangala was brutal. Ahindra was a genius, but no outdoorsman. He slipped on every moss-covered stone, tripped over every gnarled root. His arms and legs were striped with shallow cuts and mud. His coat torn. His shoes soaked.

And he had never felt more alive.

Three days passed. He drank from mountain streams. Ate ration bars. Slept on boulders beneath trees older than empires. He crossed the remnants of an ancient wagon trail—once carved by the first Anveshi brothers, now overtaken by vines and silence.

What endured was a narrow path winding through the jungle's tangle—through thorns and steam and the constant chant of unseen life. His heart pounded with each step, reminding him he was not a machine.

The final ascent to the cave entrance drained what strength he had left. But when he reached it—aching, panting, slick with sweat—he laughed. Not because the journey was over. But because he already wanted to do it again.

He lit his torch and stepped inside.

The air shifted instantly—cooler, still, and thick with the acrid sting of ammonia. His footsteps echoed into the dark. Deeper in, the odour sharpened. Then came the sound—a clicking chorus. Bats. He raised the torch. Hundreds of tiny amber eyes blinked down from the ceiling.

But he wasn't afraid. It wasn't the bats he feared.

He kept the beam low, every step deliberate. Then he saw them—footprints, softened by time, older than memory. The Anveshi and a few others had been here after them.

The cave floor slickened with guano. Insects scattered at his approach. He followed the manuscript's instructions like a sacred rite—measured turns, stone markers, ancient coordinates aligned with scripture and memory.

And then… he reached the crevasse.

There it was.

Nestled between fused stalagmites, half-swallowed by the cave wall, sat a crystal container. Its surface shimmered beneath the torchlight like a relic forged from the marrow of time—like ice that had never melted.

He knelt, brushing away the webbing.

Inside, a viscous black liquid pulsed faintly in the amber glow.

Jeeva Tatva.

His hands trembled. His mind roared.

Months of failure, of isolation, of silence—erased in an instant.

He reached forward, ready to extract the entire sample. But then—a line from the manuscript echoed in his mind:

"The Jeeva Tatva, once removed from its vessel, will begin to fade. In one lunar cycle, its essence shall perish."

He froze. Withdrew.

Instead, he carefully drew two small samples and sealed them in crystal-lined sterile vials.

One for Stanford.

One for himself.

He sat back, chest heaving, and exhaled.

This was a success.

This was the truth.

But he didn't turn back.

He turned deeper into the cave.

Something stirred in him—not fear, but curiosity.

And without a second thought, he pressed onward—further into the mountain's heart.

Ahindra continued deeper into the cave—farther than any map had charted, deeper than even the Anveshis had dared to explore. The air grew colder. Older. The kind of cold that didn't just sting the skin, but whispered of forgotten centuries. Even the echoes changed—thinner, more reluctant, as if sound itself had learned not to intrude.

He felt it immediately: this part of the cave had never been touched by humans in centuries. No footprints. No tool marks. No remnants of torches, cloth, or coins. Only stone—and silence.

Nearly a kilometre in, he reached what felt like the end.

Resting on a slanted stone dais was a wagon—ancient, weather-worn, half-consumed by the cave floor. Its wheels had fused into rock. And on top of it lay a massive casket, over twenty feet long, trimmed with faded gold and inlaid with gemstones dulled by centuries.

It wasn't the casket's size that held him; it was the mandala etched upon it—unlike anything Ahindra had ever seen. The geometry was surgical, every curve exact. Ten concentric rings circled a solid circle, each ring rendered in its own language: waves, then petals, then coiled serpents, then jagged strokes of lightning—on and on, ten in all—each band distinct yet bound to the next. At the centre, a single, unbroken disc. He lifted a hand to trace the design when his torch snagged a glint beyond—the far wall. Writing. He lowered his fingers, angled the beam, and stepped towards the script.

Someone had carved a message directly into the stone and inlaid the letters with gold. They were still sharp, untouched by time or moisture. He brushed the surface clean with trembling hands and read:

"Bhaṅgāt paścādeva sandhiḥ." To repair something, it must be broken first.

He stared, stunned. Then, just below the inscription, he saw another line—newer, unadorned, not in Sanskrit. Scratched into the stone by hand and rock. A language he recognised.

He cleared more of the wall, breath catching.

As his eyes scanned the second message, something inside him cracked.

He dropped to his knees—and wept.

High above, the bats stirred. They screeched and scattered, a black cloud erupting from the ceiling in a burst of wings and shrill chaos. But Ahindra didn't move. His shoulders trembled. His sobs were silent. Something in that message had shattered him.

Or perhaps—for the first time—repaired him.

✦

He stayed there for a long while, kneeling in that untouched hollow of the world. Eventually, he wiped his face, looked once more at the casket, and turned back. The jungle would awaken soon. And the predators would roam.

It had been seven days since Ahindra left.

Inner chamber of the mountain cave in Sri Lanka

Not unusual for him to vanish. But he always returned by nightfall. Always.

This time, he hadn't.

Panic bloomed into certainty. The living room of the mansion was heavy with dread. Dr Tara paced by the windows. Ahindra's wife sat rigid on the couch, clutching her son's hand—until her grip faltered.

The police inspector removed his cap with mechanical sympathy.

"We're past seventy-two hours," he said. "I'm sorry. The odds of survival drop significantly after that."

The words were surgical. And they sliced like blades.

Ahindra's wife broke. She buried her face in her hands and sobbed.

Their son, confused and afraid, stared at her. He had never seen his mother cry. He didn't understand the silence, the fear. So, he cried too.

Beside them, Lalit stood motionless. He knew. He had a hunch from the beginning. But he'd said nothing. Worry was contagious—and the journey Ahindra had taken was unforgiving.

The inspector offered quiet condolences and turned to leave. As the door clicked shut behind him, Dr Tara turned to Lalit. Her eyes didn't carry tears. They carried fire.

"You know where he is," she said.

It wasn't a question.

Lalit met her gaze but said nothing.

Lalit opened his mouth—ready to explain, to confess—but was interrupted by a sudden cry:

"Father is here!"

The boy had leapt from the couch and was running towards the door.

The family turned.

Ahindra stood in the entryway, covered in dirt and scrapes, grinning.

His son launched into his arms, and Ahindra lifted him easily, kissed his forehead, and stepped inside—as if nothing had happened. As if he hadn't just walked through death and darkness.

The family rushed to him.

Dr Tara extended her arms. "Give me the boy," she said.

Ahindra handed him over, still smiling.

And before he could speak—

Crack.

Her palm struck his cheek with the kind of force only a mother can summon.

It wasn't punishment.

It was grief.

It was rage.

It was love—colliding at once.

Ahindra didn't tell them the truth.

He stood in the centre of the living room—fresh clothes, the dirt washed from his skin—but the exhaustion clung to him, and so did the spark behind his eyes. He said he had gone to the United States. A sudden trip. Urgent.

"I had to collect some samples for my research," he told them, voice flat, entirely believable.

But when he said *samples*, his gaze flicked towards Lalit. He tapped his sling bag—once, deliberately.

Lalit saw. Understood. Nodded.

And said nothing.

The next morning, Ahindra sent the first vial of *Jeeva Tatva* to Stanford—packaged like a holy relic. Then he waited.

Restless. Impatient.

He filled the days with pacing and scrawling formulas across glass panels. But he refused to touch the second vial. Not until he had proof.

Not until he *saw* it.

Two weeks passed.

Then the call came.

It was his old colleague—the one who owed him too many favours to ask questions. The moment Ahindra answered, he could hear it through the line: excitement, barely restrained.

"I got the images," his friend said.

"And?" Ahindra's voice was barely a whisper.

"You're not going to believe this... It's a virus."

The call ended quickly. Clinical. Technical. To anyone else, it might have sounded like a footnote. But to Ahindra, it was the unlocking of a door.

He walked to the lab without a word, his thoughts sharpening with every step.

Of course.

Viruses.

Nucleic acids encased in protein. Nature's most efficient genetic delivery system.

Jeeva Tatva wasn't just a relic. It was a carrier—the viruses weren't designed to destroy. They were designed to rewrite.

If it could enter a host, it could rewrite the genome to resemble that of Dashanan...

At his workbench, he picked up the second vial.

Stared into its depths.

The liquid shimmered darkly—a substance older than memory, now dissolving, day by day, into entropy.

Two weeks left.

That night, he sat in the garden—his cathedral of thought. The only place where his mind could breathe.

The wind was soft. The squirrels chased each other through the lower branches. A sparrow landed nearby, tilting its head.

He watched.

Eyes narrow. Mind racing.

He remembered a passage from the manuscripts:

"Jeeva Tatva can awaken that which has passed, if the vessel is suitable."

And then—another voice. Etched in gold inside the cave wall:

"To repair something, it must be broken first."

His breath slowed.

He looked around. The garden was still. Empty.

He picked up a smooth stone.

Took aim.

And threw.

✦

The sparrow fell.

Ahindra walked to it—expression blank, hands steady. He lifted the limp creature and carried it into the lab.

On the sterile pad, he laid the tiny body gently. Drew a syringe. Pulled Jeeva Tatva into it.

With surgical precision, he injected it into the sparrow's chest.

Then he waited.

Checked its heartbeat. Examined its blood under the microscope.

Stillness.

The sparrow did not move.

He leaned closer, willing it to twitch, to gasp, to rise.

It didn't.

His jaw clenched.

He had done everything right—every precaution, every parameter.

Still—failure.

He slumped back in his chair. The silence reclaimed the lab.

Eventually, he stood and returned to the garden. He sat again. Stared at the trees. At the branches. At the stone.

And then—like lightning across his mind—he remembered.

The wall. The words.

"To repair something… it must be broken first."

Ahindra rushed back into the lab, breath ragged, thoughts moving faster than his hands.

He went straight to the containment shelf, flung open the cold box, and stared at the last remaining vial of Jeeva Tatva.

There wasn't much left.

Not enough.

But maybe… just enough.

He swept the lab with his eyes, searching for a new subject—something smaller than the sparrow. But there was nothing.

No mice. No insects. Nothing alive. Nothing sterile. Nothing usable.

Then the realisation struck him.

Himself.

If Jeeva Tatva could rebuild the dead, perhaps the key wasn't death at all but damage.

He remembered the golden inscription in the cave:

"To repair something, it must be broken first."

Of course.

The virus couldn't overwrite a whole, healthy cell. It needed something fractured.

Something to fix.

He grabbed a swab and scraped the inside of his cheek, preparing a slide.

Under the microscope, his cells sat intact. Undisturbed.

He added a drop of Jeeva Tatva to the culture.

Watched.

Nothing.

Of course.

He turned to the machine no one else was allowed to touch—the gamma-ray emitter.

A monstrous device he had bought and locked away. Designed to crack DNA like glass.

He took a second sample.

Placed it under the emitter.

Powered it up.

The machine roared.

A second later, the cells were dead.

He prepared a new slide.

Added a fresh droplet of Jeeva Tatva.

Slid it under the lens.

Watched.

Nothing.

His jaw clenched. He added another drop.

Then—life.

He gasped. Leaned closer. Laughed.

The cells were alive. Vibrant. Dividing at impossible speed.

He whispered, barely audible, as if not to frighten it:

"It worked."

But the laughter faded.

And doubt arrived.

Were they his cells anymore?

Had the virus simply revived them?

Or replaced them?

Was this his DNA…

or Dashanan's?

He isolated the DNA and initiated the amplification process. Once. Twice. Forty times.

Finally, after an hour of silent watching—

the results appeared.

The DNA was not his anymore.

Ahindra jumped in joy. It was his first success in months.

Not that he was unintelligent. But his experiments defied reason—like this one.

And now, a new thought sparked like fire through his veins:

"I have the proof of concept. Now all I need... is to inject Jeeva Tatva into a human—and turn them into Dashanan."

But there was one problem.

There wasn't enough Jeeva Tatva to transform a full-grown human.

He paused.

Ran the maths again.

Same result.

Again.

Still the same.

He stared at the vial.

The black liquid shimmered like an ancient dream—beautiful, terrible, sacred.

He was so close.

Too close.

Maybe it was ambition.

Maybe it was the cave's echo.

Or maybe—just maybe—something had entered him when he knelt before the inscription.

He didn't hesitate.

He began preparing the lab.

Quiet. Precise. Efficient.

The incubators were set.

The gene amplifiers calibrated.

The anaesthesia lined up.

Nutrient systems flushed and refilled.

Every instrument aligned.

Every movement memorised.

Every emotion buried.

Then he paused at the window.

The garden outside was silent. Still. Serene.

His son was out there, somewhere in that peace.

Ahindra watched the trees sway in the soft wind, his eyes empty of everything except one decision.

Then he turned from the light, stepped back into the lab and began preparing his own child's body to become the vessel of Dashanan.

✦

Three days had passed since Ahindra made the decision. Now, he stood with his son deep inside the cave at Rangala, surrounded by stone and dread. But for the boy, it was a day of wonder.

He moved from machine to machine, helping his father set up strange contraptions—tubes, coils, consoles—handing him tools, asking questions that only children and scientists dared to ask.

Ahindra answered them all.

Patiently. Gently.

For the first time, they were truly doing something *together*.

He had almost asked Lalit to come. Almost. He had stood frozen in the hallway that night, peeking through a crack in the door, watching Lalit laugh and play with the boy. "Uncle Lalit," the child had called him.

That was enough.

Lalit would have stopped him.

So Ahindra packed the gear himself, hired porters to ferry it to Sri Lanka, and waited for nightfall. Then, he crept into his son's room, lifted the sleeping boy in his arms, and carried him into the dark.

Now they stood at the centre of an ancient secret—surrounded by a hybrid of old-world metallurgy and bleeding-edge biotech. Generators hummed at the cave's mouth. Inside, cables glowed. Life-sign monitors blinked. A gamma-ray chamber loomed behind the tank.

And at the heart of it all: the tank itself.

An enormous cylinder of transparent alloy, filled with heavy water, rippling faintly in the torchlight.

His son stood at its edge, staring up with wide eyes.

"Want to play a science game?" Ahindra asked.

The boy's face lit up. He nodded, excited, and helped his father attach the sensors to his chest and arms. Ahindra handed him a diving helmet—specially rigged with internal comms—and a sleek, oversized glove. A small valve shimmered at the wrist.

Together, they climbed the side ladder to the tank's edge.

The boy hesitated. The water looked deeper now. Endless.

"Hold my hand," Ahindra said. "And jump backwards."

The boy did.

Inside the tank, he floated weightless, adrift in a cathedral of silence.

His father's voice echoed gently through the comms.

It calmed him.

Outside, Ahindra descended to the console.

He checked the vitals. Oxygen levels. Internal feed.

His fingers hovered above the activation pad.

"Close your eyes," he said. "And cover them as I do."

The boy laughed and copied him.

A green light blinked.

Ahindra pressed it.

With a hiss, two thick lead doors began to slide shut over the tank, sealing it from light. From sound. From everything.

Inside, the boy opened his eyes.

"Papa?"

He tried to swim upward—but couldn't.

The water was heavier now.

"Papa!"

His voice crackled through the helmet, distorted by panic.

"Why can't I see you?"

Ahindra leaned towards the glass as the child's silhouette faded behind the final sliver of light.

He smiled—not with cruelty, but with something closer to peace.

He raised his hand.

Waved once.

And the doors sealed shut.

Inside the tank, the boy flailed. His small limbs cut through water, searching for something. Some sky. Some air.

But there was nothing.

No surface.

No father.

No light.

He screamed. Again. And again.

The sound echoed into nothing.

Eventually, the flailing stopped.

His breath broke into sobs.

His helmet fogged from the inside.

He curled into the base of the tank, trembling—his tiny body folding in on itself.

And there, in the still water of that ancient cavern, the child cried until his strength left him.

Until fear became exhaustion.

Until exhaustion became silence.

✦

Back in the mansion, chaos had returned. It had been over twenty-four hours since Ahindra vanished. But this time, he hadn't gone alone. His son was missing, too.

The police had been notified again—but the tone had shifted. What began as urgency had warped into desperation. The quiet hum of concern had grown into a cacophony of panic. The Anveshi network was activated in full force. Explorers, informants, and allies mobilised across the subcontinent. Every archive was reopened. Every port was watched. Every path was retraced. Inside the great hall, people moved like pieces on a grand board. But Dr Tara Pashupati stood perfectly still—composed, contained, and burning within.

She had long sensed something shifting in her son. But this... this was not intuition. This was betrayal, cloaked in silence. She turned towards Lalit, who had remained conspicuously quiet. Her eyes, sharp and unrelenting, locked onto him.

"What are you not telling me?" she asked.

Lalit didn't respond—not out of defiance, but because he had failed. He should have seen it: the hesitations, the secrecy, the way Ahindra had brushed past oversight. The way he had tapped that sling bag days ago—his eyes brimming with something unspoken. He should have stopped him. Now it was too late.

And yet—even in the fire of his guilt—Lalit couldn't fully believe that Ahindra, distant though he was, could ever hurt his own child. He wasn't a monster, not at his core. Or at least... he hadn't been.

Hours passed like stones falling into a deep well. Then came a report.

An Anveshi explorer had flagged unusual movement near the southern coast. Vehicle logs. Port entries. Private ferry traffic. Two figures—father and son—boarding a boat from Rameswaram. No return recorded.

That was all Lalit needed.

He said nothing. Offered no explanations. He moved through the halls of the mansion with silent urgency—packing gear, checking his sidearm, pocketing a tracker, tightening the strap on his prosthetic leg.

And then, without goodbye or alert, he left. Just one man. Limping with purpose. Vanishing into the storm.

He was going to the cave.

To Rangala.

To bring them back.

Whatever it took.

✦

The boy was still in the tank. Suspended in water. Heart racing. Eyes wide with fear. Outside, Ahindra sat alone, surrounded by cables, charts, and cold blinking instruments.

He hadn't moved from his chair in hours, monitoring his son's vitals, adjusting the controls again and again. But the readings remained the same. The boy was terrified.

Ahindra glanced at the timer. Time was running out. Not just for the experiment—for everything. Lalit would come. And if he came before the procedure was complete, everything would be lost. He reached for the speaker, his fingers trembling slightly.

"Don't be scared," he said, voice low, almost tender. "I'm right here. I'll bring you out soon. I promise."

Inside the helmet, the boy could barely hear him. His throat was raw. His lips were split. But for a moment, he closed his eyes and believed. The whimpering stopped. Hope flickered.

Ahindra turned to the console. The tank was sealed. The dosage calculated. The port to inject Jeeva Tatva ready. He triggered the gamma-ray generator, aligning it with the reinforced panel—one segment of the tank wall that had been built to allow radiation to pass through.

The machine roared. It was the same sound that had once echoed through the cave yugas ago, when Pashupati's ancient device had drawn the first drop of Jeeva Tatva into its crystal vial. Now it returned—in steel and wires, in fire and faith.

Ahindra stood back, his hand hovering over the activation pad. He pressed it.

Inside the tank, the boy felt... nothing. Then heat. Then—pain. Blisters began to rise along his arms, his chest, his legs. His skin bubbled under the radiation. The scream never made it out. Only his eyes—wide, wet, pleading.

Outside, Ahindra stared at the monitor. The vitals were spiking. The pain was unbearable—but it was working. The destruction had begun. It was time. He pressed a second button.

Inside the glove—the strange, oversized glove he had built for his son—a needle slid silently into the boy's wrist. It released a single, dense pulse of Dashanan's Jeeva Tatva into his bloodstream.

Then silence.

The monitor beeped. Heart rate: erratic. Breathing: shallow. Ahindra knelt beside the tank, watching, waiting. But then—the heartbeat began to falter. The rhythm changed. The lines began to flatten.

He stared at the monitor. Flatline.

Ahindra froze. "No. No. No." He slammed his fist into the console. Then again. And again.

The tank remained sealed.

He ran to the tank, grabbed the edge of the hatch, and wrenched it open with a scream. Radiation flooded out like a silent storm, burning his skin instantly, blistering his arms.

But he didn't care.

Inside, the water had turned red. The boy's small body floated near the bottom, his skin half-dissolved, his face unrecognisable beneath the helmet. Only the right arm remained anchored—still tethered to the tank floor by the glove.

Ahindra collapsed to his knees.

"I'm sorry," he whispered. "I didn't mean... I thought... I'd save you."

The radiation began to take him. His skin cracked. His eyes bled. His veins felt like they were splitting open. But he wouldn't move. He clung to the tank, even as his breath shallowed, even as his body failed.

He stared into the water.

And watched.

Until he died.

Something was happening to the boy's right hand.

The blisters were vanishing. New skin—pink, impossibly smooth—was crawling across his arm. The wave of regeneration crept upward from his wrist to his shoulder, across his chest and spine, blooming like flame in reverse.

He was no longer floating.

He was standing now—feet planted firmly on the tank floor. His body, once ravaged, was whole again.

Inside the darkened tank, he blinked. His vision was blurry, but he saw something—a figure clinging to the lead doors.

He moved closer, squinting through the water, and saw the grotesque face of a man, skin blistered and split. It was too twisted to recognise.

He panicked. He tried to scream. And just as the healing passed through his throat, he roared.

It echoed like thunder.

✦

Far below, at the foot of Rangala, a hermit in a solitary temple looked up towards the mountain cave. He heard the roar, then saw flickers of light from the summit—strange, rhythmic, unnatural. Then the sky cracked open.

A bolt of lightning struck the generator outside the cave. Sparks flew. Power surged. The machines inside short-circuited in a storm of angry light.

Inside, the boy screamed again—louder, more primal. The tank shattered. Glass and water burst across the muddy cave floor. Another lightning strike hit the generator. The diesel ignited. Flames leapt to the cables, to the consoles, to the walls.

By the time the hermit reached the mouth of the cave, water was pouring out. He saw fire climbing the cavern's walls, wrapping around strange machines and the shattered remnants of some ancient science.

And in the centre, a boy stood atop a burning corpse. Unharmed. Unmoving. Eyes glowing beneath soot and steam.

The hermit staggered back, heart pounding. The boy bent down, gazed into the charred face beneath him, and screamed again.

The sound split the air. The man's face exploded.

A third bolt of lightning slammed into the hilltop. Everything inside the cave erupted—console, generator, metal, stone. The hermit was flung backwards by the blast, collapsing on the rocks.

But the boy still stood. Silent. Untouched by flame or fury.

At last, the boy walked forward—towards the hermit. He moved with eerie calm, like a dream walking through smoke.

The hermit couldn't move. Couldn't run.

The boy stood before him now. His body was pristine, unmarred. But his face... it was still healing—blistered, streaked with blood. The hermit stared at the boy's eyes. They were changing. Once black, now bleeding into crimson. The irises glowed like embers.

Then the blisters vanished. The face became whole. The expression blank.

He stepped closer—one foot, then another.

And then, suddenly, the boy smiled. A gentle, innocent smile. He looked into the hermit's eyes for the first time and whispered, "Thank you for saving me, father."

He reached forward. Wrapped his arms around the trembling man.

And collapsed.

Unconscious.

Alive.

Ahindra's experiment had succeeded.

His body had accepted Dashanan's **Jeeva Tatva**.

CHAPTER 03

It had been fifteen years since Devadatta, a solitary priest, found the boy outside the mountain cave. That boy had grown into a youth—tall, silent, and sharp-eyed—shaped by the discipline of the ashram and the silent weight of something ancient pulsing within him. Now he stood alone at the edge of a sea-cliff, where the night wind screamed, and the ocean glistened black beneath a silver moon. Far across the water, dim lights shimmered on the horizon like half-remembered spirits. Bharat. He did not look towards it with longing. He looked for meaning. The past had come undone in a single day, and ever since, the sea had stood between him and the truth. On his right shoulder, a scar still whispered of that night—new skin where once pain had bloomed like fire. But the wound that truly lingered was deeper. It was the memory of water. He remembered no names. No home. Just the haunting sensation of drowning in silence, screaming without sound, as light dissolved into liquid night. That memory lived inside him like a storm.

The wind howled up the cliffside, as if urging him to turn back. But he did not move. He had spent fifteen years waiting for this moment. Now he was ready. He stepped back, braced his feet into the slick rock, and shouted into the dark: "Har Har Mahadev!" The sky answered. A bolt of lightning carved it open and struck a tree behind him, the trunk splitting with flames. He smirked. Then he ran—and leapt. He plunged into the sea—dark, and endless—and disappeared beneath the waves.

✦

Fifteen Years Ago

When the boy first collapsed into Devadatta's arms, the hermit nearly dropped him—not from weight, but from what followed. A scream, unlike anything born of man, beast, or demon, tore through the cave mouth. The air had been calm one moment. The next, lightning slashed the sky as if the gods themselves had awakened in fury. Even after the boy's face healed, Devadatta never dared to look at it for too long.

And yet, in that instant, something deeper than instinct took hold. He turned, shielding the boy with his body, and stepped sideways—just as a second explosion shattered the air and a jagged shard of rock tore through the space where they had stood seconds earlier. He had moved without thinking. Too precisely. As if he had always known.

That was the moment he understood: this boy could not be left behind. Whatever he was—whatever storm he carried within—it was now Devadatta's burden too.

Without hesitation, the hermit lifted the unconscious child into his arms and began the long descent from the mountain, never once looking back.

Devadatta, a lifelong bachelor in his late thirties, was always clad in a saffron dhoti and a matching stole. Rudraksha beads circled his neck like a quiet oath. His life was one of austerity and discipline—anchored in silence, shaped by ritual, and defined by scripture. He lived alone in a secluded ashram northwest of the cave, nestled in a grove of peepal and Sal trees. It had been his home since boyhood, when he first arrived to study Jyotishya under the legendary sage, Shantinatha.

Shantinatha was no ordinary teacher. Revered across Lanka's spiritual circles, he was the living direct descendant of Dharmapaala—Dashanan's fourth disciple, the astrologer who read the threads of time. Under his guidance, Devadatta had flourished, mastering *Drishti*—the sacred gift of seeing across time and space. None among his peers could match his precision, his clarity. And yet, for all his foresight, nothing had ever unsettled him like the vision that came a week before he found the boy.

It began as a dream. Then came another. And another. Each more vivid than the last. He saw himself beneath the mountain temple as the cave above burst into flame. Every time he woke, soaked in sweat, a single certainty clung to him: this was not a dream. It was a summons. He tried to dismiss it. But the visions persisted—louder, sharper, undeniable. Finally, he confided in his Guru.

"It is not madness," Shantinatha said, stroking his long silver beard. "It is a call. And when nature calls the seer, he must go."

And so, Devadatta went.

He had been offering prayers at the temple when the cave roared. What followed defied all reason. And now, just a day later, he carried the unconscious boy through the ashram gates—his robes streaked with soot, his hands trembling from more than exhaustion. The moment they entered the courtyard, Shantinatha, seated in meditation with his students, stood. No words were exchanged. He walked straight towards them, his expression unreadable.

The boy had been placed on a medicinal bed of crushed leaves in the centre of the main hall. His breathing was steady. His skin warm. But there was something strange about him—something that shimmered beneath the surface, like his body was containing a storm.

Shantinatha's face darkened. "Take good care of him," he said softly, without removing his gaze. "Take care of Raavan."

✦

The ashram froze.

A silence fell so complete it seemed even the trees held their breath. One of the younger students dared to ask, his voice trembling, "Guruji… why did you call him Raavan? Is he… Dashanan? Is he back?"

Shantinatha turned to face the gathering students. His gaze was calm. His words were precise. "No. I called him Raavan not because of who he was... but because of what he did."

Then, turning to Devadatta, he said, "Tell them what you saw."

Devadatta met his Guru's eyes—and in that glance, he understood. Shantinatha had seen it too. Maybe even more. But he wanted Devadatta to speak. And only as much as needed.

So, Devadatta told them. Of the scream. The lightning. The cave exploding. And the boy who stood in the fire.

The students listened in stunned silence. Some stepped back in alarm. Others inched closer, curiosity warring with fear. A few peered into the boy's face, while others checked his pulse. One zealous student tried to pry open the boy's mouth, muttering that divine beings sometimes had forked tongues or split pupils.

Shantinatha, already halfway down the hall, spun suddenly on his heel—and roared, loud and sharp, directly at them. The students shrieked and scattered like startled birds.

Then he laughed. A deep, delighted, mischievous cackle.

This, too, was Shantinatha: austere in teaching, gentle in humour.

Raavan remained unconscious for two days after he arrived at the ashram. For two days, Devadatta did not leave his side.

He worked tirelessly, applying oils, smearing herbal pastes, placing heated stones at key chakras, and chanting sutras under his breath. The other students helped prepare decoctions and kept incense burning through the night, but it was Devadatta who remained—watching, waiting, whispering the boy back from the edge. And searching.

Through *Drishti*, Devadatta cast his vision backwards in time—like a thread lowered into the abyss of memory. What he witnessed shook him.

He saw Raavan's father—Ahindra—kneeling by a water tank, speaking to the boy with trembling kindness. He saw the boy's trust, the quiet obedience, his descent into the tank. Machinery hummed to life like a predator stirred from slumber.

Then came betrayal.

The gamma-ray emitter thundered. The boy's body convulsed in agony, skin cracking open as if struck by lightning from within. His mouth opened in a scream—but only bubbles rose. Devadatta flinched inside the trance, feeling the pain echo through time like a curse. Tears rolled down his cheeks.

Then came stillness.

The child's body floated, lifeless. Ahindra collapsed beside the tank, lesions erupting across his skin, clutching the glass as if sheer devotion might defy the gods.

Then came fire.

The tank exploded. A roar split the sky. A child stood atop a burning corpse, cloaked in flame—howling into the heavens. A storm born of sorrow.

Devadatta's eyes flew open, his breath ragged. He looked down. Raavan still lay before him—real, breathing, fragile and terrifying in equal measure. He touched the boy's neck.

A pulse. Faint. Steady.

Then, Raavan stirred. His eyelids fluttered open, uncertain and slow. They looked at each other—one stunned into stillness, the other reborn from fire. Raavan sat up. Slowly. Leaned forward. Wrapped his arms around Devadatta.

"Father," he whispered. "I'm hungry."

The word struck deeper than any blade. Devadatta could not speak. Could not move. He didn't know why the boy thought he was his father—but after what he had seen, he couldn't bear to correct him. Not now. Not yet.

He returned the embrace. Placed a hand on the boy's head.

"I'm here," he murmured. "I'm not going anywhere."

✦

Devadatta understood the limits of *Drishti*. It could show the past. It worked only on the living, or on those who had once been seen in life. Still, he plunged deeper, night after night, through fevered trance and exhausted meditation.

Slowly, the past took shape.

He saw the boy's birth. The house. The family. The lab. The cave. The machines.

But Ahindra's mind eluded him. He could not fathom how a father could offer his child to death. There was only one man who might understand such a paradox: Shantinatha.

But the Guru was in silence.

At nearly a hundred years old, Shantinatha often retreated into days—or even months—of stillness. No speech. No food. No water. Seated atop his sacred stone beyond the ashram, he became a statue carved from discipline alone.

The students whispered that his silence was the source of both his strength and his brilliance—even at a hundred years of age...

So Devadatta waited.

Raavan's recovery was slow but steady. His wounds faded, but fear lingered like ash in his breath. He refused to sleep without a flame nearby. Refused to bathe alone. Refused to speak to anyone but Devadatta.

He followed him everywhere—through prayers, through classes, into the quiet canopy of the forest. Every sunrise, they bathed in the river's cold bite. Every dusk, they returned with bundles of herbs and the hush of unspoken truths.

To the others, Raavan was an enigma.

To Devadatta, he was a question the world had forgotten how to ask.

Whispers stirred within the ashram. Students wondered aloud—had the boy summoned the lightning? Did his scream still echo in the clouds? Had the old stories returned?

Devadatta never confirmed it.

He didn't need to.

He believed.

But Raavan wasn't ready.

And neither was the world.

So Devadatta turned to the scrolls—to the forgotten glyphs of lost yugas, the archaic symbols etched into the margins of ancient sutras. To what had once been dismissed as myth... but now pulsed with meaning.

Where perhaps, even now, the secrets of gods and demons waited to be found.

It had been nearly a month since Raavan arrived at the ashram with Devadatta, whom he accepted, without hesitation, as his father. And Devadatta, a lifelong bachelor and hermit, accepted the role with quiet grace. He never corrected the boy. He never had to. In his heart, he had begun to believe a truth that wasn't true. Perhaps love did not require blood. Perhaps Raavan needed a father more than he needed facts.

What astonished Devadatta wasn't just the boy's resilience—it was his mind.

Raavan learned as if he were remembering.

Each evening, as they walked into the forest with students trailing behind, Devadatta would call out the names of plants, describe their properties, and point to roots and barks hidden beneath the undergrowth. But Raavan—always one step ahead, always listening—seemed to know already. He could unearth a sprig of medicinal creeper without instruction, identify poison by scent, and distinguish between herbs that even seasoned disciples struggled to tell apart.

What took others years, Raavan absorbed in weeks.

Perhaps it was instinct. Perhaps it was lineage. Or perhaps it was something deeper—the *Jeeva Tatva* itself, awakening ancestral knowledge within a vessel newly reborn.

Still, Devadatta never taught him directly. Not once.

In the ashram, teaching was a form of initiation. To guide a student was to bind oneself to their karma. And to join the ashram was not a matter of choice—it was a sacred surrender, sealed by an oath. A vow passed in whispers across generations. A vow Raavan was not ready to receive.

And Devadatta knew: the boy's path would one day lead him elsewhere.

✦

Devadatta had still not spoken to Shantinatha.

Thirty-one days had passed. Thirty-one days of deep, unbroken meditation. Devadatta had known his Guru for over three decades and still could not comprehend what truly occurred during those silences. When Shantinatha withdrew, he became more than still—he became elemental. Hunger, thirst, rain, time—none of them touched him.

And when the trance ended, he would vanish.

No one knew where he went.

Some of the younger students had tried using *Drishti* to follow him. Every attempt failed. Visions shattered into blankness. The gift turned to ash. One lost his mind. All were banished.

Drishti was never used on the Guru again.

A simple truth was accepted, though never spoken aloud: Shantinatha walked a path that no one else was allowed to see. He bore the full weight of the ashram's true purpose—a purpose older than any scripture and darker than most dared to imagine.

And one day, that burden would pass to Devadatta.

Everyone knew it. The youngest whispered it during prayer. The elders met it with silent nods. Devadatta was the heir. The chosen keeper of what lay beneath their teaching. The unspoken vow lived in him now.

And yet… he still felt unprepared.

Raavan had changed everything.

The boy, with his silence and storms, had cracked open a part of Devadatta that no mantra, no meditation, no discipline ever had.

What would Shantinatha say when he returned?

And more importantly,

What would he ask Devadatta to do next?

A full year had passed.

And still, Shantinatha had not spoken a word.

He remained seated upon the same stone slab, unmoving beneath the open sky. His eyes stayed closed. His breath, imperceptible. His presence had become legend. Birds nested near him, deer grazed at his feet, and the wind itself seemed to bend around him—as if the forest, too, dared not disturb whatever current of ancient awareness he had tuned himself to.

Devadatta visited him daily.

He would stand before the stone with palms folded, offering updates in hushed tones—the state of the gardens, the discipline of the students, the rhythm of the ashram's days. And always, inevitably, his voice would soften into concern, rising like a mist from the incense of reverence.

"I fear for your health, Guruji," he would whisper. "You are over a hundred. You've never meditated this long before."

On other days, he spoke of Raavan. Of his growth. Of his strange silence. Of the tension between innocence and something far older.

"Is he meant to stay here? Or is he destined for something beyond us?"

Shantinatha never answered. Not even a twitch of his eyelid. But Devadatta believed—no, knew—that his words reached their mark.

Still, unease gnawed at him.

He had seen it before. When Shantinatha emerged from long trances, he often disappeared into the forests, beyond the reach of sight or sound—only to return days later, his eyes holding mysteries no one dared ask about. But this time, the man was older. Thinner. Fragile.

What if he didn't return?

Raavan noticed.

Devadatta had become quieter. The light in his eyes dimmed. Though he didn't understand everything, Raavan understood enough. The man he called father was hurting.

And he wanted to help.

He had a plan.

✦

The next morning, Devadatta made his usual visit to the stone.

But the rock was empty.

Shantinatha was gone.

Though he had expected it, the sight struck Devadatta like a blow to the chest. He bowed low, offered a whispered prayer, and carried his dread into the day's teaching.

He didn't notice Raavan slip away.

For the first time in over a year, the boy did not follow him to the Ayurveda Hall. Instead, Raavan walked alone to the place where Shantinatha had sat. The stone was still warm. Raavan scanned the ground.

Footprints.

They led towards the dense forest across the river.

He followed them until the edge of the water.

Then he stopped.

The river wasn't deep. Nor wide. But to Raavan, it was an abyss. His body froze. His breath caught. The memories surged—dark water, the sealed tank, silent screams, the suffocating terror of dying without death. Pain without end. He had felt it all. Every second of it.

He stepped back.

Tears welled in his eyes—hot, silent.

Then came shame.

He had failed.

Head bowed, fists clenched, Raavan returned to the rock. But his resolve had not shattered. Only bent. He would not walk the forest—but perhaps... he could see it.

For months, Raavan had watched Devadatta teach the art of Drishti. He had sat behind the others, imitating their postures, learning the chants under his breath. He had never tried it until now.

He would do it.

For Devadatta.

For the man who had never left his side.

✦

Raavan sat cross-legged, facing the stone.

He closed his eyes.

And struggled.

His mind was in chaos—drowned in memory, flooded with fear, scattered by worry for Shantinatha and questions about himself. He couldn't find silence. His thoughts rose like weeds.

But he breathed. One breath. Then another.

And slowly, the noise receded.

Silence crept in—cool and soft, like mist on a summer morning. His thoughts fell like leaves from windblown branches. In the stillness, he felt himself lift—weightless, unbound, as though his mind no longer lived inside him, but everywhere.

He focused.

On Shantinatha.

And saw him.

Beneath a banyan tree, deep in the forest. Still. Breathing. Alive.

Raavan whispered the chant Devadatta had taught his students—to glimpse the past. He saw Shantinatha cross the river. Climb a hill. Sit beneath the tree.

Then he whispered a second chant—to glimpse the future.

And what he saw made him gasp.

His eyes snapped open.

He leapt to his feet.

And ran.

Not towards the river. But back to the ashram.

Shantinatha was in danger.

Raavan was gasping for breath by the time he reached the ashram. He didn't stop to explain. He rushed into the storeroom, snatched a handful of medicinal plants, bundled them inside a woollen blanket, and sprinted back towards the river. At the water's edge, he hurled the bundle across to the far bank—then jumped in.

The river, merciful that day, rose only to his neck. And that small mercy steadied him. He moved slowly, each step cautious, his body shivering but his resolve intact. He did not look back. Once ashore, he rubbed the crushed herbs over his arms, chest, and face, and began to run.

He ran as the wind chased him—tripping over roots, ducking under branches, legs bleeding, lungs burning. Every tree, every curve of the path, every whisper of leaf and branch matched what he had seen in his vision. He was close. Through the thick undergrowth, he saw the banyan tree. And there—seated beneath it—was Shantinatha. Eyes closed. Meditating. Unaware of the danger hovering above.

Raavan didn't hesitate. He lunged, slammed into the Guru, covered him with the blanket, and threw his own weight on top. Shantinatha, startled, began to resist—but then paused. In that moment, he used Drishti. What he saw made his breath hitch. A hive. Massive. Hidden in the canopy. Already detaching. In moments, the air would explode with rage.

Shantinatha didn't hesitate. He pulled Raavan fully under the blanket. The hive crashed to the ground with a wet, splintering thud. Then came the swarm. Thousands of bees rose like a black cloud, their droning roar deafening. They blanketed the forest, stinging the cloth with blind fury. The air buzzed with venom. Raavan shivered beneath the blanket, his breath short, his lungs aching.

Then Shantinatha smelled it—the herbs. Sharp. Bitter. Purposeful. Carefully chosen plants that repelled insects, neutralised venom, and calmed the skin. He blinked, realisation dawning. This boy hadn't stumbled into the moment. He had prepared for it.

When the buzzing finally faded and the silence returned, they emerged slowly from the shelter. Shantinatha looked at Raavan with a mix of astonishment and reverence. "Thank you, child," he said, placing a hand gently on Raavan's shoulder. "You saved me." But the warmth of gratitude cooled into curiosity. "You weren't taught Ayurveda," the Guru said slowly. "And yet you knew the plants." He paused, then asked the true question—his voice low, but sharp. "How did you know where I was?" His gaze pierced into Raavan's soul. "No one alive can use Drishti on me."

Raavan's heart dropped. He wasn't ready for this. If Shantinatha found out, he would be expelled. Devadatta would be forced to turn him away. He would be alone. Panic clawed up his chest. He searched for a lie.

"I was in the forest... looking for honey," he said, forcing each word. "I saw you by accident."

Shantinatha held his gaze. Then smiled—softly, enigmatically. "Even fate has accidents," he said. He placed a hand on Raavan's head, as though bestowing something unspoken. "Go back to the ashram. Tell no one you saw me."

Raavan nodded and turned away. Every step felt like betrayal. He wanted to run to Devadatta, to confess, to be held. But he didn't. He had lied—for the first time in his life.

✦

That night, Raavan didn't sleep. And when he did, he dreamed.

The dream was vivid—too vivid. It didn't feel like a dream at all. It felt like Drishti. Raavan saw a moonlit forest, its trees shimmering silver and swaying like silent watchers of the night. Beneath their canopy, a mob of armed men surged forward—axes, swords, and clubs glinting as they cut through the undergrowth. Their faces twisted in fury, their breaths shallow and fast. They were hunting someone. Shantinatha.

Raavan saw the old sage standing alone in a clearing, serene and unarmed. His white stole fluttered gently in the wind. The mob approached, snarling like wolves. But Shantinatha did not flinch. He didn't even raise a hand.

Raavan woke with a start. His chest heaved. Sweat clung to his skin. That wasn't a nightmare. That was a warning. He had to act.

His first instinct was to alert Devadatta. But then came the memory of his lie—the one Shantinatha had chosen to believe. If the truth were to surface, Devadatta would be forced to cast him out. So Raavan acted alone.

He crept into Shantinatha's private chamber and removed the old sword from its mount. Without another thought, he raced out of the ashram, down the path, towards the river. He crossed the water quickly, recklessly—no longer hesitating—and disappeared into the forest beyond.

For nearly an hour, he ran. The dream guided him, each landmark confirming he was on the right path. Then, as he reached the clearing, he froze. The lead bandit raised an axe over Shantinatha's neck. Raavan's breath caught.

But the axe missed. With elegant precision, Shantinatha moved—ducking, sidestepping, flowing like water through stone. Another blow came. He bent beneath it. A third. He spun away. His bare feet barely touched the earth. His robes danced like wind-wrapped mist. One by one, the bandits lunged—and one by one, they fell. Shantinatha evaded each strike as though he saw it before it arrived. His calm was unbroken.

Moments later, it was over. The attackers lay groaning across the forest floor, weapons scattered, rage extinguished. Shantinatha stood alone. Breath even. Eyes closed. Then he slowly sat beneath a tree.

Raavan stepped into the clearing, sword in hand. The old Guru looked up—and the calm vanished. His eyes burned with something Raavan had never seen in them before: fury. He rose slowly, voice sharp as flint. "How did you find me here?"

Raavan opened his mouth, but nothing came. "This place is secret," Shantinatha said, stepping closer. "No one is supposed to know it. Were you following me?"

Raavan shook his head, fast. "No. I saw it... in a dream." Shantinatha's gaze narrowed. "A dream?"

"I swear," Raavan whispered. "I only wanted to help you."

The silence that followed cut deeper than any blade. Then, without a word, Shantinatha grabbed Raavan by the wrist and began walking. Not gently.

Raavan stumbled behind him, trying to explain, but the old man said nothing. His grip was iron. They moved through the trees in silence. And Raavan, through blurred eyes, understood. He was being taken back. Back to the ashram. Back to face his truth.

And he knew—this might be the end of the only home he had ever known.

By the time Shantinatha returned, the entire ashram was awake. Devadatta had raised the alarm, summoning the disciples into the courtyard beneath the breaking dawn. He had long feared this moment—the day Raavan would leave. But he had always imagined it would come by choice, not by decree. He stood before the students, his voice trembling. "Thank you," he said, eyes wet. "For helping me search for him. I… I only wish I could have said goodbye."

Then the courtyard doors creaked open. All heads turned. Shantinatha stepped in, Raavan in tow, his hand clamped tightly around the boy's wrist. Devadatta gasped. He took a step forward, arms half-lifted to embrace the boy—but Shantinatha pulled him back, holding him like a prisoner awaiting sentence. Devadatta sank to his knees, unable to meet his Guru's eyes. His voice cracked. "Please… don't."

Shantinatha said nothing. He led Raavan to the centre of the courtyard, then turned to the gathered students. "This boy," he said, his voice like steel scraping stone, "has broken the sacred rules of our order. He followed me into the forest—to a place meant only for the Guru of this ashram. A place none of you should ever know." Gasps rippled through the assembly.

One student stepped forward. "Guruji, I saw Raavan go to sleep. He never left his room." Another added, "Devadatta was with him all evening. He couldn't have followed you." Shantinatha narrowed his eyes. He turned back to Raavan. His voice softened to a whisper. "Then there's only one way you could've known." He reached out and drew his thumb across Raavan's forehead. A glow ignited—gentle, golden.

The crowd fell silent. Shantinatha staggered back a step, as if struck by a force beyond flesh. In that moment, he saw it all—Raavan was ready. His purpose had begun to awaken.

But he couldn't say that.

So he chose to lie.

He would claim Raavan had broken the code that he must leave the ashram.

The law had to be honoured.

Shantinatha straightened.

"He must go."

Devadatta stumbled forward and collapsed at his Guru's feet. "Please," he whispered through tears. "He's still a child. He has no family. No home. He cannot survive outside." Tears spilt freely now. "I'll take responsibility. I'll teach him. Guide him. Protect him."

Shantinatha's expression was unreadable. He looked at Devadatta for a long, aching moment. Then, gently, he said, "It is because of your love that he must leave. You cannot protect him from his fate."

Devadatta froze. He didn't agree with his Guru. But he obeyed him.

Raavan's eyes filled. His face was pale, lips trembling. But he walked to Devadatta, knelt beside him, and whispered, "Don't cry. I'll be okay." Devadatta pulled him close, his arms wrapped tightly around his body, which was shaking. Around them, the students stood in solemn silence. Raavan, who had kept to himself for months, was now—if only in parting—their brother.

But Shantinatha stood unmoved. "Back to your rooms," he commanded. The students obeyed, casting one last glance at the boy they were losing.

Shantinatha turned and disappeared into the darkness. When he returned, he carried a small bundle—Raavan's only belongings. He walked to the boy, took his hand, and without a word, led him to the gates.

Devadatta stood helpless. Raavan looked back once. Their eyes met. So much left unsaid.

✦

Then the door closed. Its sound echoed in Devadatta's ears. And with it, ended Raavan's first home.

Devadatta remained kneeling in the courtyard, his eyes locked on the ashram gate that had just closed behind Raavan. His breath was shallow, his chest unbearably heavy. In that moment, he had lost his son—in every way that mattered. His fingers trembled. His eyes, red with grief, searched for answers that would not come.

Shantinatha approached quietly and extended a hand. Devadatta took it. He rose slowly, unsteadily, like a tree reeling from a storm. Shantinatha placed a hand on his shoulder. "You were fortunate," he said softly, "to walk beside him, even for a short while." There was something in the Guru's eyes—an ember of knowledge, of truth, that Devadatta did not yet understand.

Devadatta bowed, voice low. "Guruji… what do you know about Raavan that I don't?" Shantinatha stepped forward and touched Devadatta's forehead. His fingers shimmered with warm, golden light.

Devadatta's eyes rolled back. His head tilted skyward. And in a single surge of vision, the veil was lifted. He saw it all. The fire of Raavan's creation. The wars yet to come. The oceans he would cross, the burdens he would carry, the souls he would touch. Raavan was not merely a boy. He was a bearer of something ancient. A storm given form. A purpose wrapped in pain.

When the vision faded, tears of awe streamed down Devadatta's cheeks. "But he's not ready," he whispered, his voice cracking. "He needs guidance. He needs time. We must bring him back…" His emotions had clouded his mind and sight—blinding him to what the vision had already revealed. Shantinatha said nothing. He simply closed his eyes and placed his palm once more on Devadatta's head. This time, there was no vision. Only silence. Stillness. Then—light.

Devadatta's body began to glow. His breath slowed. His eyes dimmed—then flared open, blazing with clarity. In that moment, he transcended. His Sūk⊠ma Śarīra—his subtle body—rose from flesh, drifting beside Shantinatha, and together they floated over the ashram, gazing down on their mortal selves.

They soared like thoughts across the land—weightless, silent. Forests blurred beneath them. Rivers shimmered like snakes of light. "Where are we?" Devadatta asked, breathless. Shantinatha pointed to a forest below, dense and gleaming with emerald light. A small hill rose at its heart.

"That hill," he said, "is not mere stone. It is a fragment of Dronagiri—the mountain Lord Hanuman lifted during the Lanka war. When it broke, a shard fell here. And from its soil grow the rarest herbs on earth. Some of these… Pashupati used to create Raavan's Jeeva Tatva." Devadatta gazed down, reverent.

"For generations," Shantinatha said, "Dharmapaala's line has guarded this place—the stream, the hill, the plants. And we will continue to protect it… until the day comes when it must be burned down for the greater good. That responsibility now passes to you. Along with the duty to elect the final Guru of this ashram."

As the words settled in Devadatta's soul, they began to descend.

Their spirits returned to flesh.

Devadatta now wore the white robes of a Guru. Shantinatha, once more in saffron, smiled. "It is done," he said. "You are now the Guru of this ashram. Guard the hill. Guard the flame." And with that, the old master turned and walked away. Devadatta did not follow. In the space of a breath, he had lost his son—and now, his Guru.

✦

That evening, deep in the forest, Raavan gathered branches. He was building a small shelter—just close enough to glimpse Devadatta when he came to harvest herbs. He wasn't ready to let go. Not yet. He still carried one unanswered question. Who was his mother?

He had asked before. And each time, Devadatta only said, "When the time is right." But the time had run out.

As he stacked the final branch, a rustle in the underbrush made him freeze. He turned, ready to flee, expecting a wild beast. Instead, Shantinatha emerged from the trees. He looked different. No white robes. No staff. Just the simple clothes of a hermit.

Raavan stiffened. "Devadatta is a bachelor," Shantinatha said, without preamble. "He took a vow of celibacy. You're not his son. You never were."

Raavan's world shattered. He dropped to his knees.

Shantinatha stepped closer and placed a hand on the boy's shoulder. "You feel lost," he said gently. "But you are exactly where destiny placed you. You were born for a reason—perhaps to correct something left unfinished. Your road will be long. You will ache. You will lose. You will wander. And one day... you will die."

He paused.

"But right before the moment you die, you will know why you were born. And when that day comes, you will be at peace."

Raavan did not understand what Shantinatha said. He wiped his tears and asked the one question that was burning within him. "Will I ever meet my mother?" he asked, his voice trembling.

Shantinatha hid his pain behind a gentle, comforting smile. "No," he said softly.

He opened his arms. Raavan stepped into them. Shantinatha held him close, resting the boy's head against his chest—like a father might a son.

Neither spoke.

Only the wind moved, and the forest listened.

Then Shantinatha pulled back. His eyes searched Raavan's. There was no suspicion. Only awe. He exhaled slowly.

"Raavan," he whispered, "no one alive can do what you did." He paused again. This time, his voice was almost reverent. "Tell me, child… how did you use **Drishti**?"

CHAPTER 04

Ten years had passed since Devadatta became the Guru of the ashram. In all that time, he rarely spoke to anyone, except, in his thoughts, to Raavan. The boy he once called son was gone, yet never truly absent. Devadatta spent his days in meditation, as if every answer he sought now whispered to him in stillness. And every evening, he would walk to the riverbank to listen.

At first, there had only been screams, raw, guttural cries echoing across the water. Later, the screams were followed by flashes of lightning. Though Devadatta had seen all of it unfold in his Drishti, he never missed an evening by the river. It was Raavan. Everyone in the ashram knew it. The boy was training with Shantinatha, deep within the forest.

Devadatta never once crossed the river to see him. Not since the day Raavan was expelled. He longed to embrace him, to teach him, to call him son again, but he never did. He knew the boy's destiny. He knew his role in it. And so, he watched in silence. He used Drishti to observe Raavan each day—eating, training, weeping, healing, transforming. It was enough. It had to be.

Across the river, in an ancient temple swallowed by trees, Raavan lived and trained under Shantinatha. Gone was the jovial sage he remembered from the ashram. This Shantinatha was austere, relentless. A master of Drishti, Ayurveda, and Kalarippayattu—and now, Raavan's teacher.

Raavan had no one else. No family. No friends. So, he gave his Guru everything—obedience, reverence, love. His training began the day he was cast out. Shantinatha wasted no time.

Every morning before sunrise, Raavan fetched cold water from the river and bathed. From dawn until noon, he lived like a Brahmin. From noon to sunset, he became a warrior—practising Drishti and Kalarippayattu until his limbs burned and bled. But his trials truly began after nightfall.

That was when he trained in Rava—the scream that summoned lightning.

Shantinatha knew time was short. He had taken two decades to master the three disciplines; Raavan had only ten years to master them all—and something far rarer.

Remarkably, Raavan did. By the age of twenty, he had become Shantinatha's equal in recitation, combat, and Drishti. A prodigy unlike any before him. Yet, when it came to Rava, he failed. Again, and again. And it broke him.

Not because he craved power. Not because he feared failure. But because he wanted to be seen and loved by his Guru.

Raavan screamed until his throat bled. He screamed until he fainted. On those nights, Shantinatha tended to him with the care of a father—but never the warmth of one.

Raavan never stopped trying. But Shantinatha never gave him what he longed for. Because he wasn't trying to raise a son, he was forging a storm.

✦

Shantinatha, on the other hand, was fading. His body had grown thin, his steps slower, but his will remained ironclad. He had one task left before death could claim him: to complete Raavan's training. He had tried everything to teach him Rava—the primal scream that summoned lightning—but failed every time. He could sense Raavan's confidence eroding, his spirit beginning to crack. The boy was starting to doubt that the power within him could ever be awakened.

Desperate, Shantinatha turned to the one gift he still possessed: Drishti. He peered back into Raavan's past—into that terrible night in the cave with Ahindra. The moment Raavan had truly screamed. The first time, lightning obeyed. What he saw made his blood chill. The rage. The pain. That scream had not been a learned response—it was fury incarnate. It was the howl of betrayal and the shattering of innocence. It wasn't taught. It was born.

Shantinatha opened his eyes, trembling. He now knew the truth: Rava was not a skill to be learned. It was a storm waiting to be broken open.

He rose and walked into the sanctum of the ancient temple. The air was cool and heavy. In the centre stood alone Shiva Lingam, silent witness to centuries of devotion. Shantinatha bowed low and whispered, "Shankara… give me strength. Heal the boy from the wounds I may leave. I place his future in your hands." He smeared his fingers with Vibhuti from the base of the Lingam and stepped back into the light.

Raavan was near the temple pond, practising with the Urumi. Flexible blades cut through the air like liquid flame—deadly, elegant, relentless. He moved with the precision of years of training. But beneath the power, there was sorrow. He had mastered Drishti, and Kalarippayattu—but not Rava. He had done everything to earn Shantinatha's pride. And yet, what he longed for most—his Guru's affection—remained just out of reach.

Then Shantinatha called his name.

Raavan turned, sweat clinging to his brow. Shantinatha walked slowly towards him and, for the first time in years, embraced him.

"My time has come," the old man said softly. "I won't be here to see your victory. But you'll find me, whenever you need, within yourself." He pressed the Vibhuti to Raavan's forehead and pointed to the Lingam in the centre of the pond. "He is the only one who will never leave your side. When the road ahead is lost… call upon him. He will answer."

Then, with a quiet "Shankara," Shantinatha began to tie his shikha.

Raavan dropped to his knees. "Don't say that. Please. Tell me what herb you need. I'll find it. Just don't talk of dying—not yet."

But Shantinatha only smiled. "It's not illness, Raavan. It's time. And time comes for all."

Raavan was still, as if understanding what Shantinatha was trying to say. Raavan, who was still in his youth, did not think about death yet.

"Take me to the water, I need to bathe first," Shantinatha said. "We can talk about my death later."

Raavan silently agreed and helped his Guru down the temple steps and into the pond. Shantinatha waded slowly towards the Lingam at its centre. The setting sun cast a golden glow across the water.

He turned west. He dipped once. Then twice.

On the third dip, he turned to Raavan, and their eyes met one final time.

Then—silence. Shantinatha did not rise.

Raavan stared, breath frozen in his chest. The ripples spread across the pond, touched the stone edges, and returned... but the surface stilled again.

Shantinatha was gone.

Raavan stood there for a long time, unmoving.

He panicked when he saw nothing beneath the surface of the water. He stepped down to the last stone ledge of the pond, peering through the lily leaves and rippling surface, hoping to glimpse Shantinatha. But the water was silent. Still. Empty.

He scrambled up the steps for a better view—nothing. He ran around the pond's edge, heart pounding, eyes scanning. On his second round, he saw it—a figure beneath the lilies near the northern bank. He raced down the steps. Even standing at full height, he couldn't reach him.

Without pause, he sprinted to the temple and tore through his equipment for a rope. He bolted back, the fastest he'd ever run, thorns slicing his feet, sweat burning his eyes. At the northern ledge, he tied the rope to a rock, shoved it towards the lower steps, and with a final push, it tumbled down and landed on the last step, partly submerged in water.

Raavan tied the other end of the rope around his waist, took a deep breath, and dove in.

The clear water tore apart the lilies as he entered. It stung his eyes and filled his nose. He flailed, rising for a breath, then dove again—towards the still body of his Guru.

Shantinatha floated beneath the surface, eyes closed, wrapped in a stillness that terrified Raavan. He waded through the water and grabbed Shantinatha's arm. They rose together—but stopped. Raavan looked down.

His Guru's leg was entangled in thick stems.

He dove again, struggling to free himself. The stems wouldn't budge. He yanked and twisted, but the air in his lungs thinned. He swam up—gasped—and went down once more. Still entangled. Still breathless.

Then, something shifted.

He saw movement. Shantinatha's eyes opened—calm, clear. In his hand was the rope.

✦

Raavan's face lit up. He opened his mouth in relief—only to let water rush in. He gagged, panicked. His body thrashed, limbs weakening. The rope had slipped from his own waist—now only his Guru held it.

He reached forward, desperate to grab the rope or his Guru, but a sudden push—a pressure, like an invisible current—shoved him away.

Raavan sank.

Entangled in stems, limbs numb, lungs on fire, he drifted downward. The pond above glimmered faintly, moonlight flickering through floating leaves.

Still, his gaze remained fixed on the mandapam at the centre of the pond—on the silent Shiva Lingam.

He didn't think of escape. He didn't scream. He didn't curse. He simply stared, waiting for Shantinatha to return and pull him free.

His chest burned. His vision blurred. Consciousness thinned.

But even now, in the drowning dark, he trusted his Guru.

His last act was not to struggle—but to see.

With the final flicker of his mind, Raavan used Drishti—not to save himself, but to make sure Shantinatha was safe.

And then—everything stopped.

The pond fell silent. Still. Timeless.

Raavan's body floated in water, hair billowing around his face, eyes closed, skin pale.

In the realm of vision, he saw Shantinatha—drying his robes, looking calmly at the sunset, holding the rope in one hand.

No panic. No urgency.

Raavan's chest did not tighten in fear.

It ignited in fury.

Why hadn't he come?

The surface trembled. The stillness cracked.

Something ancient stirred within him.

The fear of water vanished. The pain receded. His limbs, moments ago numb, pulsed with a new force. Not strength of muscle—but of will.

His eyes snapped open. They had changed—gone dark as obsidian, flecked with red. He sank deeper, then bent his knees.

His feet touched the muddy bottom.

And Raavan stood.

He looked up at the mandapam once more, joined his palms, and bowed.

A silence passed.

Then, he turned away from the Lingam, eyes blazing with fury, and bent low.

With a burst of motion, he leapt.

The stems tore like threads.

The roots ripped from the soil.

Raavan shot upward—through lilies, through water, through light.

And then—

He broke through the water's surface.

Ten feet into the air.

A cry burst from his lips—not a scream, but something deeper, guttural, laced with rage and revelation.

The air quivered.

The pond rippled.

Clouds swirled.

And somewhere, high above—lightning stirred.

The first true spark of Rava had awoken.

✦

Shantinatha stood by the pond, offering his prayers to the setting sun, his rope tightly wound around his forearm. His posture was proud. Serene. Though he had not used Drishti, he didn't need to. He knew Raavan would rise. He had trained the boy. He had prepared him.

And he was right.

Behind him, a shadow emerged—taller, darker, changed.

Raavan landed with a splash behind his Guru, steam rising from his wet form. His eyes were entirely black—not just the pupils. His body trembled with fury, fists clenched, breath ragged. This was not the boy Shantinatha had trained. This was something else. Something ancient.

Shantinatha turned. The pride on his face vanished.

He had only heard of such eyes—from his own Guru, in whispers.

A terrible, reverent silence fell between them.

Then Raavan charged.

He leapt through the air with the grace of a warrior, fist aimed for Shantinatha's face. Shantinatha ducked. The punch missed by an inch.

Another came—closer. And another.

Each blow roared with power. Shantinatha dodged them all, but just barely. He could feel the heat pulsing from Raavan's skin. Then, Raavan let out a scream—and lightning cracked through the sky, striking the earth where Shantinatha had stood just a moment earlier.

Shantinatha knew what was coming next.

As Raavan inhaled for another scream, Shantinatha kicked him squarely in the chest. Raavan stumbled back, falling hard onto the stone.

But before he could rise—snap!—a rope coiled around his neck.

He gasped.

The noose tightened.

He clawed at it, choking. His feet flailed against the ground.

The other end of the rope hung from a banyan branch. Shantinatha, now far behind, was pulling it with both hands, muscles taut, face solemn.

Raavan struggled.

His eyes glowed like burning coals.

"I kept my promise," Shantinatha said, his voice shaking. "I taught you Rava."

Raavan thrashed harder. His Guru couldn't hold the rope much longer. But if he let go, Raavan—consumed by rage—might kill him.

Shantinatha began speaking. Softly. Urgently.

He reminded Raavan of their first lessons together, of early mornings in the forest, of meditating under the Bodhi tree, of the time Raavan healed a sick deer without hesitation.

Still, nothing changed.

The boy's fury did not wane. The rope cut into his neck, but his eyes burned with even deeper rage.

Then Raavan looked down—and in his hand, a sword appeared.

It shimmered into existence.

Its hilt gleamed with ancient gems, the grip wrapped in dark leather. The blade was massive—too long for any ordinary man. In its steel, cryptic inscriptions glowed faintly.

Shantinatha froze.

He had only seen such a weapon in prophecy.

Raavan raised it high—and with a single, effortless swing, sliced through the banyan branch.

The rope snapped.

He landed on his feet, blade in hand. The sword's tip kissed the ground. It was too large even for him.

Then, Raavan dropped it—and it vanished before it touched stone.

He lunged again, fists flying. Shantinatha dodged, but slower this time. He was weakening. As Raavan advanced, Shantinatha used the rope like a whip—looping it around Raavan's arms mid-strike. One punch. A loop. Another. Tighter. Raavan's arms were bound.

Shantinatha kicked him in the chest once more. This time, Raavan flew backwards, crashing near the pond's edge, suspended again. Shantinatha dropped to one knee, clutching the rope. He looked up at Raavan—dangling, restrained.

"Stop," he said.

"You've won.

You've done it.

You have Rava."

Raavan didn't respond.

He snarled, thrashed, eyes still red.

Then, he looked to the sky—and screamed.

Shantinatha's eyes widened. "No!"

A bolt of lightning tore through the heavens.

Shantinatha rolled away—barely.

The lightning struck where he had been standing. The impact burned his arm, seared the stone. He gasped, eyes filled with pain.

Still, he held the rope.

Still, he would not give up.

He crawled to the edge of the pond and peered down. Raavan was still hanging there, eyes wild, limbs jerking.

Another scream.

Another bolt.

This time, Shantinatha did not move.

He simply looked Raavan in the eyes and whispered:

"Shankara."

The sky split.

Lightning slammed down.

It struck Shantinatha directly.

Raavan saw it all.

He watched his Guru take the strike.

He saw Shantinatha close his eyes and release the rope.

Raavan fell.

He hit the water with a crash, sank to the bottom of the pond, limbs limp.

The rage drained from him.

His eyes returned to normal.

The silence in the pond wrapped around him like a burial cloth.

And then—it all came back.

Every moment. Every scream. Every strike. Every step. Every word Shantinatha had spoken.

Raavan opened his eyes underwater, staring up at the surface, heart shattered.

He realised what had happened.

He had used Rava.

And he had killed his Guru with it.

✦

The sun had long set, and dusk was breathing its last. Raavan emerged from the pond, ashamed, shivering, haunted by the storm he had unleashed. A heavy silence hung over the temple as he pulled himself up the steps, breathless, soaked in sorrow.

The air reeked of burned flesh and smouldering hair. It led him to the still form by the water's edge.

Shantinatha lay on his stomach, his robes charred, smoke rising from his body. Raavan dropped to his knees. With trembling hands, he turned his Guru over. His face was blistered, the skin peeling in folds, but beneath the ruin, a calm remained—as if peace had taken root in pain.

Raavan let out a wail that cracked the sky. A bolt of lightning struck the pond behind him.

And then—Shantinatha stirred. His eyes fluttered open. A faint, broken smile crossed his lips.

"See?" he whispered. "You used Rava."

Raavan wept. He clutched Shantinatha close, sobbing into his chest, words of apology spilling between breaths.

"I'll fetch herbs—I can still save you."

But Shantinatha only smiled deeper.

"No," he said, voice thin as wind, "my task in this life is complete. It's time I leave this body behind."

Guilt tore through Raavan. He looked away. "I did this to you..."

"You did nothing," Shantinatha interrupted gently. "I saw the bolt. I chose not to move."

He coughed, blood trailing down his lips. He reached for Raavan's ear, pulled him close.

"Stay here. Five more years. Your destiny will find you."

Raavan's tears splashed onto his master's face.

"You've only tasted one power," Shantinatha murmured. "More will come. Master them. Use them wisely."

Raavan kept crying. He didn't care for powers or destiny. All he wanted was this man, alive.

Shantinatha placed his hand on Raavan's cheek, eyes dimming. "When you scream, see your target. The lightning will obey."

They could no longer see each other in the dark. But Shantinatha, with his last strength, traced the lines of Raavan's face like scripture.

"I'm proud of you," he said. "You're the finest student I've ever had."

Lightning cracked again, striking the very branch Raavan once cut with his conjured sword.

Shantinatha smiled at the sound.

"I go now," he whispered, voice fading.

With that, he closed his eyes.

Raavan clutched him, broken and howling into the void.

Across the river, Devadatta stood motionless by the water, watching the smoke rise, listening to the scream.

A scream that echoed through the mountains and clouds.

A scream that shook the Gods.

A scream that was no longer just sound—

It was Rava.

✦

Raavan lived alone in the temple after Shantinatha's death. The jungle, once an exile, had become his crucible. Each morning, he wielded his Urumi, the whip-blade slicing air with a rhythm born of obsession. Each evening, he practised Rava, his voice calling out across the valley in screams that split silence and sky alike. Days bled into years. Five years.

In that solitude, something monstrous and divine was being forged.

His strength had become unnatural. He could lift boulders that would crush an elephant, leap across ravines like a Rakshasa born of wind, and sprint with the raw grace of a cheetah hunting. But these were not gifts—they were discoveries, buried in his blood. When lightning answered his scream, tearing across the twilight sky, Raavan knew he was no longer just a boy in exile. He was becoming something else. Something ancient.

Far across the river, Devadatta watched through Drishti. He saw the transformation unfold in silence: the scream, the bolts, the sheer force in Raavan's movements. It made him proud. And it terrified him. Though fifteen years had passed since he had exiled the boy, Devadatta still loved him like a son. He had wanted to guide him after Shantinatha's passing. But the oath that bound him as Guru chained him in place. All he could do was watch and wait.

Like Shantinatha before him, Devadatta now meditated for days upon the rock near the riverbank. The students saw little of their Guru, and on one such evening, he vanished entirely.

That same night, Raavan was by the forest pond, practising Rava. He had learned to shape the lightning and aim it. But he had not yet learned to stop it once called. As the sun dipped beyond the mountains, he ended his training, bathed in the river, and returned to the temple.

But the forest wasn't right.

The chirping of crickets and hoots of owls—night's familiar song—was absent. In its place was motion. Monkeys leapt in agitation, tree to tree. In the distance, yellow flickers lit the night—not fireflies, but torches. And something in his gut turned cold.

Raavan ran.

He raced through the forest towards the riverbank, heart pounding. Through the trees, he saw the ashram glowing orange, silhouetted by firelight. He stopped, breath caught, remembering the place he once called home.

At the riverbank, he saw him—Devadatta—fighting in a blur of white. He looked like Shantinatha reborn, younger but just as radiant, his robe stained with ash and moonlight. Around him, chaos. Bandits. Armed with strange rods that spewed flame and sound. Each blast is like a war cry from the underworld.

But Devadatta danced through them like a god, dodging before the fire erupted, slashing with precision, killing without pause.

Raavan's heart surged. Devadatta! He leapt into the fray, landing with thunderous force. His punch shattered a bandit's ribs—the man shrieked and fell. Devadatta turned—but his gaze was blank, unrecognising. The man Raavan once knew did not see him.

The moment stunned Raavan.

It had been fifteen years.

He moved towards Devadatta, calling out—but then pain shot through his shoulder. His right deltoid burned, hot and wet. Blood flowed. He screamed—calling for the sky.

Nothing.

Again, he screamed, louder. No lightning came.

A sharper pain pierced his chest. Something had gone straight through. He staggered, fell to his knees, eyes wide in disbelief. The bandits kept fighting. Devadatta kept moving. But Raavan was already slipping.

"Devadatta..." he tried to say, but blood filled his mouth.

He crawled.

Every inch was agony—his chest gushed with each heartbeat, limbs heavy and numb, skin stung like bees gone mad. His breath came in rattles, his sight blurred. But he dragged himself forward, hand outstretched, leaving behind a trail of blood in the dirt.

He reached Devadatta.

A blinding spark. A crack. Something struck his back.

Raavan collapsed, breath stolen. His mouth gaped, but no sound came. Blood pooled beneath him.

And there, as Devadatta kept fighting—never turning, never knowing—Raavan's body gave in.

The forest fell into silence.

✦

Raavan jolted awake, drenched in sweat. Gasping, he looked around – he was lying on his straw bed, tucked in the temple's shadowy corner. A dream. Just a dream. Yet everything had felt so real.

He stared at his hands, then at his chest. Intact. No wounds. No blood. Still breathing.

He rose and stepped outside. The forest stretched before him—still and familiar, yet uneasy. Distant flames flickered just like they had in the dream. The air trembled with the same tension. He turned, sprinted back into the temple, and grabbed his Urumi. He lit a torch and began gathering more weapons into a cloth bag.

Then he paused.

His death. He had seen it—lived it—moments ago. His eyes widened, but his feet didn't stop. There was no fear, only clarity. The thought of dying stirred nothing in him. But the thought of seeing Devadatta again—that brought warmth to his chest.

From what he recalled, there were at least thirty attackers. He packed with precision, slung the bag over his shoulder, gripped the torch, and dashed into the night.

The forest was darker than usual, howls echoing between trees, branches cracking like bones. But something was off. The noise wasn't coming from the riverbank, where he had seen the battle in his vision. It came from deeper within the forest—the opposite direction.

He froze.

If the dream was a warning, the riverbank should be where destiny awaited. And yet, that path was calm, untouched.

Then he heard it: a deafening boom, just like in the dream—followed by the cry of an elephant. Not a call—a scream.

He didn't hesitate. He turned towards the cry and ran.

He left behind the hope of seeing Devadatta, choosing instead the unknown disaster unfolding in the shadows. After nearly fifteen years in the forest, he could tell the difference in animal cries. That trumpet was a wail, heavy with pain. And if those thunderous instruments were the same as in his vision, then time was running out.

He ran faster.

So, the flame in his torch began to flicker. From a distance, he looked like a streak of golden light—a serpent of fire slithering through the dark.

The trees around him became familiar. This was the same path he'd walked the night he saw Shantinatha fight—just hours before his expulsion. His memory surged back: the elegance of Shantinatha's movements, the devastating calm in his strength.

The torch gave one final sputter.

And then darkness swallowed him whole.

Raavan arrived at the same clearing where, years ago, he had watched Shantinatha fight. Now, it was alive with fire and noise—torches lit the perimeter, freshly felled trees lay in stacks, and hunter dogs strained against leashes. Nearby, an elephant lay dead.

He moved silently to the animal's side. Its massive forehead bore several wounds, still bleeding. Something about them tugged at his memory. He crouched and inserted a finger into one of the wounds—and pulled out a piece of metal.

His eyes narrowed. The bandits' weapons fired those pieces.

Footsteps approached. Raavan slipped behind the elephant, crouching low. A group of fifteen men appeared, some carrying baskets brimming with uprooted plants, others armed with axes and spears. They dumped the baskets near the logs and turned back towards the woods.

Raavan crept forward and examined the plants. His breath caught.

Sandhanakarani.

He had never seen it in the wild before, but the leaf's shape and the stem colour matched perfectly with the drawings in Shantinatha's old manuscripts. This was one of the four divine herbs said to have been used by Sushena to revive Lakshmana. And it was Shantinatha's sacred duty to protect the forest that nurtured such plants—rare, powerful, and ancient.

Now, everything from his dream made sense: the intruders in the sacred forest, the battle, Devadatta's rage.

But one detail still didn't fit. In his dream, the fight was near the riverbank—yet here, in the heart of the forest, stood the real threat.

A growl shattered his thoughts.

One of the leashed dogs had seen him—barking, snapping at the air. The others joined in, and soon the bandits turned. They returned to the clearing and released the dogs.

Raavan stood, cornered. The dogs lunged towards him. He could have drawn his Urumi and sliced them down in silence. But he didn't.

Instead, he picked up a thick tree branch and hurled it at the dogs. The log crashed to the ground just ahead of them, thudding like a warning. The pack scattered—yelping, retreating into the trees.

He didn't kill them.

But the damage was done.

The bandits now knew exactly where he was.

✦

They raised their weapons and circled him.

Raavan remained where he stood, his Urumi coiled in one hand, a cloth bag in the other. He looked at them with calm eyes.

"I'll ask only once," he said gently. "Leave the Sandhanakarani. Leave the logs. Go to the ashram and surrender."

The bandits looked at each other—and burst out laughing.

To them, he was just a solitary hermit in his mid-twenties. Shoulder-length hair partly tied, a white dhoti in Kalarippayattu warrior style, a janeyu across his chest. Tall, strong, but not monstrous. A gentle moustache, a peaceful smile—even now.

He was alone.

But one bandit, standing behind Raavan, lost patience. With a grunt, he hurled his axe towards the back of Raavan's head.

Raavan didn't flinch.

As the axe neared, he flicked his wrist. The Urumi snapped open mid-air—three razor-thin blades slicing through the weapon like it was paper. The shattered axe head fell in fragments around him.

The laughter stopped.

The bandits stared, stunned.

The man who had thrown the axe roared and grabbed another from a comrade, charging at Raavan with a few others behind him. Others raised weapons from afar, preparing to strike.

Raavan waited.

When the attacker was only feet away, he smiled.

He dodged the strike with fluid grace and lashed his Urumi. The triple blades sang through the air, severing the man's arm clean from his body. The axe fell. The bandit kept running a few steps, looked down, and screamed when he saw his severed limb on the ground.

Before the echo of his wail faded, Raavan disarmed three more—in a whirlwind of slashes. Blood spattered his face, but his gaze remained calm, focused.

Panic set in.

Then a voice barked, "Attack together!"

The bandits regrouped, forming two concentric circles around him—the inner ring armed with axes, the outer with spears.

Raavan stood alone in the middle, his Urumi coiled once more.

Waiting.

His other hand slid inside the cloth bag. Calmly, he drew a second Urumi, gripping one in each hand.

"I'll ask again," he said, voice even. "Leave the forest. Surrender at the ashram."

The leader sneered and barked an order.

Axes flew. Spears lunged.

Raavan didn't move. His eyes shimmered as he summoned Drishti. The world slowed. Attacks unravelled before they landed. In a blur of motion, he intercepted every strike—blades singing, sparks erupting as metal clashed mid-air. He sliced spearheads from their shafts and swatted axes aside like autumn leaves. It was a deadly dance in firelight.

Then he screamed.

Lightning answered, striking down a hidden archer before his arrow could fly. The bandit leader froze. That scream—it wasn't human. This was no hermit. His resolve cracked. He dropped his spear and fled.

Raavan kept fighting—not to kill, but to disable. Each strike targeted only the weapon-bearing arm. Cries of pain rang through the clearing. One by one, the men fell—some broken, others unconscious.

The remaining bandits adapted. They doused the torches, casting a cloak of darkness over the forest. Their black clothing melted into the night.

A stone struck Raavan on the back of his head. Sharp pain flared. He spun around but saw nothing—only darkness.

More stones came, pelting him from all directions. Raavan winced. So did the bandits. No one could tell where the stones came from… or where they vanished.

Raavan used Drishti—but the sight showed only darkness. No forms. No movement. Just a thick, impenetrable void.

He punched. Kicked. Fought the air. Every strike landed on nothing.

Then a chain whipped around his neck.

The bandit leader had returned, striking from behind. He yanked the chain tight. Raavan choked, breath strangled. More men rushed in. Arrows rained. Limbs pinned him. He couldn't move. Couldn't breathe.

An arrow scraped his shoulder.

The dream… It's happening again.

Sadness gripped him—not for death, but for not seeing Devadatta one last time.

Then a rock struck his temple.

Darkness.

✦

Sound returned first. Barking dogs. Muffled voices. Raavan swayed. His mouth was gagged, hands were bound. He opened his eyes—he was hanging upside down from a tree.

Torches flickered beneath him. Dogs growled. Men milled around. The leader stepped forward, axe in hand.

Tall, heavily tattooed, his body scarred from battles with beasts, he looked more demon than man.

The axe rose.

Another bandit stepped in. "Let me cut his fingers first."

The leader grinned. "Your fingers for their arms," he said, nodding to the maimed men.

Cheers erupted.

One of them approached, dragging an axe across a wet stone. "You'll feed them well tonight," he told the dogs.

They barked, frenzied, straining their leashes.

Raavan groaned behind the gag. He twisted. Fists clenched. The bandit tried prying them open.

Raavan resisted.

Frustrated, the man pressed the blade into Raavan's thumb. Blood welled. The pain was sharp and deep. Raavan gritted his teeth, groaning.

The dogs snapped.

Then they broke free.

With a thunderous growl, they lunged—ripping into the bandit, tearing flesh from bone. Screams erupted. Blood splashed the tree trunk.

And the chaos spread.

From the canopy, owls dove with slicing talons. Insects swarmed, biting, stinging, blinding. The forest exploded with fury.

Then trumpets.

Elephants.

Bandits shrieked. Some loosed arrows in blind panic. Others turned to run.

But the trees parted—and a titan emerged.

A bull elephant, furious. It smashed skulls with its trunk, gored men on its tusks, trampled bones underfoot. Nothing could stop it.

Raavan watched in awe, helpless and upside down. The elephant turned to him, stared with dark, unblinking eyes. It let out a deep, guttural trumpet—and approached.

Raavan's body froze. His mouth was still gagged, breath shallow.

The elephant raised its trunk.

With a single strike, it snapped the branch. Raavan crashed to the ground, gasping for air.

Then—stillness.

All the animals—dogs, birds, insects, the elephant—stood around him. Silent. Watching.

He could hear his own heartbeat. And theirs.

Then, as one, they turned—and vanished into the jungle.

✦

Raavan lay motionless, stunned.

Why did they save me?

In fifteen years, the forest had never looked at him this way.

He rose slowly. Blood streamed from his scalp and shoulder - but the wounds closed quickly. He touched his thumb.

No cut. No scar.

But the memory of pain remained.

He turned towards the fallen bandits, but a shiver of remembrance stopped him.

The dream.

These men were not the same. He narrowed his eyes and, for the first time in fifteen years, turned to use Drishti on Devadatta.

What he saw shattered him.

Devadatta—surrounded. Bleeding. His robes gone. His body slumped. Fallen.

Raavan ran.

Towards the riverbank.

Towards the flames.

Towards Devadatta.

Raavan ran through the forest, guided by memory. He didn't stumble once—every root, every branch, every rock was exactly where it had been in his dream. The booming sound grew louder. The trees parted.

Devadatta lay on the riverbank, bleeding into the sand.

Far off, a boat sped down the river, carrying the attackers away. Raavan tried to scream, but choked. Tears poured down his face as he sprinted to Devadatta, collapsing beside him, cradling him in his lap.

Devadatta looked up and smiled faintly. "You've grown stronger... I saw you every day. I wish I'd been there with you. I'm sorry, Raavan."

Raavan's tears didn't stop. He hugged him tightly. "I wanted to save you. I'm sorry, Father. Let me make medicine—let me save you."

He began to rise, but Devadatta grasped his wrist.

"There's no time," he said. "You need to know the truth about your birth."

Raavan froze. "Not now," he whispered. "Tell me later. Let me heal you."

Devadatta slapped his cheek gently. "I know how you feel. But I'm leaving soon. Listen."

Raavan nodded, still crying.

Devadatta held his hand. "You came from a land far away—Bharat. Your father was a scientist. During an experiment, a fire broke out in the mountain cave. He died, but you survived. You walked out, untouched. I was there. You hugged me, called me 'Father'... and I couldn't let go."

Raavan sobbed harder. "You are my father."

Devadatta wiped his tears. "Shantinatha had the strongest Drishti since Dharmapaala. He believed you were reborn to correct the mistakes of a past life. We both agreed you needed training—that you were the key to peace."

He pulled a map from inside his robe. "Take this. Go to the cave before sunset. Your journey begins there."

Raavan's voice broke. "Why me? What mistakes? I don't know anything. Don't leave me..."

Devadatta smiled. "Shantinatha died for you. We believe in you. The cave will give you your answers."

The sun neared the horizon. Devadatta whispered, "Place me facing east. I want to see the sunrise, one last time."

Raavan lifted him gently and rested him against a boulder.

Golden light touched Devadatta's face. His body had grown cold.

"You scream a lot, Raavan," Devadatta murmured, eyes half-lidded. "Next time... think of lightning in your mind. It will happen."

Then—silence.

✦

His eyes remained fixed on the sun, unmoving.

Raavan shook him.

No response.

He pulled Devadatta into his arms and wept like a child.

He didn't know how long he sat there. But then, a hand rested on his shoulder.

Raavan turned.

It was Divyateja, a senior student from the ashram, dressed in the Guru's robes.

He embraced Raavan. "I'm sorry. But you must reach the cave by sunset. Do it for Devadatta. And... if you reach in time, you may avenge his death."

Raavan's eyes burned. He bowed low, touched Devadatta's feet, and ran—towards the mountain where it had all begun.

He ran without rest. Sweat drenched his body, his eyes red with fury. Devadatta had taken a full day to reach the ashram from the cave. Raavan reached it in half.

At the mountain's foot, he looked up. A large box hovered near the cave entrance, stirring the air. Rage surged in him.

These are the ones.

He leapt from rock to rock, scaling the cliff in minutes.

At the cave entrance, he saw them—men in black, faces masked, a strange symbol on their chests. He'd never seen it before. Yet something about it felt familiar.

They held the same machines as those in his vision. Inside the cave, they scoured the rubble, searching for something.

One of them noticed Raavan and stepped forward. Without warning, he shoved him.

Raavan—already consumed by fury—grabbed the man by the throat. His fingers sank deep. The man coughed up blood and collapsed.

Four more came running, raising their weapons—pointing them at Raavan.

He stood still, rage glowing in his eyes.

He could have screamed. He could have summoned lightning.

But no.

This, he would do with his hands.

One of them moved his finger to the trigger.

Before it could fall, Raavan leapt ten feet into the air and drove his knee into the attacker's chest—fast as lightning, powerful as thunder.

The others froze.

Everything had just begun.

The remaining attackers were frozen in fear. None had seen a man move like that.

Raavan lunged again.

Before they could react, he struck the first one with a blow so forceful that the man crashed into the two behind him. All three tumbled backwards in a heap. The last attacker slipped, screaming, and plummeted off the edge of the valley.

The two survivors scrambled to their feet and fled, tossing their weapons in panic.

Raavan picked up one of their machines and hurled it. It struck one of the fleeing men in the back, slamming him to the ground. In an instant, Raavan was on him—pinning him with a foot, wrenching his arm back until the shoulder cracked.

The last man dropped to his knees, trembling. He spoke in a language Raavan didn't recognise, but the fear in his eyes was unmistakable. He was surrendering.

Then Raavan heard footsteps—slow, heavy.

He turned.

A man stood there. Unmasked. Smiling.

Raavan narrowed his gaze and used Drishti.

He saw it clearly. This was the one who had fired the shot into Devadatta's chest.

✦

Rage surged through his veins.

Before the man could lift a weapon, Raavan lunged and seized him by the throat. Both hands clenched, squeezing with the fury of loss and the wrath of a storm. The man's grin vanished. His face turned red, then blue. He struggled, gasped, and pulled a small device from his coat—he fired.

The bullet tore through Raavan's right shoulder—again.

Blood poured, but Raavan didn't flinch.

He squeezed harder. His fingers sank deeper, thumbs meeting beneath the man's neck. With a final gasp, the attacker passed out.

Raavan roared.

And with the man still in his grip, he screamed—with all the fury he had buried for fifteen years.

Lightning tore down from the heavens. One bolt struck the hovering aircraft in the valley below. Another split the pile of corpses. A third incinerated the man in Raavan's hands.

The bandit who had surrendered witnessed it—and fainted before the lightning ever reached him.

Below, the black aircraft—a helicopter—blazed in the valley. The forest echoed with Raavan's wrath as thunder rolled in from the mountains.

Raavan sat beside the unconscious prisoner, his chest heaving, his breath ragged. Rain began to fall.

The man stirred. He opened his eyes—and fainted again.

Raavan leaned over, slapped him gently until he woke.

The man stammered something in a foreign tongue. Raavan pulled off the mask. The man's skin was pale—an outsider, just as Shantinatha had described. Raavan narrowed his eyes.

"Why are you here?" he asked. "Why did you kill Devadatta?"

The man looked confused.

Raavan tried again, using gestures.

Something registered. The man nodded nervously and disappeared into the cave.

Raavan didn't follow. He knew fear well enough to know this man wouldn't try anything foolish.

Moments later, the man returned holding a small, corroded piece of metal. He handed it to Raavan with trembling fingers.

Stamped on its surface, barely legible, were the words:

PASHUPATI PHARMACEUTICALS – AYODHYA, BHARAT

The man pointed to the name repeatedly, nodding.

Raavan stared.

Ayodhya.

Bharat.

That was where the answers lay.

He closed his fingers around the metal fragment and began descending the mountain. Rain softened into a fine mist.

As he reached the edge of the slope, he turned and waved.

The man exhaled in relief and smiled.

But before he could wave back—

A bolt of lightning struck him.

Raavan hadn't screamed.

There had been no **Rava**.

CHAPTER 05

Raavan plunged from the cliff in Lanka, crashing into the cold sea below. Saltwater stung his eyes and the torn wound on his shoulder. He kicked upward, gasping for air. He was a better swimmer now—he had taught himself after Shantinatha's death—but deep water and darkness still terrified him.

He spotted lights on the horizon and began swimming towards them. Slowly at first, unsure of his rhythm. The ocean felt endless. An hour passed before he found his pace. The vastness still loomed, but it no longer felt alien.

As he swam, his thoughts drifted towards Bharat. Devadatta had said he was born in that place. Did his family still live there? His mother? He had never seen her face. He longed to see her. And for the first time in years, he felt something close to happiness. Hope.

That's when something brushed his leg.

Moonlight turned the sea into molten silver. He spun, heart pounding. Nothing. But the fear surged. He had heard stories—sharks, predators with teeth like blades. Then he saw them—a school of large fish swimming beside him. Were they hunting? He panicked, swam faster. But they didn't attack. They simply followed.

More fish appeared, encircling him. Big and small. None touched him. He remembered the jungle—the time animals had gathered around him when he was hanging upside down, heart racing. They had come when his pulse surged and left when it returned to normal.

Was it happening again?

He stopped swimming, floating still. The fish circled gently, making no contact. He waited. His breath slowed. So did his heart. The fish dispersed, vanishing into the depths.

Astonished, he tested it again—swam fast, raised his heartbeat, then stopped. Again, they returned.

This was no accident.

The animals were drawn to the rhythm of his heart—the Jeeva Tatva. He laughed aloud, a strange, manic sound echoing across the waves. He had found an answer.

But it birthed a new question.

Why was he chosen for these powers? He thought of Shantinatha and Devadatta—who had whispered of destinies, of restoring balance, of being born for a great purpose. He had never believed them.

Until now.

Now, he wanted to believe. But belief wasn't enough. He was still afraid. Still alone. No Guru. No father.

He missed them both.

Raavan drifted in thought until the horizon blushed with dawn. He started swimming again. Bharat's coastline rose ahead—the land of his ancestors. A place he had never known, but now had to call home.

His feet touched sand.

Raavan stepped ashore, feeling the soil of Bharat beneath him for the first time. The beach was empty. Just him and the rising sun. He sat in the warm sand and watched it lift from the sea—golden, serene. He had never seen the sun rise from water before. Its warmth revived him.

He stood, took one last look at the ocean, and walked inland—into Bharat.

✦

Everything felt strange.

He had spent his life in a forest temple, untouched by the outside world. Now, walking through a town, he was overwhelmed. People. So many people. Their clothes made no sense—dhotis, pants, shirts, sarongs knotted at the waist. Women adorned in colours and ornaments he had never imagined. Carts moved without horses. Metal chunks on wheels roared past, belching smoke.

Raavan stood still, stunned. The noise, the speed—it unnerved him. He had no words for what he saw.

And he was scared.

He questioned everything—his decision to leave, his search for a family he didn't know, his hope for answers in a world that didn't welcome him. All he had was a corroded metal tag that read *Pashupati Pharmaceuticals*. He didn't even know if "Pashupati Pharmaceuticals" was real.

The farther he walked, the more lost he felt.

His face betrayed him—confusion, helplessness, fear. He wandered until noon, hungry, anxious, utterly alone. He had no money. No plan. In the forest, hunger meant climbing a tree or foraging. Here, it meant nothing but pain.

He saw women selling fruit. His stomach growled. But shame stopped him. He was strong, muscular, fearsome—but inside, he was still a child.

His steps slowed. The world grew heavier.

What was he even doing here? Searching for a mother he had never met?

He looked down at his feet. The answer came, quiet but clear.

I don't want this.

He turned around.

He would return to the forest, to the temple, to the silence.

By dusk, he was back at the shore. He would swim at sunrise—once was enough in darkness. Starving, he climbed a coconut tree, brought down a few coconuts, cracked them open, and ate slowly. The ocean breeze cooled the storm in his chest.

For the first time that day, he smiled.

He lay down on the sand, listening to the waves, watching the stars drift into view, and drifted into sleep.

Raavan was sweating, his body twitching in restless sleep until he jolted awake, gasping.

Everything was dark.

Too dark.

He could hear his own heartbeat. The sky above was full of stars, but the night was so black it seemed to merge with the land. There were no waves, no wind—just silence.

He sat up, confused.

Where was he?

Behind him loomed a massive structure—the largest he had ever seen. It towered like a stone god, its silhouette swallowing the sky. He couldn't remember arriving here. The last thing he recalled was falling asleep on the beach.

He walked towards it. With every step, the silence thickened—heavy, unnatural.

And then it clicked—that silence. He had felt it before. Once, in a terrifying temple dream. Again, in the forest before the ambush.

The same silence.

This had to be a dream.

✦

Still, he moved forward. At the front steps, a massive door stood open. He hesitated, then knocked. The knock echoed—sharp, hollow. Inside, the building was cold and lifeless, hollow as if no soul had ever dwelt within. He stepped through the doorway. Three corridors stretched ahead: to the left, to the right, and straight.

Suddenly, a sound shattered the stillness—a groan. Deep. Guttural. Agonising. His heart skipped. He turned to flee—but the door behind him was gone. In its place stood a stone wall. On it, painted in red, was a single number: 3.

Panic surged. He pounded the wall. Solid. No hidden door. No escape. Another groan followed—louder, closer. He froze. It was behind him. He didn't want to turn. But something—some force—compelled him. He spun and punched the darkness. Nothing. Then silence again. And then the groan—closer now, more broken. More human. But it felt... familiar.

Raavan took a deep breath. This was a dream. He remembered now. And with that, the fear loosened its grip. He steadied himself, tuned into the sound. It came from the left corridor.

At its end, a flickering yellow light appeared—wavering like a candle on the verge of death.

He moved quickly down the passage, his footsteps echoing through the gloom, until he reached a room. Inside, the only light came from a lone torch on the far wall. In its glow, he saw her.

A woman—kneeling on the floor. She wore a tattered green saree. Her arms were shackled to opposite walls. A metal collar bound her neck to the ceiling. Blood seeped from her wounds. Her fingers were blackened, nails long and curled. Her head hung low, hair veiling her face. Raavan's heart clenched.

Beside her stood a man cloaked in black, facing her in silence. He made no move to help—only watched her groan, as if her pain fed him. Raavan didn't know her. But he couldn't bear her suffering. His fists clenched. His eyes burned. He rushed forward and grabbed at the chains—his hands passed through them like smoke. He stumbled back, stunned. Again, he tried to touch her shoulder, to lift her face. Again—nothing.

Then, in an instant, the black-robed man turned and ran at Raavan. His hand clamped around Raavan's throat. Raavan stared into what should have been a face. There were no eyes. No nose. No ears. Only a mouth. Smiling.

Raavan struck him—fists flailing, desperate. But his blows passed through like air. Yet the grip on his throat held tight.

How is he touching me if he's made of smoke?

Raavan dropped to his knees beside the groaning woman, clawing at the fingers tightening around his neck. His lungs screamed. The groaning intensified—louder. Rhythmic. Not groaning—chanting. And then, through the haze, he heard it clearly: "Ayodhya."

It wasn't random. It was a word. He turned towards the faceless man. That smile had widened. Monstrous. His lips moved again. "Ayodhya."

Raavan smiled—barely, through the pain. He had the answer now. "Ayodhya," he whispered.

And collapsed.

✦

The sun was just about to rise. Raavan lay asleep on a beach near Rameswaram, his head shifting from side to side, murmuring a single word:

"Ayodhya…"

His hands twitched. His breathing was restless. The dream still gripped him.

Suddenly, a splash of water struck his face.

He sat up, startled.

An old man stood beside him, holding a copper vessel in one hand and a worn satchel in the other. He was short and thin, but his face radiated a soft glow. He wore an orange shawl inscribed with *Jai Sri Ram*, and his matted hair was tied in a knot atop his head.

"I thought you were having a bad dream," the man said with a smile.

Raavan nodded quickly, still disoriented. "Yes... I was dreaming."

The old man chuckled. "You were dreaming during Brahma Muhurtam. Be sure to act on what you saw."

Raavan stared at him, unsure how to respond.

The man didn't wait. He set down his satchel and walked to the sea to offer *arghya*—water to the rising sun.

Raavan sat up fully, still shaken by the dream. He kept thinking about the woman in the green saree. He hadn't seen her face, nor the man's—but he had felt her pain. Her word had become his path.

"Ayodhya…" he muttered again.

"I'll beg for food," he said aloud. "I'll walk to Ayodhya if I have to."

The old man, returning from his prayers, laughed. "It would take you twenty days to walk there. I've done it myself, years ago. Wouldn't recommend it."

Raavan looked at him, stunned. "I don't have money... or food. How do I get there?"

The old man tilted his head. "Who are you, son? Where are you from?"

Raavan hesitated. "I was raised in an ashram. I'm looking for my family... in Ayodhya."

The old man's eyes softened. "I'm on a pilgrimage. Ayodhya is on my way. Come with me."

Raavan blinked. "Aren't you afraid I might rob you? I'm a stranger."

The man laughed again. "I have nothing for you to rob. Only faith in Sri Ram. He takes care of me."

Raavan folded his hands in gratitude, picked up the satchel, and walked beside the old man.

They journeyed together for twenty days.

Sometimes walking. Sometimes buses. Sometimes trains. Once, even a boat.

Travelling with the old man opened Raavan's eyes to the world—democracy, currency, bicycles, and highways. He was full of questions. He inquired about everything: roads, clothing, buildings, machines, food, and the government.

He especially noticed clothing. Back in the ashram, everyone wore the same dhoti. Here, men wore fabrics of all kinds stitched together. Women wore colours he'd never imagined.

The old man answered every question with patience—sometimes with wisdom, sometimes with laughter.

He sang when he was happy. Spoke truths when he was silent. Once, he told Raavan he had served in the army. Another time, he recited stories from the *Ramayana* under the stars.

Raavan had never known such peace. His heart grew lighter each day. Fear left him.

They passed through many Indian states. Thanks to Shantinatha's teachings, Raavan could understand every dialect they encountered.

On the twentieth day, they walked into the outskirts of Ayodhya.

Raavan had never seen the city—only read of it in ancient texts. He expected palaces, floral gardens, roads dusted with sandalwood, and people descended from Lord Ram's lineage.

But as the city approached, the memory of the dream returned.

The faceless man.

The woman in chains.

His joy dimmed. Anxiety returned.

The old man, walking beside him, noticed. "What's wrong?" he asked gently.

Raavan opened his fist and showed him the corroded metal he had carried since the cave.

"This is all I have. My only clue."

The old man took the metal piece and read the faded engraving.

His expression changed.

Raavan leaned in. “You know it?”

The old man pointed across the river, just outside the city.

A compound stood among tall trees. Its walls were high. A new building stood at the centre.

A large sign read:

PASHUPATI PHARMACEUTICALS

Raavan stared.

This wasn't the building from his dream. But it was the place he'd meant to find—before the dream changed his path.

He turned to the old man and bowed deeply. “Thank you.”

The man smiled, pulled a white kurta from his satchel, and offered it. “I know you'll find your family. Take this. May Sri Ram guide your journey.”

Raavan accepted the gift with humility. He had admired kurtas ever since they began walking.

He looked at the old man. “Where will you go after Ayodhya?”

The man finally answered. “Badrinath. Then Varanasi.”

Raavan touched his feet, hugged him, and whispered, “Thank you... for everything.”

The old man smiled, blessed him, and turned towards Ayodhya.

Raavan watched until he disappeared behind a bend in the road. Then he looked at the metal piece, slipped it into his pocket, and walked towards the compound.

✦

The building had seemed close when the old man first pointed it out. But as Raavan walked towards it, he realised it was much farther than it appeared. And when he finally reached the compound wall, he understood how deeply he had underestimated its size. The facility was enormous—a fortress of stone and glass rising from the wilderness at the edge of Ayodhya.

The wall itself was twice his height. Inside, Raavan saw a remarkable range of flora—trees he recognised from his herbal training. Neem. Tulsi. Medicinal plants, cultivated with care. This was no ordinary compound.

He stood near the gate but did not enter. Instead, he began walking around the perimeter, alert. For all he knew, this could be the lair of the men who once ambushed him near the cave. He had to be sure.

It took nearly an hour to complete a circuit around the walls. He used Drishti to observe the people within. They didn't seem like soldiers. No weapons. Some operated large machinery that pressed pellets from powders. Others tended to plants, worked with rabbits and mice, or scribbled into thick notebooks. He watched closely until he was certain—this place wasn't dangerous.

He returned to the main gate. A knot of guards stood at the entrance; one, leather-skinned from years in the sun, stepped forward. "Where are you going?" he asked, gruff. Raavan smiled, almost boyish. "Inside." The man's face hardened. "Do you work here?" The smile fell. Raavan shook his head. "Then why do you want to go inside?" the guard pressed.

Raavan reached into his pocket and pulled out the corroded piece of metal. "I found this in a cave in Sri Lanka," he said. "My father took me there when I was a child. He died in a fire. I survived. I'm here to find my family."

A senior guard overheard and walked over. The two exchanged glances—and then, unexpectedly, began to laugh. Raavan blinked, confused. While they chuckled, he quietly tried to slip past them.

They blocked his path.

"That's a good story," one of them said. "But you can't go in without an appointment."

Raavan pleaded. "I've come from far away. It took me over twenty days to get here. I don't have anywhere else to go."

The head guard frowned but shook his head. "I understand your situation. But rules are rules."

Raavan tried again, this time softer. Still, the answer remained no. His shoulders sagged. He had come so far—only to hit another wall. With a heavy heart, he turned and began walking away.

The head guard went back inside.

But the younger guard—the one who had been silent all this time—watched him go. Something stirred in him. He glanced around, then ran after Raavan, catching up just before he vanished from view.

Raavan turned, surprised.

The young guard panted, his hands resting on his knees. "No, I still can't let you in," he said, catching his breath. "But... we can't stop you from asking the workers who leave through the gates. Maybe one of them knows about your family."

He pointed behind him. "There are four gates. Wait near each. Ask them."

Raavan's eyes lit up. "Thank you, Anna!"

The guard called over his shoulder as he ran back, "They leave at 4 p.m.! Ten minutes from now!"

✦

That evening, Raavan stood near the west gate. In his hand, the corroded metal piece. As workers streamed out, he approached each one with the same question:

Did they know of a man who might have worked for Pashupati Pharmaceuticals and died in a fire accident in Sri Lanka?

Some replied curtly with a "No." Others just shook their heads. The crowd thinned. By sunset, no one remained.

He had spoken to every worker at the west gate—and found nothing.

Still, he wasn't ready to give up. There were three more gates.

He sat under a tree near the gate, watching lights in the guard's office. His stomach churned—he hadn't eaten all day. A hand pump stood nearby, but even water felt too far. Exhausted, he lay beneath the moonlight and dozed off.

The next morning, he woke early, drank some water at the hand pump, and headed into Ayodhya. He wandered the streets, asking strangers about his father. Each answer brought a fresh layer of disappointment.

By 4 p.m., he reached the north gate. As before, he waited for the workers and asked each one his question. Again, no one knew.

Two days without food. Still, he didn't ask for alms. He wanted only one thing—his family.

That evening, he sat beneath a tree outside the north gate, weak and starving. He had barely closed his eyes when someone tapped his shoulder.

Raavan sprang up, fists raised.

"Whoa! It's me!" the man shouted, shielding himself.

Raavan blinked, lowering his arms. It was the same young guard—the one who had given him the idea.

"Sorry," Raavan said, panting. "I lived in a forest too long. I thought you were an animal."

The guard gave a half-smile and lowered his hands. "Looks like you still haven't found your family."

Raavan exhaled. "Four hundred and thirty-nine people at the west gate. Three hundred and ninety-nine at the north."

The guard's eyes widened. "That's... exactly how many people use those two gates. I've worked here for a year. You asked every one of them?"

Raavan nodded.

Now, the guard understood. This man wasn't mad. He was serious.

He sat beside Raavan and extended a hand. "I'm Karan. I got my father's job here. He... died in a fire. Fifteen years ago."

There was silence between them.

Karan broke it. "You said your father died in an accident, too. I know how it feels. Let me know if I can help."

Raavan tried to speak—but his stomach answered for him.

It growled.

Karan laughed and handed him a stainless steel container. "Eat this. I'll find something later."

Raavan hesitated, but hunger won. He took the box with both hands, eyes full of gratitude.

"Thank you," he whispered.

Karan smiled and walked away towards the south gate.

The next day, Raavan followed the same routine—but this time, he asked for alms in Ayodhya. At 4 p.m., he stood at the east gate, asking every worker who walked out of the compound. Yet again, no one had heard of his father.

That night, he slept with anxiety coiling in his chest. Only one gate remained.

If he didn't find an answer tomorrow, he would have to come up with another plan.

The following day, he repeated everything. As evening approached, he stood near the south gate, watching the workers stream out. He asked nearly everyone he met, but the responses were all the same.

"No. Sorry."

As the sun set and the lights inside the compound flickered on, Raavan watched the gate begin to close. Tears welled in his eyes. He had asked everyone. And still… nothing.

The metal piece felt cold in his palm—heavy with failure. It had led him across the ocean, across a country, across hunger and rejection… for this?

He turned away and walked towards the river.

The sky was dark. The only light shimmered from Ayodhya in the distance. Raavan stared towards the town, eyes full, and whispered:

"I hope you're somewhere around, Mother."

Then he began walking.

✦

The next morning, Pashupati Pharmaceuticals buzzed with chatter.

Workers at every gate were talking about a young man—tall, quiet, intense—who had been asking everyone about a father who died in a fire accident. No one had been spared his questions. The story spread fast. Clerks murmured about it outside the Director's office.

And then the Director heard.

He rushed out, catching the conversation mid-sentence. The two clerks, long used to seeing their Director composed and unreadable, froze when they saw his face.

His jaw dropped. His lips parted in disbelief.

He turned without a word, slammed the office door behind him, and within minutes, sent out a swarm of guards—on bicycles, in cars—across Ayodhya.

Inside, the Director sat alone, staring at a framed photograph of a family.

"You're alive..." he whispered.

Unaware, Raavan was still walking through Ayodhya's streets. But something inside him had shifted. The stress of the previous night was gone. The town filled him with a strange, stubborn hope.

He kept asking elderly women sitting on stoops, shopkeepers, and children playing in the dust.

In the beginning, hearing "No" had pierced him like a knife. Now, it barely registered. What hurt more was when someone asked:

"What's your father's name?"

And he had to answer, "I don't know."

That answer wounded deeper than any rejection.

Still, he kept asking. From morning till sunset. At night, he returned to the river, building a small shelter from logs and branches. As he arranged the logs, he saw a car approaching in the distance. Men stepped out and began walking towards him.

He didn't stop working.

One of them shouted, "Are you the man looking for his father who died in Sri Lanka? The company's Director would like to meet with you. Please come with us."

Raavan dropped the logs and rushed forward. "Does the Director know about my father?"

One of the men replied, "I don't know. But we were asked to find you. Maybe you'll find something."

Raavan's eyes lit up.

He climbed into the car. But instead of heading east—towards the factory—the vehicle turned west.

Raavan noticed and asked, "Why are we going this way? The factory is on the other side."

The driver responded, "We're going to the Director's home."

They reached a massive iron gate. The driver radioed the guard, and without a sound, the gate slid open. Raavan couldn't wait—he leaned forward, peering through the widening crack.

A grand, well-lit building stood beyond. A fountain sparkled in the moonlight. The car rolled forward down a long driveway lined with manicured lawns and flowering plants.

It stopped at the entrance.

The driver looked at Raavan. "Go on. He's waiting inside."

Raavan jumped out and ran to the front door.

A man stood there, leaning on a cane. As soon as he saw Raavan, he limped forward and—without a word—wrapped his arms around him.

Raavan froze. Then slowly, he embraced him back.

"I'm Raavan," he whispered. "Are you… my father?"

The man pulled back, looking into his eyes. Then he shook his head gently.

"No. I'm not your father. But I knew him well."

He placed a hand on Raavan's shoulder.

"I'm Lalit, the interim Director of Pashupati Pharmaceuticals. I've been the caretaker of the Pashupati estates, waiting… until I found the rightful heir."

He paused.

"And after years of searching, I finally found you. You are the heir."

Raavan stared at him blankly. There was no joy in his face. No greed. No awe.

Just questions.

"Do you know my parents?"

"Can you take me to my mother?"

The excitement drained from Lalit's face. He stepped back, quiet.

Then he said softly, "Yes. I can take you to her... tomorrow. You look tired. Have dinner. Rest for the night."

Raavan couldn't stop smiling. He stepped forward and hugged him again.

Lalit returned the embrace, more gently this time.

This—this was all Raavan had ever wanted.

Not wealth.

Family.

✦

The servants led Raavan to his room—and he was awestruck.

It was vast, the largest space he had ever stepped in. A luxurious bed stood in the centre, its white covers glowing under soft golden lights. Intricate paintings adorned the walls. Expensive wooden furniture, polished to shine, stood on either side. A lavish bathroom opened in one corner, and beyond it, a balcony overlooked the vast gardens of the estate.

He sat on the bed. The mattress sank beneath him, cradling his body like a cloud. He had never imagined such comfort.

His first bath in the bathroom felt like a blessing. The water was clean—perfectly soothing. He bathed slowly, letting it wash over weeks of hardship. When he stepped out, he found the finest clothes laid out for him.

A servant escorted him to dinner. Every person he passed bowed with respect. Though unaccustomed to this attention, Raavan liked it.

The dining hall was magnificent. Crystal chandeliers hung above a table lined with silver and gold. As Raavan entered, every servant greeted him in unison.

He greeted them back—and they were visibly surprised.

At the far end of the table sat Lalit, smiling broadly. He had instructed the kitchen to prepare everything Raavan might enjoy. Meat, vegetables, soups, rice, roti, pickles, curries, sweets—the table was overflowing with options.

When Raavan sat beside him, Lalit refused to let anyone else serve. He personally filled Raavan's plate with generous portions, watching eagerly.

But Raavan didn't eat.

He stared at the food, overwhelmed. All his life, he had eaten forest fare—fruits, roots, tubers. Nothing like this. Behind him, the cooks exchanged anxious glances.

Finally, Raavan broke the silence.

"Can I get some fruits, please?"

Lalit—always so serious—burst into laughter. The cooks chuckled. Even Raavan laughed. The tension lifted.

As Raavan slowly began to eat, Lalit began to speak—stories about the Pashupati family, tales spanning centuries.

He spoke of his great-great-great-great-grandfather who started an Ayurvedic trade, and how that enterprise grew into one of India's largest pharmaceutical companies. He spoke of land, legacy, and leadership—and then, at length, about Dr Tara, the visionary who brought the company into the modern age.

Raavan listened, wide-eyed.

Until yesterday, he had no family.

Tonight, he had a history.

In the middle of Lalit's tale, Raavan interrupted, eyes sparkling.

"Where is my grandmother? Is she in another town? When can I meet her? And what about my grandfather?"

Lalit paused. The joy on his face softened.

"It's getting late, Mr Pashupati," he said gently. "I'll take you to them tomorrow."

Raavan nodded. "I'll wait... but please, call me Raavan. That's my name."

Lalit smiled. "Good night, Raavan. Rest well."

Raavan wandered the halls before bed, overwhelmed by everything—the chandeliers, the soft rugs, the portraits on every wall. Generations of Pashupatis stared down at him from painted eyes.

He searched the faces for someone familiar. During dinner, Lalit had told him his parents' names—and now, he desperately sought their portraits.

But he couldn't find them.

Not in any of the hallways.

No photograph of his father.

No painting of his mother.

No grandparents either.

His heart sank.

Still restless, he returned to his room, crawled into bed, and tried to sleep. But it was impossible. The thought of seeing his mother the next day consumed him. He tossed. Turned. Got out of bed. Sat back down. Stared at the moonlight spilling across the floor.

More than once, he marched to the door, meaning to knock on Lalit's room—to ask if they could go now. But each time, he stopped himself.

Finally, near midnight, he couldn't resist.

He slipped out of his room and walked through the dim corridors. The ancestors on the walls seemed to watch him as he passed. Still searching, he scanned every frame—but found nothing that resembled his parents.

Then, suddenly, he realised—he was already at Lalit's room.

He knocked softly.

The sound echoed through the long corridor.

No answer.

He knocked again, a little louder. Still nothing.

He hesitated. What should he call him? Lalit-ji? Sir? Uncle? He didn't know. Social customs were still strange to him.

One more knock—harder this time.

Still, no response.

Just as he raised his fist again, a servant hurried over.

"Mr Pashupati," the man whispered, "Mr Lalit takes medicine to help him sleep. If it's not urgent, it would be best to speak with him in the morning."

Raavan gave a polite smile. "Thank you."

He turned and began walking back to his room.

The smile lingered on his face—but only for a second.

As soon as the servant turned away, Raavan's expression shifted. His walk turned into a stride. Then a run.

He rushed back to his room.

He wasn't going to wait until morning.

He had a plan.

He was going to find his mother tonight.

Raavan returned to his room and locked the door behind him. Lalit had promised to take him to his mother the next morning—and if that were true, Raavan could use Drishti to see his future and confirm it.

He sat in the centre of the room, legs crossed, and closed his eyes. With deep focus, he steadied his breath and began chanting the mantra to view the present.

The moment the chant ended, his vision shifted.

✦

The space was shrouded in darkness. No discernible features. No landmarks. He frowned, puzzled. Then it occurred to him: Lalit must be asleep.

He shifted to the mantra that allowed him to see the future and moved forward—minutes, then hours. But still, darkness.

Raavan's lungs began to ache. He could hold his breath only for so long. After re-entering, it always started from the present; no skipping ahead.

Only the Guru of the Ashram had mastered the art of breathing within Drishti. That knowledge was never shared.

Just before his breath gave out, something changed. Light flickered on.

Raavan saw Lalit sitting on a bed. But something was wrong. His leg—there was only one. And that was chained to a metal frame.

Before Raavan could process what he was seeing, his lungs screamed for air. He gasped and jolted upright, panting.

Without thinking, he burst out of his room.

His footsteps thundered down the hallway, echoing through the still mansion. He reached Lalit's door and slammed into it with his shoulder. The lock shattered. He stumbled in, breathless.

He didn't turn on the lights.

He sprinted towards the bed and yanked the blanket off.

Lalit, jolted awake, reacted on instinct. He elbowed Raavan in the throat—a precise, brutal move.

Raavan crashed to the floor, groaning. But he rose almost instantly, breathing calmly.

Lalit blinked, stunned.

That strike should have left Raavan unconscious. With only one leg, Lalit had still been a soldier—and his elbow was trained to disable.

He stared at Raavan, breath caught.

"What are you doing here at this hour?"

Raavan didn't answer. He rose slowly and glanced towards the broken door. Servants were already gathered outside, wide-eyed.

He looked back at Lalit, unable to speak.

Then, after what felt like forever, he muttered:

"I had a nightmare. I wanted to make sure you were alright."

Lalit's frown eased into a smile. He stepped forward, patted Raavan on the shoulder, and said softly:

"This is our home, Raavan. We are safe here."

He turned to the servants. "Go back to bed."

Raavan walked back to his room.

But his heart was racing.

Something didn't make sense.

Drishti never went wrong.

He paced in circles. Doubt gnawed at him. Had he chanted the wrong mantra? Was something interfering?

He closed his eyes and reviewed the verses he had learned from Shantinatha. Every syllable was right, which meant that what he saw was real.

To confirm, he used Drishti again—this time on the chef he had passed outside Lalit's room earlier that evening.

The vision came quickly.

In the present, the chef is asleep. In the near future, he will prepare breakfast.

Raavan opened his eyes, startled. If the chef's future was true, then so was Lalit's.

A cold wave passed through him.

He had to be sure.

He closed his eyes again and used Drishti on Lalit, pushing forward rapidly to the point where he had last seen the strange room.

This time, he gained a few more seconds.

The lights came on. Lalit was there, in the same dingy cell—only now he looked much worse. Pale, hollow-eyed, bones pressing against skin. He sat silently on a bed, chained by the leg.

The room was decaying. Paint peeled from the walls. Rust stained the corners. And on one wall, strange tally marks—hundreds of short lines carved by hands. His bare hands.

The wall was smeared with blood. Skin fragments clung to the scratches. He looked at Lalit's fingers—some were missing nails. One was bleeding.

Raavan's lungs began to burn again. He looked up one last time.

On a wall in that room was a symbol. The same one worn by the attackers near the mountain cave.

His breath collapsed.

He emerged from Drishti, choking.

He fell to the floor, gasping. His thoughts raced. His chest heaved.

Nothing made sense.

Lalit was in the mansion. But Lalit was also imprisoned? How?

Raavan tried to reason with himself, but every thread of logic unravelled as soon as he pulled on it. The mansion's silence felt heavier now—less like peace, more like a lie.

His body gave up. He crawled onto the bed and lay flat, staring at the ceiling.

He didn't want to think.

But he couldn't stop.

Not about the missing portraits.

Not about the blood on the wall.

Not about the truth that flickered just beyond his reach.

Eventually, exhaustion claimed him—and Raavan drifted into sleep,

with his mind stuck on that one **Prashna**.

CHAPTER 06

Raavan was still asleep. For the first time in years, he hadn't risen before sunrise. His mind, restless even in dreams, spiralled around images of Drishti—visions he could neither escape nor understand. But when he jolted awake, clarity struck like a bell—Lalit was taking him to meet his mother today.

He leapt out of bed. The thought of finally seeing his mother washed over him, flushing out every lingering echo of the night before. After a quick bath, he rushed to Lalit's room, only to find it empty. Anxiously, he ran to the dining hall and found Lalit seated, calmly eating his breakfast.

Lalit looked up and smiled. "Join me," he said, gesturing to the table.

"I'm not hungry," Raavan replied, stepping closer. "Can you take me to my mother now?"

"Yes," Lalit said gently, "but I need to eat before I take my medicine. We'll leave right after."

Reluctantly, Raavan sat beside him. He barely touched the food. His mind wasn't in the room. The vision from the night before lingered like a shadow on his chest. Uncertain, he activated Drishti again, focusing on Lalit. The same image returned—Lalit, bound and broken in a darkened cell—just as he had seen the previous night. But here he was, right beside him. Smiling. Free. The contradiction gnawed at Raavan, making him question whether he truly understood how Drishti worked.

As soon as Lalit finished eating, they left the house. "To Pashupati Mahal," Lalit told the driver in a low voice. Raavan sat silently, his eyes fixed on the window as the world blurred past. Minutes passed. Then the car slowed to a stop in front of a towering gate. This time, there was no radio call, no announcement. The driver waited quietly. Lalit stepped out first. Raavan followed.

The compound wall loomed tall but had fallen into ruin. Vines clung to fractured bricks, moss grew wild, and trees leaned against the edges of cracked stone buildings. Nature had swallowed the place whole.

Raavan frowned, unease blooming in his chest. "Does my mother live here?" he asked.

Lalit didn't respond. He stepped forward and pushed open the rusted gate, which let out a long, aching groan.

Raavan hesitated. Something about the building felt familiar, like a dream half-remembered. The main door stirred a memory he couldn't place. Dread crept in, slow and cold.

"Why are we here?" he asked, catching up to Lalit. "Where's my mother?"

Still silent, Lalit walked on. Raavan grabbed his arm, forcing him to stop. "Why are you doing this? Take me to her!"

Lalit finally spoke, his voice calm but distant. "Let's go inside first." He gestured towards the massive door.

Raavan didn't move. The truth loomed before him, silent and heavy, like a wave poised to crash. Lalit reached the door, opened it, and stepped inside.

Raavan stood at the threshold. Something was wrong. He could feel it in the air.

He stepped forward slowly and peered through the doorway. The hall beyond was vast and unlit, dust dancing in shafts of faint light. As his eyes adjusted, he noticed dark streaks on the marble—lines that crawled up the walls like the scars of fire.

He stopped just inside the doorway. His voice came out small and trembling. "Is my family here?"

Lalit turned to him and pointed towards the far wall.

"I'm sorry, Raavan," he said softly. "I couldn't save them."

Raavan followed Lalit's gaze. On the far wall hung three large paintings. His breath caught. Legs trembling, he stepped forward until he stood before them. The portraits were of his mother, grandmother, and grandfather. Below each were engraved names, birthdates, and the same date of death.

His chest tightened. Just last night, joy had overflowed in him like a rising tide. Now, his world had capsized. His knees gave out. He collapsed onto the marble floor.

The swirling patterns he'd noticed earlier weren't decorative—they were burn marks. Blackened trails scarred the marble, climbed the walls, and stained the ceiling. He looked around in horror, then turned to Lalit and clutched his hand.

"What happened?" he asked, his voice cracking.

Lalit didn't reply. He pulled away, walked slowly to the staircase, and sat down heavily. His cane slipped from his fingers and clattered to the floor. Silent tears streamed down his face.

Raavan stood, shaking. "How did this happen?" he demanded, his voice sharp with grief.

Lalit looked up, pain etched into his features. "It's all because of your father—Ahindra Pashupati."

✦

Raavan froze. His eyes widened. "That's not possible," he whispered. "My father… he would never—"

Lalit's expression darkened with something more than sorrow—contempt. "You know nothing about your father."

He drew a long breath and began. "Ahindra was a prodigy. He earned a doctorate by fifteen. Your grandmother, Dr Tara, believed he was the future of Pashupati Pharmaceuticals. But she was wrong. He wasn't interested in the company—or in people. All he cared about was his research."

Lalit stared into the distance; his voice steeped in memory. "He rarely left his lab. So, Dr Tara arranged a marriage to the kindest woman this house ever knew. Your mother, Maya. She brought light and warmth into our lives. She cared for everyone—even him. But he never loved her. His heart belonged only to his work."

Lalit paused. "Then you were born. Everyone was overjoyed. And something changed in Ahindra. He became obsessed with you. He spent all his time with you. We thought it was a miracle. We thought… maybe he was healing."

Lalit's voice dropped. "But he wasn't. One day, he vanished—gone for a week. We searched everywhere. I entered his lab, desperate for a clue. I found his logbook. I wish I hadn't."

Raavan stepped forward. "What did you read?"

"He was experimenting on you," Lalit rasped. "Using ancient techniques to alter your body. To make you superhuman. He was rewriting your DNA. I was horrified. But I kept quiet. I didn't tell the family yet—I wanted to find him first. I traced him to Sri Lanka and left that very night. It was the worst decision I ever made."

Lalit looked down. "I searched for weeks. Came back to ashes. The house... everything inside... burned."

Raavan's eyes filled with tears.

"But your mother survived—barely," Lalit said. "At the hospital, she held on… just to see you one last time. And she told me what happened."

Lalit's voice cracked. "Ahindra returned days after I left. But he was no longer himself. He murdered your grandfather. Stabbed him in the eye. He struck your grandmother with an iron rod. Then he poured petrol across the house. Your mother tried to escape. He caught her. Tied her to your grandparents' corpses—right here, in the centre of this hall. Then he lit the match. And he stood outside. Watching. Making sure no one helped."

Raavan collapsed—at the heart of the scorched marble. His hands trembled as he pressed his palms to the blackened floor. His tears fell freely, one drop hissing as it struck the burn mark.

He raised a trembling hand. A cry tore from his throat—a scream of anguish and rage, raw and uncontainable. He brought his fists down with thunderous force. The marble shattered. Cracks exploded across the floor and up the walls.

Then—stillness.

A deep creak sounded above.

Raavan looked up.

Lalit shouted, "Raavan!"

Too late.

The chandelier broke free. It crashed down. A jagged metal shard pierced Raavan's neck, driving clean through his throat.

His eyes fluttered once. Then closed.

Silence.

✦

Lalit thought Raavan was dead. He stood frozen in shock as time passed. Then, Raavan opened his eyes. Lalit was still there, unmoving, his face pale with disbelief. Slowly, Raavan reached for the shard of metal lodged in his neck and yanked it out. Blood poured as he tried to stand, but his strength failed. Watching this, Lalit fainted.

Raavan crawled towards him, desperate to wake him. But he was bleeding heavily. His vision dimmed, and he could barely keep his eyes open. Then he noticed figures entering the room—men in black, all dressed identically. They rushed in, picked up Lalit, and carried him out. Raavan turned weakly and saw them placing Lalit into a large white van. From what he had seen in his Drishti, this appeared to be a kidnapping. He tried to drag himself towards the van, but his strength gave out. His blood pooled beneath him, and consciousness slipped away.

As he faded, images flickered before him—a dream. He was on the beach near Rameswaram, then inside a building. He saw the number three on a wall. He walked down a corridor, entered a room. A woman knelt, her head bowed. When she lifted her face, it was Maya—his mother. She whispered one word: "Ayodhya."

Voices stirred him from the darkness. Raavan tried to open his eyes, but they felt like iron. He turned his head slightly. A few men stood around him—one of them looked like Lalit. No, it was Lalit. Raavan forced his eyes open in disbelief. He tried to speak, but no sound came. Lalit noticed, stepped closer, and sat beside him.

"You're severely injured. Don't strain yourself," Lalit said gently. "Doctors don't understand how you're alive. They've never seen anyone heal like this." Raavan squeezed his hand. Around him, machines beeped steadily. Tubes connected to his body. Doctors moved about the room, along with quiet, unfamiliar servants.

Raavan gestured weakly, asking how Lalit was. Lalit smiled. "I'm fine. I fainted when I saw you like that. Luckily, the driver witnessed everything and called for help. We were taken to the hospital. I woke up in an hour, but you've been unconscious for two days. The doctors thought you would die... but you healed. They're calling you 'Miracle Man.' Rest, Raavan. We'll go home soon."

A doctor entered and asked Lalit to step out. Then, without a word, he inserted a needle into Raavan's arm to draw blood. Raavan grabbed his wrist and shook his head. "No," he croaked. Lalit returned just then and reassured him, "They're just testing your blood to help treat you. You're safe." Raavan looked into Lalit's eyes, then slowly released his grip.

Four days later, Lalit brought him home.

The mansion didn't feel the same. The old servants were gone. The new ones were strange—too quiet, too watchful. Even the chefs had changed, and the food lacked its former warmth. But Raavan barely noticed. He spent his days shut in his room, silent and withdrawn. The truth Lalit had shared about his family tormented him. His father had killed his mother and grandmother and experimented on him. Everything he was, every power he had, came from that inhuman cruelty. He wasn't a son. He was a test subject.

Hatred festered inside him.

He had no family now—only Lalit, who tried to lift his spirit every day. Lalit spoke to him about Maya and the grandmother he had never met. These moments brought faint smiles to Raavan's face. Every day, Lalit took him to the hospital for check-ups. The doctor would examine the scar on his neck, draw blood, and ask questions. Lalit also brought Raavan to their company and introduced him to the staff. Gradually, these small gestures stitched together the fabric of a new life.

Raavan began to feel less alone.

His wound eventually healed. His hospital visits were reduced to once a week. Though he had never been formally educated, Raavan's knowledge of Ayurveda—taught by Shantinatha—was vast. He joined the company's Ayurveda department and began working. The staff liked him immediately. Despite being the owner, Raavan chose to work in the lab. He enjoyed the work. It was the first time his knowledge tangibly helped people. His days became busier, filled with purpose.

And yet, every evening, he returned home in time for dinner with Lalit. The warmth of those dinners was healing in its own way. Something still felt missing—something unspeakable—but for the first time in his life, Raavan felt a sense of peace.

✦

Months had passed since the chandelier accident at Pashupati Mahal. He kept a strict routine—early mornings, long hours, always surrounded by others. But tonight was different. It was nearly 9 p.m., and he was still alone in the lab, working by the dim light of a Bunsen burner.

All the staff had left long ago, and Raavan usually left with them. But earlier that day, Lalit had asked him—just once—to prepare a remedy for his headache. It was the first time Lalit had ever asked him for anything, and Raavan couldn't refuse. He respected the man too deeply.

Focused on his concoction, Raavan stirred a mixture of herbs as the pot simmered. Then he paused. A faint voice had called out - he was sure of it. He looked around. No one.

Brushing it off as imagination, he returned to the burner. Moments later, he heard footsteps behind him—soft, approaching steadily. Instincts honed in battle kicked in. He didn't turn. He kept stirring, but his senses shifted entirely to the sounds behind him.

As soon as the footsteps reached striking distance, Raavan spun, grabbed the intruder by the throat, and raised a pen towards the man's eye.

"Easy! It's me!" the man gasped, raising both hands in alarm.

It was Karan.

"You know," Karan said breathlessly, "most people just say hello."

Raavan blinked, lowered the pen, and released his grip. "You startled me. What are you doing here?"

"I'm on night patrol," Karan said, catching his breath. "I saw the lights on and wondered who was still working."

They had crossed paths a few times since Raavan joined the company. Raavan liked him. They were beginning to form a quiet friendship.

Karan looked around. "Why are you still here this late? Most labs shut down by now."

Raavan started to answer, but Karan cut in, "Forget it. Want to grab some food? I just finished my first patrol, and I'm starving."

Raavan hesitated, then nodded. Karan's company was welcome. He began wrapping up his materials while Karan wandered the lab, ears pricking at a sound. He heard a faint beeping—one he didn't recognise.

"These machines always beep, but that one's different," Karan muttered, walking towards the noise.

Raavan, now ready, called out, "You coming? I want to eat and get home before Lalit falls asleep."

Karan turned from the sound and followed him. Together, they walked out to Raavan's motorcycle and rode towards the main gate.

They had just reached the entrance when it happened.

A loud bang shattered the air. The ground shook. Shockwaves rippled through the complex.

Raavan slammed the brakes. Behind them, the lab he had just left exploded in a fireball.

Karan's jaw dropped, stunned. His mouth hung open. He stared at the burning ruins, his eyes fixed, unblinking.

Raavan looked at him. "Karan—" he began, but the man didn't move.

The next day, the company remained closed. Lalit had declared a holiday. At home, Raavan and Lalit sat with a few police officers who had come to investigate the explosion.

The inspector asked countless questions. Lalit, visibly worn, finally lost his temper. "How many times will you ask us the same thing?" he shouted.

Raavan intervened, calming him down. He escorted the inspector to the door. "I'm sorry," he said. "He's under a lot of stress."

The inspector nodded. "Understandable. One last thing—I forgot to ask. Did you see anyone suspicious that day? Or in the days before?"

Raavan opened his mouth to answer, but a constable ran up and whispered something in the inspector's ear.

The inspector turned back. "We've found the cause. A gas leak. Likely ignited during your work. Did you smell anything unusual?"

Raavan shook his head. The inspector nodded and left.

Back inside, Raavan found Lalit seated, unusually anxious. He sat beside him and placed a hand on his. "It's okay. It was just an accident. We're fine."

Lalit looked up. "We?" he asked. "Was someone with you?"

"Yes," Raavan replied. "Karan. If it weren't for him, I'd be dead."

✦

But Lalit's face went still. "The guards saw only you at the gate," he said slowly. "They told me you were alone."

Raavan blinked. "That's not possible. I was with him—Karan."

Lalit's voice hardened. "I've worked here my whole life. I know almost everyone. I've never heard that name. And the guards said you were alone that night." He studied Raavan. "Are you alright?"

Raavan stared ahead, the memory clear, but the facts refused to fit. He knew Karan had been there. He couldn't understand how Lalit didn't know him—or why the guards swore otherwise. Silence settled.

Confusion sharpened on Raavan's face, and Lalit saw it. "Let's go to the company and ask the guards," Lalit said. "We'll hear it from them." Raavan nodded. Neither spoke again as the car rolled into the night.

The car came to a stop near the west gate of the campus, where heavy construction vehicles were clearing the rubble from the explosion. Raavan and Lalit stepped out and walked briskly towards the guard's office.

Raavan approached the front desk and asked, "Who was on duty last night during the blast?"

One of the guards replied, "There were six guards. But they're all at the south gate now."

Without speaking, Raavan and Lalit returned to the car. As they drove, Lalit broke the silence. "Why are you doing this?" he asked, frustrated. "People will think you're hallucinating. You are the future of Pashupati Pharmaceuticals. People cannot see you like this."

Raavan didn't reply. He turned his face away from Lalit and stared out of the window, jaw clenched.

When they reached the south gate, Raavan leapt out of the car and rushed to the guards' office. "Tell this man that you saw Karan with me last night!" he demanded.

Lalit entered behind him, moving more slowly and with greater composure.

The guard at the desk looked confused. "Sir... you were alone," he said.

The others agreed—none of them had seen anyone with Raavan.

Raavan stumbled back, shaking his head in disbelief. "No... no, no," he whispered.

Then something clicked. He counted the men. "There were six of you last night. Where's the sixth?"

The guard replied, "He went home early this morning. Said he had a fever after the blast."

Lalit placed a firm hand on Raavan's shoulder. "See? You were alone."

Raavan's chest heaved with heavy breaths. He looked Lalit in the eye, voice barely audible. "Karan was there..."

Lalit tried to lead him away, but Raavan resisted. "Where does the other guard live?" he asked, turning back to the group.

The guards looked to Lalit for permission. Raavan did too.

Finally, one of them said, "He lives opposite the police station... in Ayodhya."

The name hit Raavan like a thunderclap.

Without another word, he bolted. Lalit called after him, but Raavan didn't stop. Lalit got into the car and followed, but Raavan ran faster than the vehicle, weaving through the narrow streets of Ayodhya until he reached the small house across from the police station.

He banged on the door.

It opened slowly. The guard stood weak and dazed. Raavan grabbed him by the collar and pulled him close. "Did you see anyone with me last night?" he growled.

Lalit's car pulled up behind him. He didn't get out, only rolled the window down to watch.

The guard looked pale and fevered. "No, sir," he said. "You were alone."

Raavan's grip loosened.

His hand fell from the man's collar.

He turned and began walking slowly towards the car, mouthing over and over,

"Karan was with me..."

His steps faltered. His balance wavered. Lalit's expression changed. Just as he opened the door to get out, Raavan stumbled forward, vomited, and collapsed to the ground.

✦

Raavan woke to the rhythmic beep of medical monitors. He was back in the hospital. A doctor stood beside him. Lalit sat quietly at his bedside.

Raavan blinked against the light. "Did you find Karan?" he asked.

Lalit didn't answer. But Raavan could see the disappointment in his eyes.

Lalit called for the police inspector and the six guards from the previous night. They entered the room together.

Raavan looked at the guards and said in a faint voice, "Please try to remember. He worked with you. You must know him. Please... tell the truth."

The guards glanced at one another, but no one spoke.

The inspector stepped forward. "There's no one named Karan in our records. No guard by that name has ever worked at Pashupati Pharmaceuticals. I was there last night. I saw you at the gate—and you were alone."

"Maybe you hit your head during the blast," he added, more gently.

Raavan turned towards Lalit, his face a mix of confusion and desperation.

Lalit remained silent for a moment. Then, unexpectedly, he stood and faced the inspector. "Find him," he said. "Find Karan."

The inspector looked baffled. "Sir—"

"If he says Karan exists, then he exists," Lalit interrupted. "It's your job to find missing people. I'll file a formal complaint. Let's go to the station."

The inspector knew better than to argue. Lalit's influence in Ayodhya was unquestionable. He softened his tone. "We'll check again. I'll bring every man named Karan from around the region to your house, I promise."

Lalit sat back down on Raavan's bed and placed a hand on his shoulder. "I believe you. You're not alone—we're family."

Raavan's eyes filled with tears; he felt seen.

Just then, a nurse entered, handing the doctor some pills.

"You had a concussion when you collapsed," the doctor said. "I'll be keeping you under observation for two more days." Then he and the nurse stepped out.

Raavan turned to Lalit and squeezed his hand. "Thank you."

Lalit looked into his eyes. "Don't go looking for Karan again."

Then he rose and quietly left the room.

Raavan lay alone in his hospital room that night. Lalit had arranged for two servants to wait outside the door, just in case. But even with them nearby, Raavan couldn't rest. His thoughts kept circling back to Karan.

Karan had been the first person to help him in Ayodhya. If not for him, Raavan might never have found Lalit. And now, something didn't feel right. His instincts screamed that Karan was in danger.

He needed to find him.

Raavan closed his eyes and took a deep breath, preparing to invoke Drishti. He began silently reciting the mantra. But before he could finish, the door opened. A servant entered with a set of stainless steel food boxes from home.

The servant, thinking Raavan was asleep, gently nudged him awake. Raavan blinked and sat up, the trance broken. The servant asked if he should serve the food, but Raavan shook his head. The man nodded and left the room.

Raavan was about to close his eyes again when something about the food containers caught his attention. They were identical to one he had received earlier in Ayodhya—from Karan. He remembered it clearly. Karan had given him a similar lunchbox on Raavan's second night in the city. It had Karan's name engraved on it.

A surge of hope lit up his face. The box was still in his closet back at the mansion. If he could get to it, he'd find proof that Karan exists.

His eyes sharpened with purpose. He stepped out of bed and peeked through the hallway. The servant was nowhere to be seen.

Raavan crept out of the hospital room and slipped past the guards unnoticed. Once outside, he broke into a run.

✦

He stopped a few feet from the main gate of the house and ducked behind a tree. Guards stood at their posts as always. If he tried to enter through the front, Lalit would know. He didn't want to betray Lalit's trust again.

Instead, he circled the compound, stopping at the spot closest to his balcony. He scaled the wall, climbed up the side of the building, and entered his darkened room.

He opened the closet and rummaged through his belongings. After several minutes of digging, he found it—the stainless steel container from Karan.

His hands trembled as he turned it over in the light. But what he read stopped him cold.

The name engraved wasn't Karan.

It was Raavan.

And the address? "Pashupati Hospital, Room 307."

His heart pounded. His breath came faster.

"No... that's not right," he whispered. "I remember... it said Karan's name. I saw it. I know it did."

Doubt surged through his mind like a rising tide. "Is Karan even real? Am I imagining him? Did I misread it? Or... is this someone else's container? Why does it have my name on it?"

He staggered backwards, dizzy. Panic threatened to crush him.

Then—footsteps. Approaching fast.

He dashed to the balcony. Servants stood in the garden below. He couldn't climb down.

The door creaked open. A maid stepped in, looked around the room, and found it empty; she then switched the lights off again. She exited.

Raavan was now perched on the narrow ledge outside a different room's window, clutching the wall. He waited.

Inside, two men entered. The first voice was familiar, but Raavan couldn't place it.

The man was furious—shouting, accusing the other of failure after failure. The second voice pleaded, apologetic.

Then came the chilling order: "Lalit will be at the hospital tomorrow morning. Make sure you kill him before then."

Raavan froze. His rage ignited. He leapt up to see who the conspirators were—but the room was already empty.

He no longer cared who saw him. He jumped from the ledge to the balcony, sprinted across his room, burst into the hallway, and raced to Lalit's room.

He flung the door open. Empty.

He searched the bathroom. The balcony. Nothing.

Breathing hard, Raavan stood in the centre of the room, hands shaking. Drishti wouldn't work on Lalit—he had tried that before.

But then an idea struck him.

Lalit always travelled by car—and he always had the same driver.

If he couldn't track Lalit directly... he could use Drishti on the driver.

Raavan sprinted towards the Pashupati Pharmaceuticals campus. Drishti had shown him what he feared—Lalit's driver had taken him there. He didn't know exactly when the attack would come.

As he approached the gate, he saw Lalit's car. Parked beside it were four large black vans, each bearing a symbol Raavan instantly recognised—the same insignia he had seen near the cave in Sri Lanka.

Books were being loaded into the vans. Not ordinary books—these were ancient, bound in brittle leather and etched with glyphs.

Raavan pushed forward, rushing inside the building. He scoured every room, every lab—no sign of Lalit. Then he heard muffled voices upstairs.

He crept up the stairs, moving towards the sound. The voices were coming from behind a door—partially ajar. It was Lalit's private room.

Raavan leaned closer and peered through the opening. Inside, a man sat in a chair with his back to the viewer, surrounded by several others clad in black uniforms, each bearing the same chest insignia.

His heart sank. Please, don't let it be Lalit.

The man turned.

It was Lalit.

✦

Raavan staggered back, a sick knot forming in his stomach. He dropped to his knees, hands on the floor, as disbelief flooded him. In the movement, his shoulder nudged the door—it closed with a loud thud.

Inside, silence broke.

Then a voice barked: "Shoot."

Raavan panicked. He didn't know who they meant—but he feared it was Lalit.

Rage surged through him. He stood, eyes glowing, and threw his hands forward.

Lightning burst from his body, splitting into hundreds of serpentine bolts. They tore through the room, striking the armed men in waves. Some dropped immediately, their torsos burned to ash. Others fired back.

Raavan fell to the ground, shielding Lalit with his body. Bullets tore through his back. He didn't move. Blood pooled beneath him as he looked up at Lalit.

"Run," he whispered.

His eyes closed.

The shooting stopped.

The remaining men stepped closer, guns still raised. One of them asked, "Is this the one we were meant to kill?"

Lalit stepped forward. "Yes," he said coldly. "This is Raavan."

He looked down at Raavan's bloodied body. "We've collected enough blood from you. We don't need you anymore."

He smirked at the men holding Raavan. "Collect every last drop of blood from his body. The master will be happier."

The men moved quickly. They lifted Raavan's limp body into a chair and inserted a needle into his arm. Blood began flowing into a dark, metallic cylinder.

Then—crack!

One of the men jerked and dropped to the ground. A bullet had struck him cleanly in the neck.

Smoke flooded the room as a small canister rolled across the floor. Panic erupted. The men coughed, choking on the fumes.

Lalit turned to Raavan—and saw something terrifying.

His wounds were healing.

The bullets were being pushed out of his skin. Muscle reknit. Flesh restored.

Lalit knew what had to be done. If Raavan woke up now, everything would fall apart.

He reached for a blade strapped to a choking guard's back. He raised it above Raavan's neck.

But before he could strike—crack!

Another bullet tore through his wrist. The bone snapped, and the blade clattered to the floor.

From the smoke, a figure emerged.

The shooter moved like a ghost, firing one clean shot through the head of the final guard.

Raavan stirred, eyes fluttering open. His breath returned. The blood loss had stopped.

The shooter walked to Lalit, stepped on his wounded hand, and leaned in close.

"I won't kill you," he whispered.

Then he raised the gun and struck Lalit hard across the temple.

Lalit collapsed, unconscious.

The shooter knelt beside Raavan, who was slowly regaining consciousness. He gently shook Raavan's face. Raavan opened his eyes and blinked at the haze around him. The room was filled with the bodies of men in black, and in front of him stood a familiar figure.

It was Karan.

✦

Raavan lifted a trembling hand and pointed. "Save him," he said.

Karan rose silently and walked over to Lalit. He crouched beside him, then gave a few light slaps to his cheek. Lalit stirred, blinked groggily—and then his eyes snapped open, locking onto Raavan's.

"Save me, Raavan!" he cried, voice shrill with panic. "He's going to kill us!"

Before he could finish, Karan's fist cracked across Lalit's face.

The blow was brutal. Raavan gasped. For a split second, the skin on Lalit's cheek seemed to ripple—like disturbed water beneath a mask of light.

Raavan's voice cracked. "What are you doing to Lalit?"

Karan didn't answer. Instead, he knelt low, his fingers twitching with intent. "You still don't see it, do you?" he whispered.

Then—slowly, deliberately—he drove his fingers into the skin just above Lalit's brow.

"No!" Raavan tried to rise, but pain lanced through his body. His muscles refused to obey.

With a sickening squelch, Karan began to peel.

The skin didn't tear—it slid. A perfect membrane lifting from skin, as though reality itself had been wearing a mask. Raavan could only watch in horror, his breath caught, his heart hammering.

The face beneath emerged—paler, colder, unfamiliar. The cheeks were thinner. The eyes were wrong. But the grin—that was the worst part. It belonged to a stranger.

Raavan stared, his throat dry. "If he's not Lalit... then who... Where is La—"

He stopped. The pieces were falling into place. The vision from Drishti. The room. The chain.

Raavan turned his gaze, trembling, to Karan. "Who is he?"

Karan stood, holding the discarded face like a trophy. "Mayank," he said, voice like flint. "Your uncle. Maya's brother. He's been pretending to be Lalit for years."

He let the mask drop to the floor.

"And he's working for the wrong Anveshi."

Before Raavan could respond, Mayank struck.

Seizing the moment while Karan was distracted, he pulled a knife from his boot and stabbed Karan repeatedly in the side.

Karan dropped to the ground, mask still in his hand.

Raavan screamed, rushing forward. He tackled Mayank, slamming him against the wall. He didn't care about himself—he only wanted to save Karan.

He dropped to Karan's side, pressed his hands over the wounds. Blood poured through his fingers. "Stay with me," Raavan whispered.

Karan's eyelids fluttered. He grabbed Raavan's hand and exhaled.

Behind him, Mayank stood with the knife raised. "Join us, Raavan," he said. "And I won't kill you."

Raavan laid Karan gently on the floor and stood. His eyes burned.

"Why did you do this?" he asked, voice sharp.

Mayank shrugged. "He attacked me. He killed my men."

"I'm not asking about Karan," Raavan growled. He stepped closer. "Why did you pretend to be Lalit?"

Mayank hesitated, stepping backwards. "Ahindra never wanted to lead the company. Dr Tara married him to my sister so I could run it after her. I came to the Pashupati Mansion ready to lead—but no one gave me a chance. It was always about Ahindra."

Raavan narrowed his eyes, closing the gap between them.

Mayank's voice cracked as he continued, "The night Ahindra burned the house, I was at the hospital—watching over Maya. A man approached me. He said he could give me everything—Pashupati Pharma, Anveshi India—but I had to do what he said."

His voice grew hollow. "He gave me a mask. He said it would make me Lalit. Said I had to keep Maya in a coma... and kill you if we ever find you."

Raavan's fists clenched.

Mayank looked haunted. "The mask... it changed me. It gave me some of Lalit's memories, his mannerisms, his voice. Soon, I wasn't even deciding for myself. I was just... following orders. I agreed to everything. Including killing you."

✦

Raavan grabbed Mayank's wounded arm. "Who made you do this?"

Mayank trembled. "They'll kill me if I tell you."

Raavan didn't blink. He tore the knife from Mayank's boot, stabbed it into the bullet wound, and twisted.

Mayank screamed in agony.

Tears streamed down his face. "I don't know his name," he sobbed. "He's from Anveshi... Norway."

Before Raavan could ask anything more, a sharp click echoed from Mayank's chest.

A small explosion burst inside him.

Mayank's eyes went wide before his body slumped. Dead.

Raavan stared in shock, then shook him violently. "No! Wake up! Wake up!"

But Mayank was gone.

Raavan turned to Karan—but he was gone too. His body had vanished, and with it, the pouch one of the attackers had used to collect Raavan's blood.

Raavan stood, shaken. On the floor where Karan had lain, something was written in blood.

He knelt down to read it.

Go to him.

Raavan sat on the floor, his back against the wall, mind clouded with questions. None had answers. Why had Mayank pretended to be Lalit? If he'd always planned to kill Raavan, why wait so long? Who was Karan, and why had no one else seen him? What was hidden in Room 307 at Pashupati Hospital?

But for now, none of that mattered.

Like a lightning bolt, a thought struck him. His eyes opened wide. He knew where Lalit was.

Raavan rose and made his way towards Pashupati Mahal. The dilapidated mansion loomed like a haunted carcass against the new moon sky. Shadows filled its broken halls. The darkness still made him uneasy—but this time, he didn't stop.

His body had healed. Strength had returned. He stepped inside and walked the familiar path back to the hall where the chandelier had once crushed him. Cracks spidered through the floor and walls, like veins of trauma embedded in the building itself.

He searched every room on the ground floor, then moved to the first, and finally to the second. Still no sign of Lalit.

But something felt wrong. In Drishti, he had seen light in Lalit's room—yet not a single light shone now. This meant only one thing: the room wasn't part of the visible structure.

Raavan took a deep breath, closed his eyes, and used Drishti again.

Lalit appeared—sitting in a dim, windowless room, his finger dragging lines on the wall in blood. The sight chilled Raavan to the bone. Lalit paused, then bit into another finger, letting fresh blood fall, and resumed drawing.

When the sketch was finished, Lalit turned and stared straight ahead—as though he could see Raavan watching.

Then he pressed his bloodied finger to his chest... and then to a square he had drawn.

Raavan recognised it. A map. Of the mansion.

He opened his eyes.

Lalit was in the basement.

Raavan rushed to the spot where the basement entrance should be, but only found a blank wall. He pushed with all his strength—nothing. He punched and kicked it in frustration.

Then he paused. His breath was heavy. Something caught his eye: a small groove on the side.

He slid two fingers into it and pulled.

With a click, the wall slid to one side.

Behind it, six men stood on a narrow staircase, waiting in complete silence. They wore black uniforms beneath tactical vests; each marked with the same sigil Raavan had seen in Lalit's room.

Weapons gleamed in their hands—knives, batons. Their eyes locked onto Raavan.

The man in front charged. His knife slashed the air, but Raavan moved faster. He sidestepped, slammed his fist into the man's gut, and sent him collapsing on the steps.

Four more charged. Raavan met them head-on. He dodged blow after blow, then kicked one so hard he tumbled down the stairs and crashed into the sixth man, who hadn't yet moved.

The remaining three circled Raavan. They attacked in sync—but none could land a hit. He waited, let them exhaust themselves, then leapt and kicked two of them simultaneously. The third, wide-eyed, dropped his weapon and fled.

Only one man remained, frozen at the bottom of the staircase. He hurled his baton at Raavan. It hit Raavan's head with a solid crack—but he didn't flinch.

Raavan descended slowly, step by step. The man trembled. Raavan grabbed him by the collar, pulled him close, and stared deep into his soul.

The man turned pale. His heartbeat thundered in his stomach.

Raavan let go, pointing towards the hallway.

The man ran for his life.

Raavan reached down and unhooked a ring of keys from the belt of a man who was lying unconscious—just what he needed.

He descended into the hallway. It was narrow, grimy, and lined with strange rooms filled with bizarre machines. He ignored them all.

At the end of the corridor stood a heavy metal door.

He tried each key, one by one, until one clicked.

The door opened.

Lalit stood inside.

Raavan's breath caught. He rushed forward and embraced him.

"I finally found you," he said, tears in his eyes.

Lalit hugged him weakly. "Thank you for saving me. I've waited for this day... for fifteen years. You've freed me."

Lalit was frail. Too weak to walk.

Raavan lifted him gently onto his back and carried him out of that cursed basement, step by step, into the light.

Lalit was under medical care for severe skin infections. The doctors kept him under constant observation. Raavan stayed by his side, but his mind was adrift—haunted by questions.

There were things he knew he would never understand—Mayank's transformation, the mask, the deeper intentions of Anveshi Norway. But one question clawed at his chest: his name engraved on the box—Pashupati Hospital, Room 307.

✦

This was a hospital built by Dr Tara, just a few minutes from their company. It was still early—just before dawn. Quietly, Raavan walked towards the hospital...

As he approached the gate, a shiver ran down his spine.

The building was exactly as he'd seen it in his dream—the same white pillars, the same steps, the same door. Then another image returned: his second dream—the woman in the room.

His mother.

Raavan broke into a run.

He raced through the first floor, throwing open door after door. Nothing. Then he remembered the number—Room 307. It was on the third floor.

He sprinted up the stairs. The hallway was just as he had seen it in his dream.

And there it was.

Room 307.

He stood at the door, trembling.

Inside, machines beeped in a panicked rhythm. Voices shouted. A woman lay on the bed in a pool of blood. Her throat had been slit.

It was Maya.

Raavan stumbled backwards. He turned and pressed his head to the glass window in the hallway, then slammed it again—and again. "I killed her," he whispered. "I killed her…"

Blood trickled from his forehead, down into his eye.

Through the blur, he saw someone fleeing the hospital. A man in a white lab coat, blood staining the sleeves.

Raavan's eyes narrowed.

It was the doctor who had treated him.

Raavan screamed, "STOP!"

But the man kept running.

Lightning erupted all around the doctor. Bolts tore through the air like divine judgement. The doctor froze, terrified.

Raavan descended the steps with fire in his chest. He walked right up to him, grabbed him by the throat, and snarled, "Why did you kill my mother?"

The doctor was shaking. "Please—I'll tell you. Just don't kill me."

He swallowed hard and began.

"Fifteen years ago, Lalit came to my house. He pulled a gun on me, shot my youngest daughter in front of my entire family. She died in my arms. He said, 'Do what I tell you... or the rest of your family dies next.' I had no choice."

"The next day, he brought a woman. Her body was almost entirely burned—except her face. He told me to keep her alive. Not just alive—in a coma. Permanently. Medically induced. And I did it. For fifteen years."

"I couldn't go to the police. He owned them. His men watched everything."

Raavan's grip tightened, but he let the man speak.

"A few months ago, he gave me another order. He said to collect your blood. I told you it was for tests… but there were no tests. His men took it straight from me. They said they needed it—urgently."

"And the poisoning? That wasn't random. They had me mix it into your food, your water. The day you collapsed vomiting—it wasn't a coincidence."

"And yesterday... he threatened my wife and my son. If I didn't kill the woman... he would have killed them."

"I'm sorry. I had no choice. I had to protect my family..."

Raavan could barely contain his rage. Lightning danced at his fingertips.

He wanted to end the man right there—burn him into ash.

But he closed his eyes.

And through Drishti, he saw the truth.

The man wasn't lying.

Raavan let him go.

The doctor fled.

Raavan stood alone outside the hospital. Then his knees buckled, and he collapsed to the ground.

He had saved the world from conspiracies, survived death, and walked through fire.

But he couldn't save his mother.

And so, he wept—raw, broken, and utterly alone.

✦

Months passed. Raavan and Lalit lived in the same house, but Raavan never left his room.

He locked himself inside, refusing to see anyone.

Lalit was worried. Every evening, he'd stop at Raavan's door and ask if he was okay. But Raavan never replied.

Then one evening, Lalit said softly, "I have the answers you're looking for."

A soft click echoed from the other side.

The door opened.

Raavan's room was a disaster. The walls were cracked. The floor was fractured. Furniture lay broken, plates shattered, spoons twisted into grotesque shapes.

Raavan walked to the balcony. "Why didn't Mayank kill me when he found me?"

Lalit stepped beside him. "Because you're not just anyone, Raavan. You're a marvel. Ahindra experimented on you—rewrote your DNA. That's why you have powers you don't even know about yet. Mayank was your uncle. But he chose the wrong Anveshi. He worked for Anveshi Norway—a rogue faction. They're creating something terrible. I don't know what it is… but I know your blood is key to it."

Raavan didn't respond.

"They sent men to Sri Lanka to find you," Lalit continued. "You escaped. But then you came to Ayodhya… straight into their jaws. The chandelier at Pashupati Mahal wasn't an accident. Mayank lured you into place. His men brought it down to get your blood."

Raavan's eyes didn't blink.

"They poisoned you. You survived. They triggered the lab explosion. Still, you lived. Mayank kept you alive just long enough to harvest what he needed. And yet... you're still standing."

Raavan nodded slowly. "How did Mayank manage to look exactly like you?"

Lalit exhaled and turned to the setting sun. "Anveshi Norway was founded by Kanaka, an alchemist who claimed to have learned his craft from Dashanan himself. He combined alchemy with Norwegian rune metals. Created materials that behave like magic. The mask Mayank wore. It's made from a programmable nanomaterial. It reads thought. It can shift texture, shape, and colour to mimic anyone in memory. Mayank used it to become me."

Raavan's face didn't change. Still, he stared at the horizon. "What about the books in their vans? Why were they stealing them?"

Lalit turned to him. "They tried—but failed. Those books were written by your ancestors, dating back to the Treta Yuga. Ahindra used those texts to transform you. They're sacred—dangerous in the wrong hands. Tomorrow, they'll be moved to our secret library in Varanasi."

Raavan's expression finally shifted. Anger flared in his eyes.

He clenched his jaw at the sound of Ahindra's name.

Lalit placed a gentle hand on Raavan's shoulder. "I knew Ahindra well. He wasn't a monster. I watched him around you when you were a child. He loved you more than anything. I don't believe you were just an experiment. There's more to the story. He would never hurt you."

Raavan shrugged Lalit's hand off. "What about Karan? No one saw him but me. What did the guards say? Did you find anything?"

Lalit sighed, his face heavy. He turned away and walked towards the hallway. "Yes. I investigated Karan. I don't think that's his name. No records matched your description. None of the guards were lying—they saw you alone every time."

Raavan's hands curled into fists.

Lalit paused, then continued. "But when I went to Sri Lanka, searching for you and Ahindra, I heard something... a piece of folklore. They say that whenever Dashanan returns, someone else rises with him. A guardian. A shapeshifter. A shadow in disguise. No one knows his face or his name. But they said he would appear. He protects Dashanan until the day he no longer needs protection. He hides behind many forms. He can be anyone. He senses danger like instinct. And he always arrives... just in time."

Raavan's thoughts drifted through every memory of Karan. The man who fed him when he was alone. Who saved him from the explosion? Who fought off armed men. Who bled, silently.

It had always been Karan.

He blinked. "Who is he?"

Lalit turned in the doorway. His voice was quiet.

"They call him… the **Kapatadhari**."

CHAPTER 07

Someone knocked on Lalit's door—loud and insistent. It was early morning, and for the first time in weeks, he had found peaceful sleep. The knocking dragged him out of it. Grumbling, he opened the door. A servant stood outside, breathless, holding a letter. He said nothing—just handed it over and walked back.

Lalit closed the door, returned to his room, slid on his glasses, and unfolded the note.

"I read the books my father studied before he created me. Until now, I thought I was just his experiment. But now I know who I am—and what runs through my veins.

I thought Shantinatha named me Raavan because of my scream. However, the truth is that I was created with Dashanan's Jeeva Tatva.

I feel less and less human every time I think about it.

If I stay, more people will come for me. I am a threat to all of you. And I've already lost too much. I don't want to lose you, too.

I'm leaving. Don't look for me.

Thank you for answering my questions—but now I have more. And you can't answer them. Pray that I find someone who can.

I've taken some money, my motorcycle, and some clothes. The rest is yours—the property, the company, all of it.

You are a kind man, Lalit."

Lalit stood on his balcony, his eyes red with fury. A single tear rolled down his cheek and dropped onto his shoe. But it wasn't sorrow that filled his chest. It was anger—cold, aching anger.

He walked to the railing and gripped it tightly. His knuckles turned pale. He had spent fifteen years in confinement, waiting—preparing—for Raavan. Every sacrifice, every year in the shadows, had been for this. And now, Raavan was gone, leaving behind nothing but a letter.

✦

Fifteen years ago, when Ahindra vanished, Lalit had been young enough to chase him. But now, age had robbed him of that strength. Once, he had the support of the Indian Anveshi. Now he was among the last few. And the Norwegian cell was hunting him.

If they found Raavan, they would harvest his blood, dissect his secrets, and destroy him. If Raavan died, Lalit's entire life would have been wasted.

He looked out at the horizon, the sun melting into the earth, and memory blurred with grief. The rage in his eyes softened—gave way to pain.

Lalit stood alone on the balcony, the city stretching below him in golden silence. His eyes were fixed on the horizon, but his thoughts turned inward—to the sacrifices he had made for the Pashupatis. He remembered the moment clearly: the day he received word from an Anveshi explorer that Ahindra had been spotted near Rameswaram. Something told him Ahindra was heading for Sri Lanka. He left the house without a word.

Lalit was an adrenaline junkie—danger made him feel alive, but his prosthetic leg slowed him. He already knew, even before the explorers confirmed it, where Ahindra was going: the cave where Dashanan's Jeeva Tatva was hidden. He had to get there first—before Ahindra endangered himself or, worse, his son.

He boarded the fastest train to Madras. But the moment he arrived, he felt it—eyes on him. He was being followed. He didn't know who they were or what they wanted, but he knew what the Jeeva Tatva was worth—and how much destruction it could unleash in the wrong hands. A military veteran with decades of fieldwork behind him, Lalit remembered the first rule of his trade: clear your tail before reaching the target.

He sat alone on a platform bench, pretending to read a book. Hours passed. The train had arrived in the afternoon—it was now nearly midnight. A man wearing a railway uniform approached. "Where's your ticket? You've been sitting here a while now," he said. "Which train are you taking?" Lalit didn't look up at first. Then he glanced at a group of men standing some distance away and replied, "I'm with them. They have my ticket. You can ask them."

The man frowned. "They're not with you. Just tell me where you're headed." That was all Lalit needed. He had been watching them the whole time—their posture, their gait, their eyes. This man wasn't a railway officer. The group was following him.

Lalit closed his book and smiled. The thug grabbed him by the collar and yanked him off the bench. "Guys, come here! Looks like he doesn't want to talk politely." The others began walking towards them.

Lalit leaned in and whispered, "How much did they pay you? I'll double it—if you tell me who they are." The thug sneered. "You can't come close to what they're paying." That confirmed it—this wasn't a random gang. This was funded. Someone inside the Anveshi circle had sent them.

Lalit dropped his briefcase and began rolling up his sleeve. The thug laughed and shouted back to his men, "The old man's gonna fight!" They all laughed—until Lalit moved.

With one sudden shove, he threw the thug backwards. The man staggered, stumbled towards the edge of the platform—and fell. His body hit the ground, but his head hung over the tracks. A train roared past.

In a flash, the thug's head was gone. Blood sprayed across the platform. His body convulsed once, then rolled off the edge. The others stopped cold, frozen in horror. When they looked back up, Lalit was gone.

He was already on the train, leaning against the wall beside the door, his heart pounding like a war drum. For the first time in years, he felt truly alive. Lights blurred past the window, but Lalit wasn't watching them. He was thinking.

He wasn't safe. Not yet. Only one person knew where he was headed—the same informer who had tipped him off about Ahindra. That meant he couldn't trust anyone now.

✦

Suddenly, the puzzle pieces clicked into place. He remembered how the Anveshi cells from Norway and Egypt had pressured Dr Tara to crack the Jeeva Tatva, how their agents had started flooding into India. And how Indian Anveshi members were either dying in mysterious accidents—or getting suspiciously rich overnight and leaving Anveshi.

It was clear now: the global Anveshi network was infiltrating the Indian chapter. And they didn't want the Jeeva Tatva for knowledge—they wanted it for control.

Lalit's eyes widened. The Pashupati family is in danger, he thought. And the only person who could have protected them was far away. His heart clenched. His instincts screamed that Ahindra was on the verge of a mistake—but his family could be next. These were the kinds of crossroads that broke even the strongest of men.

He reached into his pocket and pulled out his lucky coin—a worn, familiar piece of brass from his days in uniform. Heads, I return to Ayodhya. Tails, I go to the cave. He flipped the coin. It hung in the air, spinning with the weight of fate—then landed.

Heads.

Lalit closed his eyes, smiled, and kissed the coin before tucking it away. He was going to save Ahindra first.

It was past noon when a passenger gently nudged Lalit awake. The man spoke in Tamil, but Lalit didn't need to understand the words—he understood the message. The train had reached Rameswaram. Lalit disembarked and made his way into a coastal fishing village. He sought the darkest, quietest corner he could find—the kind of place where rules didn't matter and questions weren't asked. Eventually, he found it: a thatched tavern where men sat beneath palm fronds, drinking toddy and eating fried fish. They were loud, volatile, and dangerous.

Lalit approached. The men fell silent and stared. He pulled out a thick bundle of cash and spoke a single word. "Ceylon." They exchanged glances. One of them—a wiry man with a jagged scar and a knife in hand—stood up and replied in Tamil. Lalit didn't understand the language, but he understood the nod. The man had agreed. He introduced himself as Selvan.

They walked to a small boat with a tattered mast. Selvan climbed in and helped Lalit aboard, then began to row. The sea was rough. Currents pulled against them. Waves slapped the sides. The sun blazed down. Neither of them spoke—which suited Lalit just fine.

Hours passed. At one point, Selvan caught a fish, gutted it with practised ease, rubbed it with salt and spices, and roasted it over a small flame. He offered a portion to Lalit with a rare smile. Lalit was starving. He accepted without a word.

Selvan began to hum a tune in Tamil—a melody of the sea, sorrowful and slow. Lalit didn't understand a single word, but somehow, it calmed him. For the first time in days, he felt a sense of peace. The breeze had cooled. His stomach no longer ached. And in the golden haze of the setting sun, the coast of Sri Lanka appeared on the horizon. He didn't know it then, but this would be the last time he felt peace for many years.

✦

As the shoreline came into view, Lalit stood up, eager to disembark. The boat rocked violently. Selvan shouted and gestured for him to sit. The moment Lalit obeyed, a bullet struck the water just ahead of them. Lalit spun around. A motorised boat loomed in the distance—larger, faster, and armed. Several figures stood on the deck, silhouetted by the sun. Rifles glinted in their hands.

Another shot rang out. The paddle in Selvan's hands snapped in two. A third bullet hit the hull, splintering wood. Selvan dropped to the deck, trembling. Lalit grabbed him by the hair and yanked him down. "Stay low," he growled. Lalit reached into his bag and pulled out a pistol. He fired—once, twice—the bullets went wide. Selvan flinched with every shot, curling deeper into the boat. Lalit fired again. Six shots in total. All missed. The enemy boat drew closer. Lalit slumped beside Selvan, heart pounding.

Selvan turned towards him, furious, and spat a curse. Lalit looked back, calm as ever, and muttered, "The boat was moving."

A spotlight flooded their faces. Men in uniform climbed aboard. Not thugs—soldiers. The Coast Guard. One of them—tall, clean-shaven, and smirking—lifted his radio. "Sir, I've found the man the Norwegians were asking about." A voice crackled over the speaker. The soldier's smile widened. He turned to his companion. "Cuff them both."

The order was carried out. Selvan struggled, but Lalit didn't resist. Their wrists were bound in front, and the boat turned back towards Sri Lanka. They docked near a secluded beach. The prisoners were marched inland, down a narrow jungle trail that led to a hidden British-era outpost. Lalit walked silently. Selvan glowered beside him. Soldiers trailed behind with rifles trained on their backs.

As they neared the outpost, firelight flickered through the trees. The squad leader stepped into a canvas command tent. Lalit and Selvan were chained to the legs of a wooden table in a nearby tent. Selvan spat another curse—low and bitter.

Lalit turned to him, smiled faintly. He still didn't understand a word.

Captain Henryson, a young British officer of the Royal Navy stationed in Ceylon, stood inside the command tent, reviewing logistics with Captain Wilson, the older and more experienced leader of the outpost. They discussed security protocols for their new prisoners and preparations for important guests who were due to arrive the next afternoon. Wilson, a veteran of the region, ordered additional tents to be raised and instructed the cooks to account for the guests in their meal planning.

After the meeting, Henryson stepped out into the thickening dusk and entered the prisoner's tent. Selvan immediately began pleading in Tamil. Though Henryson didn't understand a word, the desperation in his tone was clear—he wanted to be released. Henryson ignored him. He wasn't here for Selvan.

He walked straight to Lalit, pulled up a chair and sat. "You seem like a weak old man," he said casually, "but my commander seems very concerned about you. Why is that?" Lalit stared back, silent. Henryson shrugged. "No matter. I'll hand you over to the Norwegians tomorrow, and we'll go our separate ways. I return to London, and you... wherever they take you." With that, he left.

✦

Later, a sepoy entered with two metal trays and placed them on the ground. Selvan didn't move—either confused or imprisoned for the first time in his life. He didn't touch the food. Lalit picked up his own tray, then reached for Selvan's and placed it before him with a cold look. He gestured once—eat. Reluctantly, Selvan complied.

Outside, the fog thickened. Lanterns hissed and burned higher. The outpost was prepared for the jungle night. Tigers, leopards, and bears were known to circle the perimeter. The guards remained alert. Inside the tent, silence returned. Everyone slept. Everyone except Lalit.

He opened his eyes. Still chained to the table, he scanned the tent. A nail protruded from the wooden leg. Quietly, he pried it loose and began working on the lock. After several minutes, a click. The cuff opened. He stood, stretched, and moved slowly. He retrieved his bag from the ground, crept to the edge of the tent, and peered outside. The fog had swallowed the outpost. Guards appeared only as drifting shadows in the mist. Lalit slipped into the white veil—and vanished.

He ran through the jungle, each step thudding softly, his prosthetic leg muffled by the soil. He moved fast, driven not by fear, but by urgency. He had to find Ahindra. Eventually, the jungle gave way to a village—no more than a dozen straw-roofed homes cloaked in darkness. Every door was shut, and though the windows stood open, they revealed nothing but shadow. Except one.

A faint glow flickered from its window. A horse stood tethered outside. Lalit approached and knocked on the open frame. No answer. He knocked again.

Suddenly, a hand touched his shoulder. He spun around, already coiling for a punch. An old man stood behind him, clothed in white, with a long silver beard and a tall wooden staff. Lalit's fist flew. But just before it landed, the old man raised his staff and blocked the strike with quiet, effortless precision.

Lalit froze. "I'm sorry," he panted, stepping back. The old man smiled. "You are strong," he said calmly. "You're the right one for the task."

Lalit didn't care. "That horse—is it yours? Sell it to me. I need to get somewhere. Now."

The old man looked at the horse, then back at Lalit. "I know you want to find Ahindra and take him back," he said. "Don't. The fate of the Yuga depends on what he is doing." The name hit like a slap. Lalit's face hardened. He shoved the old man against the doorway, drew his pistol, and pressed the barrel to his chest.

"How do you know why I'm here? How do you know Ahindra? Who are you with?"

The old man didn't flinch. "I know your weapon is out of ammo," he said softly. "I've been watching you all day."

Lalit stepped back. "They call me Shantinatha. I'm the Guru of an Ashram nearby. I've been following your lives since the day I took on the post. And I'm here to stop you... from stopping Ahindra."

Lalit's expression twisted from confusion to fury in seconds. Without a word, he shoved Shantinatha inside the house and slammed the door shut, bolting it from the outside. His heart thundered in his chest. He didn't understand how the old man knew so much—and he wasn't going to stick around to find out. He leapt onto the horse and galloped southwest towards the cave.

His mind raced. The most logical explanation is that Shantinatha was working with the Norwegians, who had been sent to track him—possibly to mislead him. The wind lashed against his face, and for a moment, he felt young again. Alive. As he had once felt in the army before he lost his leg.

Then, without warning, something slammed into his chest. He flew backwards off the horse and crashed onto the ground. His sling bag flew yards away. Breathless and dazed, he groaned and looked up. Shantinatha stood over him. It hadn't been a branch. It had been the old man's staff.

Shantinatha approached, extending a hand. "I'm sorry if I hurt you," he said calmly. "All I want is to show you your place in Ahindra's son's destiny."

Lalit ignored the hand and scrambled to his feet. "Who are you? Are you working with the Norwegians?" He moved to restrain him—but Shantinatha spoke first.

"If you grab my wrist, twist, and try to lock me, I'll take a step back, pull you forward, and jab my elbow into your throat."

Lalit froze. That was exactly how he would have countered the move. He slowly lowered his hands, confused. "Who are you? Tell me."

Shantinatha stepped forward and gently placed his palm on Lalit's head. Lalit ducked, shoved him aside, and bolted towards his bag. Just as he bent to retrieve it, he was yanked backwards and slammed into the ground. Shantinatha again.

Lalit rolled, grabbed a handful of stones, and hurled them. Shantinatha dodged some, shattered others mid-air with his staff, and finally struck one back. It hit Lalit squarely on the forehead. He collapsed.

Shantinatha approached and knelt beside him, pressing against the bleeding wound to stem the flow. "Listen to me carefully," he said, voice firm but kind. "I cannot let you stop Ahindra. This must happen. You don't know what's coming—but you're part of it. Trust me. Let me show you what you need to see." He placed his hand on Lalit's forehead again.

Lalit's eyes rolled back. Consciousness slipped. He entered a trance-like state. When he came back, he was not the same.

Shantinatha had etched something into his mind—a vision filled with war, monsters, and cold that could freeze the sun. Lalit saw pain. He saw death. He saw the world freezing. His lips trembled.

Lalit lurched back, eyes wide. "Who are you? What are you doing to me?" His knees gave out, and he sank to the ground, shivering. A tear tracked down his cheek. "How is this possible?

How does stopping Ahindra from experimenting on his son destroy the world as we know it?" he whispered.

Shantinatha set a hand on his shoulder. "That boy will save us all. But before he can, he must be transformed." At once, another vision rushed up—the one Shantinatha had already shown him: Dashanan's Jeeva Tatva driven into the child's body, the white-hot agony that would follow. Lalit recoiled and shoved Shantinatha away. "He is just a child," he said, voice heavy.

Shantinatha stepped closer. "That is the child's destiny. But the child will live, I will train him. Prepare him. He is our only hope. He is the one."

But Lalit wasn't convinced. He had seen children wounded in battle—but never a child bear what he had just witnessed. And he had borne much himself: bullets, blades, even an amputation without anaesthesia. But the suffering awaiting that boy... it terrified him.

He clasped Shantinatha's hand and pleaded, "Please... help me save him."

Shantinatha's gaze darkened. "I can't."

Lalit had seen too much already. His mind throbbed with pain. He was slipping into unconsciousness. Moments later, he fainted.

✦

Lalit lay slumped against a tree, breathing heavily. Shantinatha sat quietly nearby, perched on a rock, watching him in silence. As the fog of unconsciousness lifted, Lalit gasped awake, shifting restlessly, trying to make sense of the heaviness in his chest.

Shantinatha placed a hand gently on his shoulder. "Whatever you saw," he said, "that is what will happen if you stop Ahindra now. The boy is the only one who can prevent that future. He is our only hope. Let's make sure he walks the right path."

Lalit, drained of strength and will, summoned what little he had left. He turned to Shantinatha. "I trust you," he said. "I'll let Ahindra finish what he came here to do. After that, we'll take the kid to Ayodhya. You can train him there. Come with us."

Shantinatha looked past the treetops, eyes fixed on a distant mountaintop. "He won't go anywhere just yet," he said. "He'll come to Ayodhya when the time is right."

Lalit nodded reluctantly. "Then I'll stay back. I'll help you train him."

But Shantinatha shook his head. "No. You have a destiny to fulfil, Lalit. You must stop Anveshi from reaching the cave—at any cost. They'll arrive at the outpost tomorrow afternoon. Hold them off until sunrise. They are greater in number, stronger, and better armed. The odds are not in your favour... but stop them anyway. Your part in the boy's destiny begins here."

Lalit stared at the ground, fists clenched around the socket of his prosthetic leg. His voice trembled. "I can't... fight." He had faced death before. He had fought in war zones. But since losing his leg, his confidence had bled away—one drop at a time.

"I believe in you," Shantinatha said gently. "I only wish you believed in yourself as much as I do. Never forget—you are a soldier."

That word—soldier—sparked something deep inside him. A flicker of flame from a long-buried life. He stood, back straight, eyes hardening. "I'll give them a fight," he said. "And when this is done, I'll bring the boy to you."

Shantinatha didn't reply. He turned away and stared into the sky. "You won't meet him anytime soon," he said. "Go back to Ayodhya. Keep his mother alive for as long as you can. That is the greatest gift you can give him."

Lalit's chest tightened. He stepped forward. "Maya's fine. She's safe. She's at home."

Shantinatha didn't meet his eyes. "They are not safe. Leave for Ayodhya as soon as the sun rises the day after tomorrow. If you're quick, there's still a chance to save her."

A cold shiver ran through Lalit's spine. His eyes were bloodshot, his jaw clenched with rage. "I'll keep her alive," he vowed. "I swear to you—he'll see his mother again. But when will he come back?"

Shantinatha looked into his eyes. "Fifteen years, four months, and three days from now," he said. "The day the walls crack, and you'll feel tremors in Ayodhya. On the third new moon after that, during the guard shift change, draw the map of the building you're in. The boy will find you."

Lalit didn't understand most of it. But he didn't question Shantinatha. He burned the time of the boy's return into his mind and nodded. "I'll count every single day from now on."

They smiled—for the first time that night. A quiet, heavy smile, forged from sacrifice and duty.

Shantinatha tapped his staff against the earth. The horse returned from the trees, snorting softly. He embraced Lalit one final time and whispered, "Go now, soldier."

✦

Lalit mounted the horse, tightened the reins, and looked back. "See you on the other side." Then he rode into the mist, back towards the outpost.

He reached the outskirts just as the first light of dawn crept across the horizon. He dismounted quietly and led the horse to a tree, tying it securely. Then, moving swiftly on foot, he slipped back inside the perimeter—and into the very tent where he had been imprisoned. Selvan still lay asleep on the floor, his breath deep and even. Lalit moved to the table, fastened one cuff loosely around his wrist, and lay down beside it. He didn't lock the shackle. The illusion of captivity might serve him well.

He closed his eyes, but sleep wouldn't come. Shantinatha had shown him glimpses of the future—just enough to keep him from interfering with Ahindra, just enough to prepare him for today's battle. But there was no map. No strategy. No prophecy about how to stop what was coming. One thing was certain: the Anveshi wouldn't listen to reason. They wouldn't hesitate. And neither could he. He would have to fight.

But the weight of that truth pressed down like stone. His body was weary. His mind was frayed—shaken by visions, hollowed by truths. He hadn't lifted a weapon in years. And the last time he had fought—truly fought—it had cost him his leg.

The amputation hadn't broken him. That day, he had remained calm, sealing his wound with fire, surviving like the soldier he was trained to be. But what followed—that had broken him, piece by piece. He could no longer run. Couldn't climb. Couldn't lead in the field. People had stopped saluting and started pitying each other. They called him brave, but looked at him as if he were a relic. A cripple. And somewhere along the way, something inside him had died. He was no longer a soldier. He was just Lalit.

Captain Wilson was already awake. He stood outside his tent, sipping tea and listening to his men banter about the two prisoners Henryson had brought in the day before. His own tent was stationed just behind theirs. Curiosity tugged at him.

He circled around to the side of the holding tent and peeked through the mesh flap. Selvan was closest to the entrance. Wilson smirked—just another coastal fisherman, by the looks of it. A dime a dozen. Then he noticed the second figure. Boots. Pressed trousers. One leg—metallic. A prosthetic.

Wilson narrowed his eyes. He stepped closer, leaned in, rose slightly on his toes, and peered through the mesh. And froze. His face went pale. He stumbled backwards, tripped over a guy line, and collapsed into his own tent, bringing it down in a tangled heap. Canvas and poles crumpled over him.

Soldiers rushed to help, startled by the noise. But nothing could prepare them for the look on their captain's face—blank, breathless, horrified as if he'd seen a ghost.

Wilson grabbed a soldier's hand and pulled himself up. Still dazed, he scanned the camp. Then, in a voice so low it barely reached their ears, he spoke the words that would change everything. "Kill the man before he wakes up." He swallowed hard. "He is Captain Savyasachi."

The soldiers crept towards the tent, rifles raised, fingers tense on the triggers. Captain Wilson stood behind them, sweat beading on his brow. He knew that if the man inside that tent woke up, none of them would survive. The soldiers, unaware of who lay within, stepped closer.

Then something flew from the tent. A flash of steel.

Wilson dropped. The soldiers spun around. Their captain lay on the ground, a knife lodged deep in his throat. Blood pulsed in rhythmic jets. He choked, gasped, and managed a final word. "Run."

They turned back to the tent—just in time to see the mesh flap fall away, and a man step through the slit.

They had no time to react. A table flew from inside and crashed into three soldiers, sending them sprawling to the dirt. The man leapt out after it. He moved like a storm. He yanked the blade from Wilson's throat and buried it in the chest of a nearby soldier. Then another. And another. Each strike was clean. Controlled. Lethal.

Behind him, Selvan stood frozen—wide-eyed, mouth agape. He had just watched Lalit—no, something else wearing Lalit's body—kill three men in under ten seconds. Then Lalit turned and flung the knife at Selvan. It missed him by an inch and struck a soldier behind him, right through the eye. Selvan whirled around, stunned, as the body dropped lifeless. Lalit limped towards him, fast and furious.

"I've saved you twice," he growled, grabbing the knife from the skull and shoving it into Selvan's hand.

Selvan looked down. It was his knife—the one Lalit had taken from him back on the boat and hidden until now. He still didn't move. Still couldn't speak.

Lalit bent to the fallen soldiers, gathering rifles and ammunition. He tossed one rifle to Selvan, who caught it by reflex, though he remained paralysed by shock. Lalit stood tall, blood on his hands, a pistol in each hand. He was ambidextrous when it came to shooting.

Shouts erupted across the outpost. Gunfire. Screams. The remaining soldiers had heard it all—and they came running. Some emerged from tents. Others took to the towers. Shadows flickered in the fog.

Selvan ducked behind a tree.

Lalit didn't.

Ten rifles turned towards him. He dove behind cover and returned fire. Every shot struck true. Six bullets. Six dead men. But more kept coming.

A tower guard steadied his aim. He had a clean shot. He paused. And stared. The face in his scope wasn't just familiar—it was legendary. He climbed down and sprinted across the battlefield, dodging fire, shoving past chaos, shouting, "Stop the fire! Stop shooting!"

No one listened. He reached Captain Henryson, panting.

"It's—he's—it's Savyasachi!"

Henryson couldn't hear over the gunfire. The soldier grabbed his shoulders. "It's Captain Savyasachi!"

✦

The name cracked through the chaos like a thunderclap. The field froze. Rifles lowered. Boots halted mid-step. Only Henryson kept shooting—until he noticed the stillness. He stopped and looked around.

The soldiers' faces were pale. Some dropped their rifles. Others stared into the fog, lips trembling. A whisper cut through the silence.

"Savyasachi? Wasn't he... supposed to be dead?"

The soldier who had raised the alarm nodded slowly. "I saw him. Don't shoot. If you want to live—don't shoot."

Henryson sneered. An outsider. A stranger to the legend. He raised his voice.

"You're all cowards," he spat. "Take my command—or face the same fate as him!"

He struck the soldier across the face, sending him to the ground. Then he raised his pistol and aimed it at the man's head.

"Shoot the captives!" he roared. "Or I shoot you!"

No one moved.

Henryson placed his finger on the trigger—but the pistol didn't fire.

Pain erupted in his hand. He looked down. A knife had pierced clean through his trigger finger, severing it. Blood gushed in waves. His hand twitched. And the finger dropped to the ground.

For a moment, nothing moved. Not even the wind. Then Henryson dropped to his knees, screaming.

The soldier he had struck stood up, stared at the chaos, and pointed to the mist, to the shadow rising from the smoke. He shouted one word:

"Savyasachi!"

✦

To the people of Ayodhya, Lalit was just a quiet, middle-aged man—a former soldier who had lost his leg in some distant war and faded into obscurity.

But only Dr Tara knew the truth.

She knew the legacy he carried.

His full name was Lalit Savyasachi, son of Mahesh Savyasachi, the most brilliant explorer ever to serve the Anveshi. It was Mahesh who had deciphered the ancient map, who had led the first expedition to the cave where Dashanan's Jeeva Tatva was hidden.

Ten men and women had gone in.

Only Mahesh had returned.

He had wanted his son to follow in his footsteps—to become an Anveshi. But Lalit had chosen the army instead. To the world, Mahesh died on a failed mission to Kadali Vanam. Lalit, they said, lost his leg in a foreign war.

But Dr Tara knew the truth. She knew what the Savyasachis had sacrificed—not just for the Anveshi, not just for the Pashupatis, but for people that weren't even their own. Since that day, she had treated Lalit like kin—and made him the chief of security for Anveshi India.

Now, Lalit was walking slowly through the outpost—no longer a captive, but a legend returned.

The soldiers around him said nothing. For the first time, they were seeing Captain Savyasachi in the flesh.

Henryson, humiliated and bleeding, had switched the pistol to his other hand. He raised it towards Lalit—but the knife was still jammed in the trigger. He couldn't fire.

Lalit approached him calmly. He took the pistol, removed the knife, wiped the blade on his sleeve, and handed it to Selvan without looking.

"Good to see you alive, my friend," he said quietly.

Selvan stared at the weapon, then at Lalit, stunned. He hadn't understood anything that had just happened.

Lalit turned to the soldiers. "Lower your weapons."

They obeyed.

Then he helped Henryson to his feet.

"I know the Norwegian Anveshi are coming," Lalit said. "Go to the beach. Tell them to turn back."

Henryson, seething with rage and shame, nodded stiffly and disappeared into the trees. Lalit watched him go. He knew it wasn't over. A wounded snake always returns for revenge.

And that was exactly what he wanted.

When Henryson was gone, Lalit turned to the rest of the soldiers.

"I'm sorry I had to shoot your men," he said. "I had no choice. Henryson will return—with reinforcements. Leave this place. Go home. Guide Selvan to the shore."

The soldiers glanced at Selvan, who blinked, still processing.

One of them—a Tamil speaker—stepped forward and translated everything. Selvan listened, then looked at Lalit with new understanding. He nodded.

The outpost erupted in silent motion. Men packed gear, stripped weapons, doused fires. No orders were shouted. No songs were sung. It was an orderly evacuation—carried out in reverence.

One soldier approached Lalit.

"Are you… Captain Savyasachi?"

Lalit smiled faintly.

"I was Captain Savyasachi," he said. "Now… I'm just Lalit."

The soldier hesitated, then offered him a rifle. "You said Henryson would come back. Keep this. You might need it."

Others followed—placing weapons on the table beside him. Rifles, pistols, grenades, cartridges—not as supplies, but as offerings. Offerings to a man they no longer dared to fight beside—or worse, against.

By ten o'clock, the outpost was empty.

Lalit stood alone.

He took out his pocket watch and stared at the time. Tick by tick, it moved towards something he could no longer avoid.

For a moment, he looked around—at the empty tents, the still morning air, the silence that follows reverence.

There was no one left to shield him. No more distractions. No fear of someone else's face to protect.

Only him.

He knew—with full certainty—that if that tower soldier hadn't recognised him...

If he hadn't shouted *Savyasachi*, he would already be dead.

✦

It was nearly sunset. Deep in the forest, the shift of day was changing. Birds returned to their nests and bats rose in swarms from the caves. The light dimmed. So did the air. Lalit sat at the centre of the outpost—alone. A campfire crackled before him, flames flickering like nervous tongues. A rifle rested across his lap. His eyes, fixed on the fire, glowed orange in its reflection. Above, birds on high branches looked like still leaves against the dying sky.

Then—rustling. He turned. A burst of flame streaked from the trees. A heartbeat later—pain. His chest lit up with searing agony as a gunshot rang out across the forest. Lalit had been shot. He looked down. Blinked. But didn't care. He raised the rifle to his shoulder and fired blindly towards the source. Reloaded. Fired again. Then collapsed.

From the trees emerged a man in black, the Anveshi insignia stitched across his chest.

"I found our man," he shouted. "I tranquilised him."

A squad followed. At their centre, a masked officer pulled off his covering—a Caucasian man with pale eyes and pale intent.

"How long until he wakes up?" the officer asked.

"About an hour."

The leader knelt beside Lalit as the others fanned out to guard the perimeter. He plucked the dart from Lalit's chest—and froze. The needle was bent. Not normal. He looked down at Lalit's face. Eyes wide open. Smiling.

"Too late."

Lalit pulled a shotgun from beneath his coat and fired directly at the leader's feet. The blast tore his boot, ankle, and most of his foot into pulp. Flesh and bone were sprayed across the fire pit. Burning embers exploded like stars.

Chaos followed.

Screams. Curses. Panic.

Lalit rolled behind a crate, snatched up two pistols, and began firing. Every shot precise. Every movement measured. He moved like a ghost—weaving through firelight and shadow, leaping, rolling, dodging. He used the dead as shields. He made every bullet count.

Ten had come.

Seven were dead.

Out of ammo, he grabbed a chair and hurled it—the leg slammed into a soldier's throat, collapsing his windpipe. Lalit seized the man's rifle and finished the last two with surgical calm.

Then…

Silence.

Only the fire remained.

Lalit stood panting, soot-streaked, alone in the dark.

Near the flames, the leader—Isak—screamed beside the wreck of his foot.

Lalit dragged him to a pole and tied him there. Blood soaked the soil beneath what remained of his leg.

He removed the tattered boot.

What was left was barely human—shredded meat and shattered bone.

Lalit looked at him, eyes clouded. "I'm sorry," he said.

Isak blinked through the pain, stunned.

"Your apology means nothing," he spat. "Henryson is coming. With more men. When I find the scientist, I'll cut your leg off."

Lalit froze.

He hadn't expected reinforcements. He had no grenades left. No rifles to spare. Every trap was now spent.

Isak saw the fear crack through his composure—and laughed.

"I'll gut you alive," he shouted.

Lalit turned away.

Isak kept shouting. Threats. Curses.

Lalit walked from tent to tent—methodical, silent.

When he returned, he knelt beside Isak with a bottle of water and began cleaning the wound. Isak screamed. Lalit tore strips from his shirt and wrapped the leg.

Isak spat on him. Kicked him.

Lalit wiped the spit off—and walked away.

He reloaded his pistol, his shotgun, his rifle. Filled his pockets with whatever ammo he could find. Then he crouched behind a bunker of sandbags and crates. He looked up. The moon was full—but veiled behind clouds. He looked down at the flak jacket he wore. He removed it. Then, slowly, he reached into his pocket and pulled out the coin.

"Heads... survive," he whispered. "Tails... die."

He tossed it.

The coin didn't land in his hand. It fell to the dirt. He bent to find it. But the dark was too deep. And then silence.

Isak had stopped screaming. Too suddenly.

Lalit stood. Behind the bunker—shadows. Figures. Guns raised. Henryson. Isak. And a fresh squad.

"Drop the gun!" one of them shouted.

Lalit had no choice.

He let the pistol fall.

It landed with a clink.

He looked down.

The coin had landed.

Tails.

✦

The sun was just beginning to rise. Its golden light stretched across the treetops like fingers brushing away the last veil of night. Lalit hung from the same pole where, hours ago, he had bound Isak. Now it was his turn. His body sagged, bruised, battered, bleeding. Burn marks striped his back. The Anveshi symbol had been carved into his chest—a wound not just of flesh, but of contempt. Dried blood covered him like armour.

His arms were tied high above his head, and his toes barely scraped the ground.

Isak stood before him, holding Lalit's prosthetic leg in one hand. Lalit's head hung like a wilted flower. Isak raised the prosthetic and pressed it beneath his chin.

"Tell me where the scientist is," he said coldly, "and I'll shoot you in the head. Keep stalling, and the pain will only get worse."

Lalit, through slitted eyes and a veil of blood, smirked.

"You hit like a kid," he rasped.

Isak's rage boiled over. He signalled to Henryson for a pistol and pressed the barrel to Lalit's temple.

"How about I end your crippled life?"

But Lalit's eyes widened—he wasn't afraid to die. He was afraid of not saving Ahindra. Of failing Dr Tara. Of shattering the legacy of the Pashupatis. That fear, not pain, burned in his bloodshot eyes.

Isak moved the gun to Lalit's knee and pulled the trigger. The bullet grazed flesh. Lalit screamed—a raw, primal cry. He twisted in his restraints, every nerve alight with fire. Isak shoved a burning stick against the wound, then punched Lalit on the face while he was still screaming.

"That one just skimmed," he whispered. "The next one? Right through the bone."

He pulled his hand away. Lalit panted—ragged, broken. Then looked to the sunrise and whispered, "I'll tell you... where the scientist is. Get the map... from the tent."

Isak didn't hesitate. He barked the order. A soldier ran towards the tent.

The moment he entered, an explosion tore it apart. Fire surged into the sky. The blast wave rolled through the camp like a war cry. Screams followed.

Grenades hidden in the soil detonated in sequence—wires, triggers, pressure pads—all orchestrated in advance. Men flew like ragdolls. Limbs vanished. Bodies crumpled into silence. Lalit's eyes lit with fire. He kicked the pistol from Isak's hand and stomped on his mangled foot. Isak shrieked, crumbling.

Around them, the forest erupted in panic. But the trees offered no safety. Tripwires hidden beneath brush triggered mounted guns. As soldiers ran, they were cut down by their own terrain.

Isak, crawling, turned in horror. Lalit had freed himself. Still bloodied. Still burning. But walking. He picked up a pistol and approached Isak. Shot him in the other knee.

Isak screamed—louder than before. A sound not of defiance, but of realisation.

This wasn't a crippled man. This was Captain Savyasachi.

Lalit said nothing. He turned from the carnage and limped towards the camp's ruins. Embers glowed in the broken dawn. He retrieved his prosthetic leg and strapped it back on. Then, he walked to the half-buried bunker and picked up the coin. He kissed it.

"You were wrong," he whispered.

There was no pride in his voice. He had fulfilled a part of Shantinatha's ask. The outpost was a graveyard now. But the mission was done. And yet—he knew. This had been the easy part. The real burden lay ahead. Fifteen years. Fifteen years of waiting.

He turned to leave. The sun crested the horizon, gilding the destruction in light. Lalit limped towards the northern shore of Ceylon.

Then, a voice.

"Who are you? How many of your men are in the forest?" Isak croaked, still bleeding in the dirt. "How did you kill us all?"

Lalit stopped. Turned back. His expression was blank.

"I work alone," he said. "I'm Captain **Savyasachi**."

CHAPTER 08

Raavan lay broken on the ground, staring up at the sun. His limbs were shattered, his body slick with blood, and his breath came in shallow, tremulous gasps. Dirt whipped into his eyes and nostrils, but he could not lift his hands to shield himself. His vision blurred. The world swayed.

Then the ground shook.

A low rumble rose from the horizon. It grew louder. Closer.

Through the haze, he saw them: a herd of wild beasts stampeding towards him—dozens, maybe hundreds. The earth groaned beneath their charge. So did he.

The wounds were deep. Blood loss clouded his thoughts. But he did not shut his eyes.

With his final breath, he whispered, "Mahadev."

And just before darkness took him, he remembered everything he had done—and everything he had become.

✦

A few days ago.

Raavan took his motorcycle, packed a few clothes, and left with whatever money he had. He had no destination in mind. At first, he wandered through cities, across highways, his mind spiralling through everything that had happened. The question that consumed him was no longer "Who am I?" but "Am I Dashanan?"

Before reading the ancestral texts, he could bow his head in any temple and chant Jai Sri Ram without hesitation. But now, the name brought a frown to his face. So, he left Ayodhya behind and rode westward—away from its chants and memories.

As the miles rolled beneath him, he thought of Ahindra, of Devadatta, of Mayank and Lalit—and of the mother who had died before his eyes. He questioned his dreams—visions that had once seemed surreal, but now felt real. The speed of his motorcycle matched the speed of his thoughts. He rode like a storm.

Then came a whisper from memory—Kapatadhari.

He remembered what Karan had murmured into his ear, what he had etched onto the floor in blood.

Raavan halted.

He turned north.

There was only one whom he believed could answer his questions—one he admired above all: the witness of the past, the present, and the future.

He rode towards Mount Kailash.

He didn't know the way. At every fork in the road, he closed his eyes and whispered, "Har Har Mahadev." And then, he followed the voice inside him.

He rode for hours without stopping—no food, no sleep. Civilisation gave way to dirt tracks, then to trails barely wide enough for a man. When his motorcycle finally ran out of fuel, he left it behind without hesitation. He walked through forests, across rivers, up ravines—driven not by hunger for food, but hunger for truth.

By the beginning of the fourth day, he stood on a ridge, exhausted and half-mad. And then he saw it.

The first rays of the sun struck Kailash Parvat.

The mountain shimmered—not white, but golden, as if sculpted from light itself. His hands rose involuntarily, joining above his head, and he cried out, Har Har Mahadev!

The wind stilled.

And the peaks around him trembled, as if the memory of his presence from yugas ago had stirred them from slumber.

Raavan ran. The wind turned against him. Rocks fell from above. The mountain resisted.

But he did not stop.

He dodged the stones. He pierced the gale like a falcon. When he reached the base of Kailash, he threw off his sandals, bowed low, and touched his head to the sacred stone.

Then he began to climb.

Dressed only in a kurta and dhoti, he shivered against the biting wind. But he pressed on—leaping from rock to rock, crawling through crevasses, clinging to cracks. After five hundred feet, his foot slipped. He plunged.

The fall broke his legs. He heard the bones snap. Blood pooled around him, quickly freezing into jagged red crystals under the midday sun.

He screamed—once.

Then he waited.

His bones knitted together. His wounds closed. He was healing. Within minutes, he stood again.

He climbed once more. Reaching the same point as before, he tried the same route—and fell again. This time, the damage was worse. More bones broken. More blood lost. More agony. And again, he healed.

On the third attempt, he changed his path. He climbed higher than ever before. At that height, he howled—a scream not of pain, but of pride.

He was capable.

He would reach Mahadev.

But pride has its price.

A boulder came loose beneath him.

He fell.

His legs were crushed. He screamed—this scream was different. It was pain, not pride.

Pinned beneath the rock, he tried to crawl. Then came a deeper rumble. More rocks—from the mountain itself—fell upon him. Stones struck his arms, shattering bone and flesh.

The sun now sat at its zenith, shining directly into his eyes. He squinted but could not lift his arms. They were only pulp now—meat and broken bone. His blood soaked the slope, but there was still pride in his face.

He knew.

He would heal again.

And with that final thought, Raavan closed his eyes—and fell into unconsciousness.

✦

Raavan was regaining consciousness. The sun was still high, a blazing orb that pierced his eyelids with white-hot needles. He had been unconscious for nearly half an hour—long enough, under normal circumstances, for his body to begin healing. But something was wrong. When he tried to lift his arms to shield his face, they didn't move. His legs, too, were frozen. Panic surged. Since his awakening, he had never felt powerless—until now.

The air was bitterly cold. The ground beneath him, jagged and harder than stone, sucked the heat from his bones. Every attempt to move sent waves of pain crashing through him. Exhausted, aching, and rapidly losing warmth, he gave up. He was tired. He was freezing. He was starving and parched. Curling his head away from the sun, he shut his eyes, hoping that sleep might restore what willpower could not.

But rest brought no relief. Even the gentlest breeze stabbed like needles. His mouth cracked with thirst, his stomach howled, and his body shivered violently. Anger ignited in his chest. He screamed—a raw, primal scream, uncoiling from the depths of his soul, shaking the silence with its fury. He kept screaming until his throat burned and his lungs collapsed into breathless gasps. Then, the rage dissolved. And grief took its place.

Tears spilt from his eyes. He glared towards the peak of Mount Kailash and cried out, "Either meet me here on Kailash Parvat, or meet me in Kailash after I die. I'm not leaving without the truth!" His voice cracked and splintered. The sunlight seared into his open eyes, but he refused to blink. His body was failing—but his questions were alive.

Until recently, he had believed his powers were a miracle—lightning from the skies, stones lifted with ease, wounds closing in seconds. But now, he knew. It was the Jeeva Tatva of Dashanan. That truth had shattered the illusion. If he was made from Dashanan's essence... did that mean he was Dashanan?

And if so, what did that make him?

A threat.

A Rakshasa.

Everyone he loved was in danger. There was only one who could answer the questions boiling within him—Mahadev. So Raavan stared at the mountain, even as his vision blurred and tears began to form at the edges of his eyes. Dust swept across his face, but he didn't flinch. Pain became a steady companion, sharp and ever-present. The sun devoured his sight. And still—he did not close his eyes.

Evening came. The angle of light shifted. His eyes, burned and dry, were still open. He hadn't moved. Not a blink. Not a cry. Just a silent, withering vigil. His blood had frozen in the cracks of stone. His bones remained broken. Hunger clawed at his insides. Cold crawled towards his heart. And something worse began to break faith.

Not only in Mahadev's presence at Kailash Parvat.

But in His existence.

The stories Shantinatha had told now rang hollow. Raavan no longer felt watched, protected, or chosen. He wasn't even angry at Mahadev. He was angry at himself for believing. Mahadev, he realised, was no different from the world: always watching suffering, never stopping it.

That thought scorched him more than the sun. Rage returned. He twisted his head slightly, gritted his teeth, and tried to grab a nearby rock to hurl at the mountain. His limbs didn't move. He screamed again—this time not in pain, but in defiance. He cursed Mahadev, hurled accusations at the sky, spoke names no devotee dared whisper. With every insult, another piece of faith peeled away.

And then... the fury faded. What remained was sorrow. Sorrow so deep it had no sound. He wept, but only the wind bore witness.

Then the ground trembled.

Barely conscious, he turned his head. A cloud of dust was racing towards him. The sound of hooves—hundreds, maybe thousands—rumbled like a war drum. Shapes danced in the dust, too blurred to decipher. The vibrations reached him. His broken body screamed anew. Pain flooded every nerve. He was going to die. Trampled, starved, or frozen—it didn't matter. Death was here.

And yet—he chose to face the mountain.

His gaze flickered towards the peak. Sightless. Burned. Empty.

Still, he did not close his eyes.

His body was numb. His thoughts, scattered. But from somewhere deep inside, he summoned one last breath. And with it, a whisper—

"Mahadev."

And then, he fainted.

✦

Raavan remained unconscious through the night. When the sun rose, the skies above Mount Kailash were streaked with soft white clouds, drifting like sheets of snow around the sacred mountain. The peak, high above the cloud line, gleamed golden in the newborn light, while cold winds howled like a pack of wolves.

It wasn't the light that woke him. It was the thudding of his heart—the same steady rhythm that had echoed in his chest all night, a relentless reminder that he was still alive. He wanted to rise, to see if his body had healed, but exhaustion pinned him down. Slowly, painfully, he opened his eyes.

He was lying on his back, but there was no sky above—only darkness, threaded with slivers of light. It felt like he was wrapped in a thick, ragged blanket. He raised his hand to push it aside and realised, to his surprise, that his arms had healed. He shoved harder.

The rug grunted.

Light broke through as the weight shifted. Raavan blinked against the sudden glare—then his vision adjusted. Towering above him, their thick brown fur glistening, stood massive yaks. They had been lying on and around him, their warmth cocooning his broken body. Now, disturbed by his stirring, they began to shuffle and groan.

He turned his head. More legs. Hooves. Tails. Horns. Even smaller animals nestled nearby. Birds flapped lazily away. Panic struck. He tried to sit up, but his legs remained numb. They hadn't healed. Frustrated, he shouted and shoved at the yaks, desperate to free himself.

One of the yaks stumbled, jostling the others. A ripple of movement spread through the herd. Hooves clattered like thunder. Horns swung in wild arcs. Dust exploded into the air, choking his lungs. Raavan coughed violently. A hind leg struck his face, splitting the skin across his cheek. Another hoof narrowly missed crushing his ribs as he rolled aside. The chaos lasted only a moment before the animals calmed, and again he found himself pinned, flattened beneath the bulk of fur.

Lying still, breath ragged, Raavan cursed himself for provoking them. "If I could stand," he muttered, half-angry, half-defeated, "I could lift one of you off the ground." But his legs and lower back still refused to give him relief. The thought remained just that—an empty threat hurled into the dark.

Then, something unexpected. He noticed it wasn't cold.

For the first time in days, warmth soaked into his skin. Not mystical, not divine—but real. Animal. The yaks' bodies had trapped the heat around him, turning this pile of flesh and fur into a living shelter. He let himself enjoy it. The ache in his muscles dulled. The tremor in his jaw faded. His mind began to think again.

A shaft of sunlight pierced the herd nearby, illuminating a path out. It was far, but reachable. Gritting his teeth, he began to crawl—dragging his broken legs behind him, inch by inch. Hooves, horns, and warm bodies surrounded him. He weaved through them all, moving like a wounded serpent towards the light.

Then he stopped.

Something felt familiar. The thumping in his chest. The hum beneath his skin. His heartbeat.

It was loud—too loud. He could feel it in his ribs, echoing through his spine, pulsing in his skull. And suddenly, he understood.

That's why the animals had come.

Not for warmth. Not for shelter. But for the sound. For the rhythm. For the ancient pulse that now lived inside him.

They were attracted to the rhythm of Dashanan's Jeeva Tatva pulsing in Raavan's heart.

Raavan lay still, trying to calm the storm in his chest. Gradually, the thunder of his heartbeat softened. Around him, the animals that had gathered—drawn to the rhythm pulsing within him—began to stir from their trance. One by one, they turned and walked away. And as they did, the warmth departed with them. The cold of Kailash crept back in, coiling through the cracks on the icy ground, reaching for his skin.

He braced himself on his palms and slowly lifted his torso. In every direction, he saw the herd retreating—yaks with thick brown coats, shaggy marmots, white-limbed gazelles, Tibetan foxes with glassy eyes, and mastiffs that looked more like bears than dogs. He had drawn them all, as if summoned by something primal. And now, whatever that was, it had faded.

Then he heard it.

A voice. Distant. Human.

✦

He turned around, heart pounding. A single yak still stood nearby, unmoving, its back to him. Beyond the beast's curved horns stood a man—tall, pale-skinned, dressed in layered sweaters and a windproof jacket. A woollen cap hugged his head, gloves covered his hands, and a sturdy backpack clung to his shoulders. From one glove, a rope ran through the yak's nostrils. A trekking pole was planted firmly beside him. A walkie-talkie dangled from a cord around his neck, bouncing gently as he moved.

Raavan stared.

The man was gently patting the yak's head, speaking in a language Raavan didn't recognise—soft, syllabic, and foreign. But the yak wouldn't budge.

Raavan didn't think. He shouted, voice raw and desperate: "Please help me!"

The man looked up sharply. His eyes widened. He dropped the rope and jogged towards him, crunching over snow.

This was the first human Raavan had seen in days.

The man crouched beside him, scanning his broken form—torn clothes, bloodstained fabric, bruises blooming across skin like spilt ink. "Are you hurt?" he asked, breath quickening.

Raavan didn't speak. He just glanced down at his legs.

The man followed his gaze. He lifted the shredded cloth and recoiled. Deep gashes ran down Raavan's thighs and shins. Flesh torn. Bones exposed. Blood frozen in thin lines across the ice.

"How are you still alive?" the man muttered under his breath.

Raavan's lips cracked as he whispered again, "Please help me."

The man reached into his backpack and pulled out a metal water bottle. "Who are you? What are you doing here?"

Raavan didn't answer. His eyes drifted towards the peak of Mount Kailash. Then back to his mangled legs.

The man followed his gaze and understood.

He unscrewed the cap and held it to Raavan's lips. "Drink slowly," he said.

The water was icy. Raavan's throat, parched and torn, spasmed at the first sip. He coughed, choking. The man gently patted the back of his head, voice lowering. "Were you trying to climb? Did you fall?"

Raavan, still sipping, nodded faintly.

The man exhaled sharply. "I don't know why people keep doing this. They come up here chasing visions, testing faith, chasing death. Then someone like me ends up pulling them back."

His voice was tinged with weariness, but Raavan didn't understand the words.

Then, the man paused, studied his face, and tried again—in Hindi.

"Why are you here? What do you want?"

Raavan's eyes lit up.

Finally, something he understood.

He looked at the man and said, "I want to know who I am."

There was a pause. Even the yak grunted, then slumped to the ground, sending the instruments strapped to its saddle clattering into the snow. The man jumped at the sound, rushed over, and began checking the gear, muttering curses under his breath.

"Lakhs of rupees... wasted," he groaned, fumbling with tangled cables and bent metal parts.

Raavan watched him in silence. After a moment, he asked, "Can you help me reach the top of Mount Kailash?"

The man turned, eyes drifting to Raavan's bloodied legs. He shook his head. "Your legs are broken. You don't have proper clothes. Honestly, I'm shocked you survived this cold."

Raavan looked down. His legs were still torn. Unhealed. And that terrified him more than anything else. His strength was supposed to return by now. The silence of his body felt like a betrayal. Almost ashamed, he whispered, "Can you at least take me to a hospital?"

The man hesitated. His eyes went from the yak to his battered equipment. Helping Raavan meant abandoning everything—his gear, his plans. It meant using the yak not for transport, but for rescue.

After a long pause, he sighed. "There's no hospital nearby. But... there is a healer. I can take you to him."

Raavan could see the reluctance on his face. But there was no other way.

Without another word, the man unzipped his thick jacket and handed it over. "Wear this. You'll freeze otherwise."

Raavan slipped into it slowly. The warmth enveloped him, heavy and overwhelming. It wasn't just protection—it was kindness. It felt like salvation.

The man began unloading the gear from the yak's pouches, making space. Then he dragged Raavan closer and hoisted him onto the saddle. Raavan tried to sit upright, but his back couldn't support him. They adjusted, laying him face-down across the yak's back—awkward, painful, but far better than the frozen ground.

And then… they waited.

The yak didn't move.

It sat where it was, head bowed, eyes empty. It looked old. Tired. Spent.

The man tugged the rope, patted its thick side, and barked commands. Raavan, too, reached out—not physically, but with something deeper. Still, the yak didn't budge.

Eventually, the man collapsed beside it, leaning against the warm fur. Sweat glistened on his brow. He had tried everything—tugging, pleading, even cursing—but nothing worked.

"How did you even get it here in the first place?" Raavan asked, still watching from the saddle.

The man didn't answer at first. Then, slowly, he looked into the yak's eyes and said, "I was transporting research equipment from my office in India to a new facility—just fifteen kilometres from here. We were almost there when the yak suddenly turned. It refused every command. Just walked… here. And stood still."

He exhaled and shook his head, as though still trying to believe his own story.

"It felt like something was pulling it. I've been here all night, trying to move it. But it won't listen. And the strangest thing—last night, I saw animals everywhere. Predators, prey… all mingling. No fear. No aggression. Just silence."

Raavan knew why.

He looked at the man beside him—frustrated, exhausted—and felt a quiet sympathy.

Then, his eyes drifted to the yak's head. And he remembered something.

A lesson Shantinatha had once taught him. A technique so subtle, so advanced, that even his Guru had barely mastered it. A method of projection—not through words or force, but through sparks of lightning.

Raavan had practised it in secret. It had never worked.

Until now.

✦

He took a deep breath and gripped the saddle with one hand. With the other, he reached towards the yak's forehead—not quite touching it, but close enough for the hairs to tremble. He began to chant under his breath. His veins bulged. The space between his palm and the animal's fur shimmered with a faint blue glow.

Tiny golden sparks crackled through the air like static.

The man didn't notice at first, though the hairs on his own arms began to rise. Raavan had tried this technique before—deep in the forest, on wild beasts and domesticated animals from the tribal outskirts. It had never worked. But back then, he couldn't summon lightning.

Shantinatha had called the technique a form of *Dhi*—the ability to channel the bioelectric charge of living beings through one's own body, encoding thought into mantra and transmitting it into another creature. It was communication beyond language. A technique only a few chosen ones could attempt.

Raavan had failed each time. Worse, his last attempt—on a dog near the tribal lands—had nearly led to disaster. Some believed the ashram's dwellers were sorcerers who drained sacred power from trees and stones. He had been called a witch. The memory of that word still stung, especially when whispered against Shantinatha's name.

But this time… something shifted.

The yak's forehead glowed—soft and blue, like a winter moon.

The man beside him leaned back, startled by the light. For a moment, he saw it clearly—Raavan's outstretched hand, the shimmer in the air, the quiet hum of power.

Then the yak stood.

The movement knocked the man backwards. He scrambled to his feet, stunned. "What… what did you do?" he asked, stepping closer.

Raavan quickly withdrew his hand. He didn't want to be feared—or worse, exposed. Outsiders didn't understand *Dhi*. And they feared what they didn't know.

But the man didn't look afraid.

He looked amazed.

Gripping the yak's rope, he said, "Who are you? What was that?"

Raavan, still lying flat across the saddle, couldn't see the man's expression—but he could hear the awe in his voice. Still, he deflected.

"What are you talking about?" he muttered. "Please… My legs are killing me. Take me to the healer."

The man knelt beside him, more gently this time. "I know what I saw. A blue light from your hand. And then the yak stood up. I'm not going to tell anyone. I just want to understand."

Raavan avoided his gaze.

Then, suddenly, he slipped from the saddle and collapsed into the snow.

Pain shot up his legs like fire. He groaned, dragging himself from the heap of scattered gear. The man rushed over, crouching beside him again.

"Do you want me to take you to the healer?" he asked, glancing at the knife he'd earlier used to cut the saddle straps.

Raavan saw something different now in the man's eyes—not just concern. A need to understand.

And he realised he couldn't lie anymore.

He turned towards the man and asked, "Who are you? What's your name?"

The man adjusted the strap of his backpack. "Kranti," he said. "I'm an astrophysicist. I work here in the mountains, studying the origin of the universe."

Raavan looked at the scattered equipment in the snow. It made sense now.

Then he asked, "Do you believe ancient chants have the power to manifest?"

Kranti smirked. "Well then, Mr Witch. What's your magic trick?"

Raavan placed a calm hand on his shoulder. "I'm not a witch. And this isn't magic. It's ancient knowledge. There's logic in every mantra. You can deny it—but that won't make it less real."

✦

Kranti's smirk faded. He nodded, slower this time. "Alright," he said. "Tell me what you did. Tell me what you chanted. We'll try explaining it through science."

Raavan hadn't expected that. He'd never seen his powers through a scientific lens—only through the teachings of his

Guru. But now, with Kranti's curiosity, something inside him stirred.

"First," Raavan said, "help me back onto the yak."

Kranti nodded. He reattached the saddle, repacked his gear, and with great effort, lifted Raavan into position. By the time he finished, he was panting. Raavan noticed—and appreciated—the effort.

Kranti tied him in place and gave the yak a command.

To his surprise, the animal obeyed instantly.

Kranti stared, stunned. This was the same stubborn beast he had pleaded with all night. Now it moved without resistance.

It was the first time Raavan had ever successfully used *Dhi*.

A surge of pride bloomed in his chest.

And a pang of sorrow.

He wished Shantinatha had lived to see it.

As they walked, Kranti asked, "So... what exactly were you doing to the yak?"

Lying flat on the saddle, Raavan watched the path pass beneath them. "My Guru taught me how to summon lightning," he said. "But more than that, he said I could gather electricity from the world around me and channel it into a chant. That chant carries a command, encrypted with intention. If it works, the animal hears it—not with ears, but inside its mind."

He paused.

“This is the first time it’s ever worked.”

Kranti halted. The yak stopped beside him. He walked back to Raavan, crouched at his side, and looked him in the eye.

“If you don’t want to explain, that’s fine,” he said, his voice low. “But please... don’t tell me you control animals with chants and spells. That sounds like witchcraft.”

Raavan flinched.

He hadn’t expected that from Kranti. Not after everything they’d just been through.

He turned his head towards him, but Kranti had already stood and walked back to the front, wordlessly urging the yak forward.

“I’m not lying,” Raavan called after him. “I’m telling the truth. I’m not a witch!”

Kranti didn’t answer. His voice, when it came, was cold. “Don’t worry. I’ll take you to the healer.”

But after that, he said nothing else.

Raavan’s heart twisted. He grew desperate.

“If you don’t believe me,” he shouted, “I’ll prove it. I’ll make the yak stop—right now!”

He placed his hand on the animal’s head and began the chant again.

Nothing happened.

The yak kept walking.

Kranti didn't turn around, but Raavan could see the slight glance over his shoulder. There was no glow. No spark. Just silence.

Raavan tried again. Then again. Over and over.

Still nothing.

He wasn't just trying to prove himself to Kranti anymore. He needed to believe it, too.

They walked away from the mountains and deeper into the forest. The terrain began to change. Tall trees lined the trail, their branches swaying above. Raavan heard birds rustling in the canopy. The air grew denser, thicker. Kranti looked around, noting the shift.

Then, without warning, a faint blue glow flickered across the air.

Kranti spun around.

"Wait—!" he shouted.

Too late.

A bolt of lightning burst from Raavan's palm, striking the ground inches from the yak's face.

The beast reared in panic, bellowed, and slammed Kranti aside with its horned head. The rope tore free from his hand as he hit the dirt, dazed and winded.

The yak bolted.

✦

Raavan was still strapped to the saddle. He bounced violently, clinging for dear life. Dust erupted behind them, swallowing the trail. Kranti vanished from sight.

Raavan screamed. He tried again to command the beast, to calm it, but the technique failed. Again.

His legs scraped the dirt. He was slipping. Each jolt ripped pain through his back. He reached for the saddle horn, but the yak veered sharply—off the path, into the trees.

Then he saw it: a sharp-edged tool wedged in the saddle pouch.

Clenching his teeth, he twisted his body, grabbed the tool, and sliced through the rope binding him to the saddle.

He slid off.

Hit the ground.

Rolled.

The yak thundered ahead, disappearing into the woods.

Raavan lay in the dirt, coughing. His legs screamed. His arms were scratched raw. Dust caked his tongue.

But he was alive.

He sat up slowly, pain flaring with every breath.

And then, Shantinatha's words came back to him:

"People outside the ashram will never understand the ancient knowledge we hold. When you try to prove you're not a magician, you'll only hurt yourself."

Raavan looked back.

Through the thinning dust, a figure was running towards him.

Kranti.

He came running through the trees and dropped beside Raavan, panting, coughing from the dust. "Where's the yak?" he gasped.

Raavan looked towards the forest with a heavy expression. Kranti understood—the yak was gone.

He spotted a few pieces of his equipment scattered on the ground, some of them cracked, and one of them beeping. He crawled to it—a handheld device flashing red, the beeping intermittent. He tapped it gently. The sound sharpened, and the red light intensified.

His eyes widened.

He moved the device towards Raavan. The beeping grew louder. The red light burned brighter. He pulled it away—

the beeping softened. Closer again—it flared. Kranti repeated, testing it like a child discovering a new toy.

Raavan watched, confused. He didn't understand the device, but he could feel something: his lower back had healed. He sat upright slowly. His legs, however, were still numb and burning.

"How far is the healer?" he asked, voice low.

Kranti barely heard him—still entranced by the device. He dropped to all fours and scurried back to Raavan. "How did you accumulate that much charge?" he demanded, eyes gleaming.

Raavan paused. He remembered Shantinatha's warning—never try to explain what others won't understand. He gave a crooked smile and said, "I'm sorry I lied earlier. I didn't do anything to the yak. I was trying to trick you."

Kranti scoffed. He moved the device closer—it beeped violently, the red light flaring before the bulb burst with a crack. Smoke curled from its edges.

"You can lie to me," Kranti said, holding the ruined device, "but this can't. That was an EMF metre—and it thinks you're charged. I saw the light in your hand. I saw lightning. You weren't lying."

He crouched, almost reverent. "Tell me the truth. Who are you?"

Raavan reached out and took the broken device from Kranti's hand. It shrieked, sparked again, and went dead. "People call me Raavan," he said softly. "And my guru taught me how to summon lightning."

✦

Then he told Kranti everything—how he drew electricity from the life around him, encrypted a command into a mantra, and channelled it into another living being. Kranti listened, eyes wide with disbelief.

He wanted to dismiss it. But the EMF metre had already told him what he needed to know. No trick, no bluff, no sleight of hand could fake what he had just seen.

When Raavan explained that it was his heartbeat that had drawn the animals to Mount Kailash, Kranti just nodded. This time, he didn't question.

Without a word, he stood and said, "I'm going to find the yak. I'll come back for you."

His face was pale. His voice was hollow.

He turned and walked into the forest.

Raavan called after him. "It'll be dark soon. Stay close. We can search at sunrise."

But Kranti didn't respond. He kept walking until the trees swallowed him.

Raavan sighed. His legs still ached, useless. He dragged himself towards a nearby tree and leaned back against its trunk, watching the forest where Kranti had vanished.

The sun dipped behind the mountains. The cold returned.

He gathered dry twigs and branches scattered nearby. He would need fire. He didn't have the strength to search for more later.

Pulling his legs in, he grunted in pain. The skin was red and torn, blood dried along the edges. He wrapped Kranti's jacket tighter around himself and waited beneath the growing dark.

He rubbed two sticks together. Again and again. He had done this a hundred times in the forest temple—but his strength was gone. No smoke. No warmth.

Desperate and exhausted, he piled the wood in front of him.

A bolt of lightning crashed from the sky and struck the wood.

The fire roared to life.

In the glow of the flames, Raavan looked up—and saw Kranti standing in front of him, the yak by his side.

✦

Raavan had expected Kranti to take much longer to return. The forest was pitch black, and Kranti had neither fire nor light to guide him. By all logic, he should have been gone for hours.

But there he was—already back, standing before Raavan with the yak, smiling.

Raavan looked up at him. Something had shifted. When Kranti had left, he was cold and confused. But now, there was a calm on his face—almost bliss. It was as if the darkness had given him time to think... and accept what he had seen.

Before Raavan could speak, Kranti said softly, "It's time to take you to the healer."

He helped Raavan to his feet and onto the yak. Raavan winced as he settled on the saddle, pain shooting through his legs. Kranti patted his back gently. "We should reach by midnight."

And so, they walked.

Kranti led the yak by its rope, and Raavan rode in silence. The only sounds were the crunch of footsteps and the wind howling through the mountains.

After a while, Raavan asked, "How are you able to navigate in the dark?"

Kranti didn't look back. "I've been here a long time. I've taken many people to the healer—people like you. Pilgrims of Kailash."

That comforted Raavan. At least they weren't lost.

A long silence followed until Kranti asked, "Why were you going to Kailash anyway?"

Raavan hesitated. He didn't want to share the full truth—not yet. A part of him feared Kranti might abandon him again.

But before he could come up with a half-truth, Kranti pressed again, his voice firmer this time.

Raavan looked ahead at the man guiding him. "I wanted to find Mahadev on Kailash," he said. "I want to know who I am."

Kranti laughed—loud and long. His voice echoed off the ridges, rebounding across trees, rocks, and valleys—like the mountain itself was laughing with him.

Raavan chuckled nervously. "Why are you laughing?"

The laughter faded. Then Kranti said, "Who told you Mahadev is on Kailash?"

Raavan answered carefully, "Someone close to me met him there."

He didn't explain. He didn't mention Dashanan of the Treta Yuga.

Kranti kept walking, voice steady. "And when you meet him... how will you recognise him? Do you know what he looks like?"

"Yes," Raavan said, without pause.

He described the vision he had always held: a fair man with matted hair tied high, a blue throat, ash smeared across his skin, garlands of skulls, snakes curled around his limbs, draped in elephant hide, holding a Trishul, and bearing a vertical third eye.

Kranti drew closer and asked, "Then why do some say he is Nirguna Brahman—without form, without qualities?"

Raavan was caught off guard. He hadn't expected such a question from a man of science.

After a moment, he nodded. "You're right. He is Nirguna Brahman."

Kranti gave a thoughtful nod and walked on. Raavan could feel the next question forming.

It came: "Then why do people worship a Lingam if he's formless?"

Raavan blinked. Kranti's knowledge ran deeper than expected.

With effort, he answered, "Because Mahadev is in everything—the five elements. The lingams represent his presence in all matter, all states of being."

Kranti nodded again. The questions stopped.

Raavan felt a flicker of relief. His body and mind were frayed. He just wanted to rest, to float into sleep.

But then, Kranti asked—softly, clearly, as if piercing straight through him: "If Mahadev is in everything—air, fire, earth, water, sky—why did you come looking for him on Kailash? Why not look within yourself? Do you not believe what you say?"

Raavan's eyes widened.

He had no answer.

He had known that Mahadev was everywhere. But, at that moment, he realised that he didn't truly believe it—not deep down. He had come looking for a form, a figure, a saviour. Not a presence within.

Tears spilt silently from his eyes.

He didn't blink.

Dust blew across his face. But still, he didn't close his eyes.

He kept his gaze locked on the sky, caught in the echo of Kranti's question. His mind was quiet, yet full—ringing with a realisation he had never dared confront.

Kranti turned, saw him staring upward, and spoke gently. "Do you know how this universe began?"

Raavan didn't respond. He heard the words, but he was still floating in silence.

Kranti continued anyway. "This entire universe—the galaxies, stars, oceans, trees, animals, you and me—was once the size of a pinhead. A singularity. Then, billions of years ago, an unknown force caused it to expand. That expansion became everything we know. Everything around you—every drop of blood, every grain of sand—was once that one point."

He paused. Letting it settle.

"I came here, to these mountains, to study that force. The one that caused the Big Bang."

Something shifted in Raavan.

He blinked slowly. Then turned to look at Kranti. And suddenly, he understood.

He understood *Tat Tvam Asi—That Thou Art.* Not just as a chant. But as truth.

He realised the same force that birthed him had birthed the mountains. The stars. The yak. Even Kranti.

Everything came from the same source.

And everything would return to it.

He thought of what Shantinatha had once taught him. The universe was born from consciousness. From the formless *Para Brahman*. The sages called it Shiva. They called it Vishnu. They said: *You are that.*

Raavan had always known it.

But only now did he believe it.

In that moment, he understood: he was no longer just the son his father had experimented on, nor the Raavan forged by his Gurus, nor even the Dashanan whose Jeeva Tatva burned within him. He was a fragment of Mahadev, and Mahadev was a fragment of him.

Goosebumps rippled across his skin. Tears flowed without shame. He looked up.

And the sky answered.

It was the most beautiful thing he had ever seen.

The night stretched forever, filled with stars. Shooting stars streaked across like divine messengers. The Milky Way arched overhead like a cosmic river. A crescent moon glowed low and golden, hanging like the eye of a god.

Raavan didn't blink.

He was in a trance.

The wind vanished. Footsteps faded. Even the yak's breath was silent.

All he could hear was the rhythm of his own heartbeat.

He felt as if he were the only soul alive on the mountain, facing the universe.

The pain disappeared. The cold dissolved. His senses were suspended—consumed by wonder.

And then, he saw Mahadev.

In the moon.

He rubbed his eyes, thinking it was an illusion. But the image remained.

He looked again—at the stars, the earth, the trees, the yak, the wind, and Kranti.

And he saw Mahadev in all of them.

Something opened inside him.

His breath slowed. His heartbeat stilled. His eyelids grew heavy.

And he fell—slipping from the yak, body limp, eyes open to the stars.

He hit the ground softly.

And fainted.

✦

Raavan stirred awake, his eyes blinking slowly. Above him, the ceiling was ancient and cracked, etched with an inscription that read: *"Prathamo Daivyo Bhishhak"—The First Divine Healer*. He smiled. He was at the healer's home.

The clarity he had felt before fainting hadn't left him. It was still fresh, like a light burning softly within. He laughed to himself, softly—at the absurdity of searching for Mahadev on Kailash, when Mahadev had always been with him. Within him.

He felt warmth in his chest, energy pulsing through him like never before.

For a moment, a question arose: *Am I the reincarnation of Dashanan? Is that why I possess these powers?*

But before the thought could fully form, the answer emerged—not as a sentence, but as knowing.

His body was not that of Dashanan.

It was a vessel. A shell. Modified by Ahindra, yes—infused with Dashanan's Jeeva Tatva—but it had no bearing on who he was within.

He knew now: he was not Dashanan.

He was a part of Mahadev.

Peace spread across his face. For the first time in a long while, his pain began to ease—as though he was finally healing.

Now he understood where his powers came from. Perhaps they were born of Dashanan's Jeeva Tatva.

But it was Mahadev who had made everything possible.

He turned his head to take in the room. It was dim and quiet. A small oil lamp flickered near his feet. The air smelled of herbs—pungent and healing. He was lying on a rough bed, legs coated in a thick green paste. He scraped some with his fingers, smelled it, and recognised the medicine. The texture, the scent—he knew this formulation.

He tried to move his legs—they responded. The pain was faint, almost gone.

With effort, he swung his feet to the floor and tried to stand.

The moment he put weight on his legs, he collapsed—knocking over a pot of water beside the bed.

The crash echoed through the small chamber.

A man entered swiftly—elderly, his body smeared with ash, clothed in a saffron dhoti, rudraksha beads on his neck, and thick matted hair on his crown. The healer.

He helped Raavan back onto the bed and handed him a steaming bowl.

"Drink this," he said in a deep, slow voice. "You'll be walking soon."

Raavan drank it. The taste was bitter and familiar.

The healer observed him and said, "Your wounds have healed faster than I've ever seen. I thought it would take months. But here you are—three days later. Looks like Mahadev healed you from within."

Raavan blinked. *Three days?*

He sat up, eyes wide. "Where's Kranti? The man who brought me here?"

The healer looked confused. He was about to answer when another man burst into the room—younger, dressed like the healer, perhaps his student. He bowed and said, "A group of nomads brought someone in. They found him in the forest—unconscious. He needs help."

The healer nodded. "Bring him here."

Raavan stood up slowly and cleared space on the bed.

The student returned with a nomad, both carrying a limp figure. They laid him gently down as the healer checked his pulse and began issuing instructions—for pastes, for decoctions.

The nomad left.

Raavan stepped closer, curious.

And then he saw the face.

It was Kranti.

✦

Unconscious. Lips cracked. Clothes dirty. His skin pale, almost grey.

Raavan stood there in silence, his heart heavy, watching the man who had once led him… now needing to be saved.

Raavan rushed to the bed and knelt beside the healer. "This is the man who brought me here," he said urgently. "He saved me. He brought me from Mount Kailash on his yak."

The healer looked surprised but said nothing. Calmly, he gestured towards the door. "Leave the room."

Raavan didn't move. He tapped Kranti's face gently, trying to wake him.

The healer's patience snapped. "Take him out," he barked at his student.

The young disciple grabbed Raavan's arm and dragged him from the room, closing the door behind them.

Before Raavan could speak, the student said, "You were brought here on a yak. But not by that man. It was your twin brother."

Raavan froze.

The student continued, reaching into a satchel hanging on the wall. "He left a note for you. Asked me to give it to you when you woke up."

Before the student could hand it over, Raavan snatched the cloth from his hands and unrolled it.

I know you won't go back to Kailash looking for Mahadev. I hope you found the answers you were seeking. Now that you understand who you truly are now it is time for you to discover what lies in your destiny. Read the books your ancestors wrote. Go to Kāsi.

There was no name.

Raavan looked up, eyes burning. "Please... try to remember. Who brought me here?"

The student said nothing. He took Raavan by the hand, led him to a mirror on the far wall, and made him stand before it. He dipped his fingers into a bowl of ash and, with care, smeared the ash across Raavan's forehead.

Then, softly, he said, "The man who brought you here... looked like this."

Raavan stared at himself.

And he smiled.

The student stepped back and said, "Looks like you're healed. There's no reason to stay. Take this twice a day for two days."

He handed Raavan a bottle of green concoction, along with his old clothes and the jacket.

Raavan took the potion and his clothes, but returned the jacket. "Give this to the man inside," he said, and got dressed.

Outside, a sandstorm was approaching.

Raavan stepped into it, walking south—destination Kasi.

But his next stop would be Ayodhya. There was unfinished business waiting there.

He climbed the first hill along the path and turned back. The healer's house was vanishing into the haze. A group of pilgrims stood nearby, gazing towards the distant peak of Kailash, chanting:

"Har Har Mahadev!"

Raavan joined in. But he did not look at Kailash. He looked within.

And he smiled—not because he had found all the answers, but because he had found **Mahadev**.

Somewhere in the foothills of Mount Kailash

CHAPTER 09

It was past midnight when Raavan arrived at the gates of his home in Ayodhya. The guards were stunned—unable to recognise him beneath layers of ragged clothing, a thick beard tangled with dust, and hair matted from weeks on the road. Dirt clung to him like a second skin. One guard hurried inside to alert Lalit, while the other struggled to unbolt the heavy gate. Raavan had travelled mostly on foot from Kailash. The journey had been long, intentional, and deeply solitary.

Now he stood at the threshold of what was once home, but he didn't cross it. Not until he had seen Lalit. The guard offered him water and urged him to come inside, but Raavan refused, shaking his head gently. And so, the guard stood beside him in silence, sharing the stillness of the night.

Inside, the house was quiet. Lalit's sleep was broken by hurried knocking. He opened the door, bleary-eyed, only to hear a single sentence that pierced his mind like a thunderclap: "Raavan is at the gate."

He froze. The words took time to land. Then, suddenly awake, he grabbed his cane and rushed into the courtyard. The path was dark, but halfway to the gate, he saw a silhouette—tall, worn, unfamiliar in form, yet unmistakable in essence. Raavan.

Relief surged. Then worry. Then anger. As he reached Raavan, words failed him. His hand rose and, without thought, slapped him across the face. The sound cracked through the courtyard. Even the guards flinched.

Raavan didn't react. He met Lalit's eyes with calm. "I know I shouldn't have left without telling you," he said quietly. "But it was necessary. I went to Kailash. I had to meet Mahadev."

Lalit's voice trembled with pain. "I would've taken you myself."

Raavan looked down, guilt thick in the space between them.

Then Lalit stepped forward and pulled him into an embrace. Raavan hesitated, then held him back. It was the first warmth he'd felt in weeks. Lalit pulled away after a moment, wrinkling his nose. "When was the last time you bathed?"

Raavan gave a tired smile. "The day I left for Kailash Parvat."

✦

The next morning, Raavan sat at the breakfast table, devouring his first real meal in weeks. The staff moved around him quietly, eyes filled with disbelief. This was not the boy they had known. The man before them looked as though he had walked through a storm—his beard wild, his hair unkempt, his gaze older, deeper. Even during his years in the forest temple, Raavan had always maintained order. Now, he looked like someone who had touched something vast and dangerous—and survived.

Lalit studied him from across the table. Then, trying to disguise his worry in sarcasm, said, "Are you going to do something about that beard? You look... unrecognisable."

He leaned in, more serious now. "You said you went to meet Mahadev. Did you find him?"

Raavan swallowed his final bite and looked up. "I didn't meet him. But I now know where to find him." He tapped his chest. "Here."

Lalit sat back, stunned. This wasn't the same man who left for Kailash a few days ago. This was someone transformed—by silence, by truth, by revelation.

The pause between them grew. Then Raavan spoke again. "Can I go to Kasi? I want to read all the books written by my ancestors. I want to learn the legacy of our ancestors."

Lalit didn't respond immediately. He was still trying to process the shift in Raavan—this new stillness, this sense of purpose.

Raavan reached out and touched his shoulder gently. "Lalit?"

"I can have someone bring the books here."

Raavan shook his head. "I've always wanted to see Kāsi. This way I'll get to go. I promise I won't be long. Once I understand who I truly am—and what they intended me to become—I'll return."

Lalit hesitated. The thought of letting Raavan wander again unsettled him. But he nodded.

As Raavan stood to leave the table, Lalit reached out and caught his hand. "Be careful. Come back soon."

Raavan turned and embraced him again. "I'm sorry I left for Kailash without telling you. It won't happen again."

Back in his room, Raavan began to pack. This was not going to be a short visit—he would be in Kāsi for weeks, maybe months. As he sifted through his clothes, his fingers brushed against a familiar cloth bag. He lifted it, feeling its weight, and opened it. Inside lay his Urumi—the coiled, flexible blade that once made him feel invincible. He held it in his hands, letting memories of combat, training, and fire return for a moment. Then, quietly, he set it aside. He wasn't taking a weapon to Kāsi. Not this time.

Just then, a knock echoed on the already open door. Lalit stood there. Raavan gestured for him to enter. Lalit stepped into the room, scanning the nearly empty closet with an ache in his heart, though he said nothing. He walked up to Raavan, placed a firm hand on his shoulder, and said quietly, "I know you're strong, and you can protect yourself. But that doesn't stop me from worrying. You're all I have."

Then he handed him a small wooden box. "This contains the address, the instructions... and one of only two keys to the Pashupati Granthalay. The library has quarters for you to stay in."

Raavan opened the box, barely glancing at the address or the documents. His eyes locked onto the key—a heavy, transparent coin etched with the Anveshi symbol. Nearly five times the diameter of a one-paise coin and much heavier, it was encased in a silver hexagonal frame. Two black lines ran vertically across the surface, intertwining like strands of fate. The darkness of the etching was so pure it seemed to swallow light. The coin pulsed with a strange gravity—as if it bore the weight of a buried world.

"Is this the key?" Raavan asked, turning it over in his hand.

Lalit gently took it from him and held it up. "Never lose it. Only two remain. This place houses the legacy your ancestors protected for centuries. It must never fall into the wrong hands."

Raavan nodded solemnly, returning the coin to its box and the box to his bag. They left the room together and walked towards the waiting car. But at the threshold, Raavan paused. He looked at the car, then at the sun overhead—high, hot, unrelenting. He turned to Lalit and said, "I want to walk to Kāsi."

Lalit hesitated. The thought of Raavan walking alone again unsettled him. But he didn't stop him. He reached out, placed his hand on Raavan's head, blessed him, and watched silently as Raavan walked away—bareheaded, unarmed, and radiant with purpose.

✦

Kāsi.

The city where time folded in on itself. The first city—not built by man, but consecrated by Mahadev. Older than memory, older even than the word 'history', it stood like an eternal sentinel on the banks of the Ganga. For millennia, seekers had journeyed there—some in search of truth, others for moksha. It was said that those who died in Kāsi would never be reborn. Liberation wasn't earned—it was given.

Raavan walked for nearly two days, stopping only when necessary. But the closer he came to Kāsi, the lighter he felt. He passed clusters of sadhus and Aghoris heading the same way—men who had shed the world, seeking only essence. When the city finally revealed itself, his breath caught.

But he didn't go straight to the Granthalay.

Something else pulled him.

He wandered through the serpentine alleys, asking directions in Hindi and Sanskrit. After what felt like a pilgrimage, he saw her.

The Ganga.

She shimmered before him, holy and infinite. Raavan dropped his bag and ran—barefoot, unthinking, like a child returning to his mother. He plunged into the river, and the cold wrapped around him like a blessing. He submerged once. Then again. And a third time. When he emerged, he felt reborn.

As he walked back towards his belongings, he noticed a figure standing beside his bag.

An Aghori.

His body was coated in ash. His hair, long and matted, reached his hips. He wore nothing but a loincloth. In his left hand, he held a human skull filled with ashes.

Raavan slowed.

The Aghori turned, extended the skull towards him without a word.

Unsure of what to do, Raavan joined his hands in a respectful greeting. Then, hesitantly, he reached into his bag, pulled out a few notes, and placed them into the skull.

The Aghori threw the money away.

Still holding the skull, he stepped forward, dipped his right hand into the ashes, and smeared them across Raavan's face. Then, without warning, he overturned the skull and poured the remaining ashes over Raavan's head.

"Har Har Mahadev!" he bellowed, his voice crashing through the air like thunder.

Raavan gasped, coughing as ashes entered his nose and mouth. He rubbed his eyes to see again—but the Aghori was gone. Vanished into the crowd like a spirit returning to dust.

Raavan didn't wipe off the ash.

He let it cling to him.

And from there, cloaked in ash and silence, he made his way to the library.

✦

Raavan wandered through the dense, winding streets of Varanasi for over an hour, asking locals for directions. Most only gestured vaguely towards the river. Eventually, the path led him to the banks of the Ganga, where an old two-storey structure stood—worn by time, wrapped in vines, and cloaked in silence. Built of dark grey stone, the building looked abandoned, a relic from another age. A low stone wall enclosed it, but the gate was missing. The whole place felt forgotten.

He paused at the threshold, unsure. This couldn't be the Pashupati Granthalay. Lalit had described something powerful, secretive, sacred—not this crumbling house half-eaten by time. Still, Raavan stepped inside. A lone cow lay in the shade cast by the house. It lifted its head as he passed, but quickly returned to chewing, indifferent. In Varanasi, such creatures were hardly unusual.

He circled the perimeter. The north wall faced the road but bore no windows or doors. Finally, on the eastern side—beside the cow—he found a narrow doorway sunk into shadow. As he approached, the cow locked eyes with him, unmoving. He met its gaze briefly, then entered.

Inside, the room was vast, dark, and stale. Dust floated through beams of faint sunlight that seeped in from the open door. The air smelled of stone and centuries. A narrow staircase to the south led upward. He climbed, only to find a smaller, darker chamber—no signs of life, no windows, no light. Disappointed, he returned to the ground and stepped into the heat.

Leaning against the wall, Raavan stared out at the Ganga beyond the eastern edge of the compound. He vaulted over the wall and sat beside the river, defeated. This couldn't be it. The Pashupati Granthalay was supposed to be a sanctuary of secrets, a fortress of forgotten science—not this ruin.

Frustration rising, he opened the box Lalit had given him and pulled out the coin-key. Underneath it lay a card he had ignored earlier, labelled Instructions. He skimmed it. Then stopped. His lips curled into a quiet grin. He had missed something essential.

He packed up, clutched the coin and rushed back to the building.

Once inside, he shut the main door from within, plunging the room into complete darkness. The first instruction was complete. He ran his fingers along the inside of the door until they found a small knob. Pulling it open to a narrow slit. A thin ray of sunlight pierced the room, landing on the opposite wall.

He followed the light. Kneeling, he splashed water over the dusty surface where the beam had landed. The grime parted, revealing a mirror embedded in the wall. The reflected beam jumped to another mirror, then another—until thin threads of light crisscrossed the room, illuminating dust particles suspended like stars in a frozen constellation.

He raced upstairs.

The instructions had said the final beam would land on the north wall. It did. He approached it and saw a faint circular depression carved into the stone—the exact size of the Anveshi coin.

Raavan poured a few drops of Ganga water into the groove and pressed the coin into place.

The wall began to tremble. The floor vibrated softly. Stones groaned, rearranged themselves. A seam of golden light split the wall, and then it slid open—revealing a hidden chamber and two staircases.

One spiralled up. The other, down.

He frowned. The building had no floors above. Cautiously, he reached towards the upper stairs. His fingers met cold glass. It was a flawless mirror—the upward staircase an illusion. The true path was below.

Raavan descended slowly. As he spiralled downward, he glanced at the mirror. It showed him climbing upward—as if he were being split into two: one version ascending, the other sinking into the earth.

At the base of the stairs, the narrow corridor opened into a cavernous hall.

The chamber stretched far and high, bathed in soft light. Yet there were no flames, no bulbs, no skylights—the radiance came from the air itself, as if the space breathed light. At its centre stood a circular table surrounded by ten chairs. But it was the walls that stole his breath.

Towering bookshelves loomed in every direction, packed tight with scrolls, manuscripts, and ancient tomes. They rose twenty feet high, maybe more. Time thickened in the air—sacred, weighty, alive.

This was it. This was the Pashupati Granthalay.

✦

Raavan stood frozen and breath held. Before him stretched the greatest collection of knowledge he had ever seen—shelf after towering shelf of books, scrolls, and manuscripts, some rising over twenty feet high. He stepped forward cautiously, his boots echoing softly across the marble floor, and approached the circular table at the centre of the chamber. The air smelled faintly of sandalwood—soothing.

He reached towards a nearby shelf and ran his hand along the polished wood. Red sandalwood—fragrant and aged. Each shelf was marked with a date range; the one before him read: 1000–1500 AD. It was just the beginning. Beyond it stretched centuries—perhaps millennia—of collected wisdom. The weight of it all made him dizzy.

"It would take me a lifetime to read this," he whispered, eyes wide with awe.

He turned towards the crystal table, intending to set down his bag—but something caught his eye. The table was made from a transparent, crystalline material; its centre was etched with the Anveshi symbol, but he wasn't sure what it truly meant. But here, it felt like it belonged.

Drawn by instinct, Raavan wandered to the farthest edge of the chamber, to a shelf labelled Treta Yuga. The first book had no title—only a single number: 1. It looked modern, its binding clean and crisp. But when he opened it, the pages revealed high-resolution photographs of palm-leaf manuscripts—not the originals, but precise, curated replicas.

He began to read.

Time vanished. Minutes blurred. His eyes darted across the images at astonishing speed—a gift he had carried since childhood. Within seven minutes, he had absorbed nearly two hundred pages. When he finally paused, he flipped the book over and caught something faintly etched on the back cover, half-buried in dust.

Pashupati.

Raavan's breath caught. His fingers trembled as he brushed away the dust. It was the name of their founder. The name of his lineage. For the first time, he felt a great pride in his ancestry—not because of honour or myth, but because of truth. This was real.

Reverently, he returned the book to its shelf and picked up the next ten in the series, cradling them like sacred relics. As he walked back towards the crystal table, his mind reeled.

The first volume alone had shattered every preconception. In it, Pashupati detailed his arrival in Ayodhya—but more importantly, he spoke of his Guru. His inspiration. His master.

Dashanan.

Raavan froze at the name.

He remembered Shantinatha once quoting Hanuman's reluctant praise for Dashanan—for his strength, brilliance, and dauntless spirit. But Pashupati's description went further. He portrayed Dashanan not as a Rakshasa, not even as a king, but as a cosmic being. A master of Yantra Shastra, Rasayana, Vimana Shastra, Ayurveda, Yuddha Neeti, Dhanurveda, Samaveda, and more than ten other disciplines. To Pashupati, Dashanan wasn't just a teacher.

He was knowledge itself.

And then, towards the final pages, Raavan stumbled upon a list.

Ten names.

Pashupati named himself among Dashanan's ten disciples—and one of his four closest students, alongside Dharmapaala, Kanaka, and Veerabaahu.

Raavan nearly dropped the book.

Dharmapaala.

The name struck like lightning. He had heard it before. From Shantinatha. In the teachings of Drishti. In Jyotishya. In Rava. These weren't simply Vedic practices. They were Dashanan's creations.

His hands trembling, Raavan dropped the books on the table and sprinted back to the shelf. He retrieved the first volume and flipped rapidly to the passage listing the disciples. His finger hovered over the name again: Dharmapaala.

A cold shiver coursed through him.

Everything suddenly aligned—Shantinatha's cryptic lessons, the dreams, the vision in the blizzard, even Devadatta's final words. It had all been part of a larger transmission. Not a reincarnation—an inheritance. Raavan wasn't destined to become Dashanan. He was meant to awaken the fire that Dashanan had seeded.

He returned to the table and collapsed into one of the ten chairs, mind spinning, heart thunderous.

That's when he heard the sound.

A bell.

He looked up sharply. Near the stairwell stood a black rotary telephone—jarringly modern amid the mythic silence. It rang again.

Cautiously, Raavan walked over and picked up the receiver.

"I hope you reached safely and that you've settled in," said Lalit's voice, calm but urgent.

Raavan exhaled slowly. "Yes," he whispered.

"You can live in the house above the Granthalay," Lalit added. "But clean it first. And keep a low profile. No one must know you're there."

A pause.

"Okay," Raavan said softly.

The call ended.

Still dazed, Raavan walked out into the sunlight and made his way to the Ganga. He stepped into her sacred waters and submerged himself fully, hoping the cold would quiet the storm inside.

✦

Days passed in the Pashupati Granthalay, and Raavan rarely emerged from its depths. He read voraciously, moving from one manuscript to the next. Within a short span, he had completed nearly two full shelves. Each book was a universe unto itself, brimming with mysteries that defied logic and science. The subjects ranged from arcane branches of medicine to the mystical sciences that had once defined ancient Lanka.

He uncovered remedies for forgotten diseases, intricate methods to trace plague vectors across centuries, battlefield chronicles where shattered limbs were regrown, and formulas for tinctures that granted strength beyond mortal limits. Some could neutralise every known poison for hours. Others could awaken dormant senses, or accelerate healing so fast it flirted with resurrection.

But the texts weren't limited to science.

There were treatises on governance, strategies once used in the courts of Lanka, and battle records of campaigns fought not just against humans, but against gods. One manuscript chilled him to his core. It chronicled Dashanan's final days—and the events that followed. The desperation. The defiance. The resurrection attempt.

For the first time, Raavan began piecing it together: how Pashupati, along with Kanaka and Veerabaahu, had stolen their Guru's body and vanished into the caves north of the capital. There, surrounded by hope and shadow, they had placed Dashanan's corpse and preserved him close to the crevice where his Jeeva Tatva was entombed.

And they had failed.

Raavan turned the page, breath held. The manuscript continued—describing how, with Vibhishan's rise to power, the disciples' mission collapsed. They were hunted. Cornered. Forced to flee. And from their failure and exile, the Anveshi Saubhratra was born.

As Raavan continued, the manuscript shifted into narrative—a memory preserved in ink. It transported him to the day the three disciples fled Lanka. A grey morning. Pashupati,

Veerabaahu, and Kanaka walked the broken paths towards the northern coast, fear clinging to them like mist. They had not only lost their Guru. They had lost their homeland.

Pashupati led the way, silent and grim. The other two followed, hollowed by grief and exhaustion. Then, suddenly, he stopped. An idea sparked behind his eyes.

"We still have allies," he said. "Not in Lanka. Not in Bharatakhand. But in Shakadvipa. In Pushkaradvipa. Researchers. Not rulers, but people we can trust."

Veerabaahu frowned. "They're not kings. They can't protect us. Vibhishan's reach is long. He'll find us."

Pashupati's voice remained steady. "He won't expect us to vanish into places we once visited only for knowledge. These aren't political allies. These are brothers in science. Quiet men. Devoted men."

Kanaka nodded, hope flickering through his fatigue.

Veerabaahu still hesitated. "Even if I disappear," he said, "they'll track me through Bharatakhand. I have no one outside."

Pashupati placed a hand on his shoulder. "Then go where they'll never expect."

When they reached the northern coast, they split.

Kanaka departed first, boarding a ship to Shakadvipa—the frozen northern lands, where one of his fellow alchemists lived near the mountains and studied Odin's cosmologies. Kanaka's features would help him blend. He left without a word, with only one purpose in his stride.

A second, smaller boat had been prepared—one bound for Pushkaradvipa. Pashupati stood beside it, staring at the horizon. Veerabaahu helped load the supplies, his face now calmer, almost serene.

Then Pashupati spoke quietly. "I can't go to Pushkaradvipa. I have enemies there—ones who still remember me. If I arrive, I'll bring danger to our ally. But you—you'll be welcomed. He worships Ra. He lives on the banks of the Nile. He'll treat you like family."

Veerabaahu turned sharply. "And you? You'll die in Bharatakhand. Vibhishan's spies are everywhere."

"I'll take that risk," Pashupati said. "I have to. I need to carry this failure alone."

Veerabaahu's jaw clenched. "No. I won't let you die alone."

Pashupati's voice cracked. "Please. Let me do this."

There was silence. Then, slowly, Veerabaahu nodded.

That was how the disciples of Dashanan—once united by fire and vision—scattered across the world. Not to abandon their purpose, but to preserve it.

✦

Raavan closed the manuscript.

His chest felt heavy. His fingers trembled. In these pages, he had unearthed more than history. He had seen the broken souls behind the legend. Their failure. Their exile. Their bond.

They were not just students. They were warriors of knowledge.

And now, their burden—their vow—had passed to him.

Days blurred into nights, and Raavan's life in Kāsi became a sacred loop. He rose before sunrise, bathed in the Ganga's icy embrace, offered silent prayers at the ghats, and returned to the library at dawn. He barely ate, surviving on the prasad from the temples nearby. He never bought food, never cooked, and yet never felt hunger. The city fed him. The river cleansed him. And the books devoured him.

One morning, while wheeling a cart stacked with manuscripts towards the central table, something caught his eye—a book unlike the others. It had no numeric tag, no binding signature. The cover bore only two words: Experimental Log.

That was unusual.

Every book in the Granthalay followed a precise system. This one stood apart. He placed it on the cart with the others, intending to read it later. But by the second page of the book, he had started; his curiosity overruled him. He closed it, reached for the log, and opened the cover.

The first word he saw struck like lightning.

Ahindra.

His chest tightened. Breath faltered. Fists clenched. Tears sprang to his eyes even as his face flushed crimson with rage.

Beneath the name, a note was scrawled in ink: I love you, my son.

A scream tore from his throat—raw, guttural, unfiltered. The stillness of the library echoed with it. He stood, trembling, roaring until his fury collapsed into sobs. He fell back into the chair, heaving, broken.

Ahindra. The man who had torn his childhood apart. The man whose shadow haunted every nightmare. Raavan remembered little of those early days—but what he remembered was enough. Pain. Drowning. Chemicals that burned like fire. The helplessness of a boy turned into a vessel. The smell of steel and blood. The terror of being touched by science, not love.

And now, it was here—written out. The log chronicled everything. The first theories of Jeeva Tatva. The texts Ahindra consumed. The expedition to Rangala. The slow unravelling of reason. Every chemical. Every hypothesis. Every test. Until the final act, the gamma ray fired into his son's body.

Raavan read in silence, a storm building behind his eyes.

Then, a line stopped him cold.

When Ahindra first entered the sacred chamber in Rangala, he found something carved into the stone above Dashanan's resting place.

To repair something, it must be broken first.

Raavan froze.

He had read the ancient manuscripts—Pashupati's, Kanaka's, Veerabaahu's. None of them mentioned any such inscription.

He sprang from his chair and rushed to the relevant shelves, flipping through the accounts, scanning every passage that described the cave. He checked again. And again.

Nothing.

He returned to the log. The line was there. Clearly described.

His jaw tightened.

Ahindra wasn't just a monster.

He was a liar.

Raavan slumped back into his seat, mind churning. He tried to return to reading—another manuscript, another story—but the betrayal had left an ache he couldn't swallow. Eventually, his body gave in. Head drooping, limbs heavy, he drifted into sleep.

And then, Cold.

Not the kind from the river or the morning wind—this cold was deeper. An ancient, bone-cutting frost. He opened his eyes.

✦

He wasn't in the library anymore. He lay on the ground—except it wasn't ground. It was ice. A blizzard screamed across a desolate white desert. Mountains rose like fangs in the distance. He gasped and sat up, the wind slicing into his skin. He looked down.

In his hand—the Urumi. But two of the blades were broken.

His blood ran colder than the air. The Urumi was indestructible. He had tested it against stone, steel, and time. And now… it was fractured.

He looked at his body. Torn clothes. Blood-soaked fabric. He pulled back his robe and saw three deep cut marks raked across his chest. The pain flared instantly—searing and raw. Something had mauled him.

He knew then, this was no ordinary dream. But knowing didn't make it easier. The pain was still pain. The wind still carved into his flesh. The fear still twisted in his gut.

He began to walk. One step. Then another. Pushing forward through the blizzard with no direction, no goal—only the sense that if he stopped, something worse would happen. He walked for what felt like hours.

And then—he woke up. Gasping. Drenched in sweat. Heart pounding in the silent library. The candle beside him had burned low. The book lay open on the table. The cold was gone—but not the dread.

It was the first dream he'd had in months. And like all his dreams, he knew—it meant something.

He sat up straight, replaying it over and over. The ice. The broken Urumi. The blood.

It was a warning. A vision. Something was coming.

And this time, he had to understand it—before it was too late, like it had been with his mother.

The answers were somewhere.

In the silence.

In the dream.

In the cold.

In **Kāsi**.

CHAPTER 10

A week had passed. Raavan, who had devoured the books on the first two shelves within days, now managed to read only three in the entire week. His mind was no longer on the pages. It was trapped in a single dream—a dream that refused to let him go. Unlike the violent ones of his past, this one was quiet, recursive, and incomplete. It always ended the same way—with him walking towards a rock, and then waking up. But each night, the dream stretched further. First, he saw the rock from afar. Then, he stood beside it. And most recently, he had walked past it. He was going deeper—and that terrified him. A part of him felt elated; progress, after all. But another part knew that each step forward might mean someone, somewhere, was inching closer to death.

Raavan abandoned food, sunlight and routine. The library became his world. His body thinned, his thoughts grew frantic. He read distractedly, slept erratically and dreamt obsessively. One evening, as he sat to meditate in an attempt to distract himself from the dream, the phone rang. He sighed, opened his eyes and answered it. "Lalit," he said. It was. Lalit had made it a habit to call every few days, always asking the same things: Was Raavan well? Was he eating? Was he healthy? Raavan always lied. Said he was fine, that he ate daily at the temple. That his health was good. Lalit would respond in kind, and they'd hang up—ritual complete, affection unspoken.

But today, something was different.

"How are you doing?" Lalit asked, gently. Raavan hesitated, then offered a weak lie. "I'm doing well." It rang hollow.

"You don't have to hide anything from me, Raavan. We're family," Lalit said. Silence followed. Raavan considered telling him about the dream—would it even make sense? He stayed quiet too long. Lalit softened. "Take your time. Talk to me when you're ready. I'm here."

Before the call could end, Raavan found himself speaking. Slowly, haltingly, he described the dream—how it differed from the others, how it returned night after night, how it lengthened each time. He admitted he was scared. On the other end, Lalit said nothing at first. The silence was thick—uncertain, perhaps disbelieving.

"I know it sounds crazy," Raavan added. "If I wasn't having them myself, I wouldn't believe me either."

More silence. Then Lalit spoke, his voice low and steady.

"I believe in you, Raavan. I always have. I don't need to understand it to know that it matters. If it's part of your path, your destiny will lead you to it. Just… don't wear yourself down."

Raavan closed his eyes, letting those words sink in. It wasn't new wisdom—but coming from someone who loved him, it landed with grace. The weight on his chest lightened, if only a little. He whispered a quiet thank you, ended the call, and turned towards the third shelf.

It was time to begin again. Not to escape the dream—but to understand it.

It had been nearly a month since Raavan arrived in Kāsi. In that time, he had read through almost twenty shelves of books, each one peeling back a new layer of the world. Though he hadn't yet tested everything he had absorbed, he felt ready—confident that when the time came, he would be able to apply the knowledge. He attributed some of his learning to focus and memory, but most of it, he credited to the brilliance of his ancestors. They wrote with such clarity and intention that even the most complex ideas felt intuitive. Their words didn't just inform—they transformed.

The collection was astonishing in its breadth. Some books offered cures for rare ailments; others unravelled the language of animals. A few explained how to detect tremors before an earthquake, while others delved into the chemistry of flowers and herbs. The more he read, the more the world around him changed. After studying a manuscript on native flora around Varanasi, Raavan began planting saplings around the house. Within weeks, butterflies and birds returned—bringing colour, music, and movement. He began to understand animals at a glance: their moods, their needs, even their grief. One cow, in particular, would sit by the gate each day, staring at the front door. Eventually, Raavan understood. She was waiting for someone—her owner, who had not returned.

Just as Lalit had hoped, the dream that once consumed him had begun to loosen its grip. Immersed in study and service, Raavan found himself healing. The rhythm of life returned—mornings spent in the library, evenings by the Ganga's ghats. But peace, for Raavan, was never a final destination.

That night, the dream returned.

He knew the sensation the moment it began—the weightless clarity of waking inside a dream. He braced himself. The cold. The snow. The silence. He began walking again, boots crunching through the frozen crust of a landscape he had memorised. But this time, the dream changed.

Before him lay a vast, frozen lake—the surface smooth, clear, and eerily still, beneath the ice, thousands of fish were suspended mid-motion, like pale ghosts drifting through crystal. It was beautiful. And suffocating. Then a ripple. A single tremor beneath the surface. Something was swimming below, fast and fluid, slicing through the stillness towards the centre of the lake. Without thinking, Raavan ran. He sprinted across the ice, the wind tearing at his skin, the cold carving into his lungs. His feet pounded the glassy surface, chasing the blur beneath, until it vanished. He stood alone on an endless white sheet, surrounded by silence. The lake stretched out in every direction. The mountains were gone. Even the familiar rock had disappeared.

Then it came.

A sound.

Not a roar, not a scream, but something far more ancient. A howl of impossible volume and vibration, as though the sky had been ripped open, and the soul of the world was howling through the wound. It came from all directions—above, below, around. It shook the ice, rattled his bones, screamed in his skull. He dropped to his knees, clutching his head, trying to retreat into himself, but there was no shelter, no escape, no pause. Only the sound.

✦

And then he woke up.

His body was drenched in sweat. His breath came in ragged bursts. His chest heaved. He was back in the house in Varanasi. Safe. Alive. And utterly shaken.

It was almost dawn. Raavan rose from his makeshift bed and stepped outside. Varanasi was already stirring. Boats drifted across the Ganga, ferrying pilgrims and traders across the sacred waters. The streets pulsed with the sound of bells, hymns, and the soft murmur of morning prayers. The city was waking to worship Lord Vishwanath—and like so many others, Raavan prepared to bathe in the holy river.

But his mind was elsewhere.

The dream clung to him like frost—the frozen lake, the beast beneath the ice, and that scream that had rattled him to his bones. The images looped through his thoughts as he walked barefoot to the river, stepped into its cold embrace, and began his morning ritual.

Waist-deep in the Ganga, he closed his eyes and started reciting a mantra, but the words dissolved on his tongue. His lips stopped moving. Disoriented, he opened his eyes and stared into the rising sun. This had never happened before. Not once in his life had he forgotten a prayer.

He submerged himself, hoping the water might restore him. But when he emerged and tried again, the words slipped even faster like mist fleeing sunlight. One more dip, this time in silence. No mantra. No clarity. Only the dream. Only the scream. Only the fear.

Frustrated, he rose and slapped the water's surface, sending droplets flying. Then, with clenched fists and flared nostrils, he screamed—a raw, feral burst of sound that tore through the morning calm. It echoed off the river like a memory returned. His chest heaved. His breath came in gasps. The water surged around him, as if stirred by something stronger than wind.

When he looked up, people were fleeing. Priests, pilgrims, and bathers backed away, their faces etched with fear and judgement. Their silence pierced more than their words ever could.

Shame washed over him.

He dipped into the water once more—not for ritual, but refuge—and began walking towards the shore, dripping and breathless.

That was when he saw him.

An Aghori was approaching—the same one who had once smeared ash upon him. Raavan froze. Every instinct screamed to leave. But the Aghori's gaze held him in place. He walked slowly, eyes never blinking, steps sure. When he reached Raavan, he didn't speak. He simply extended a burning chillum, the embers glowing red, smoke curling upward like a question.

Raavan hesitated.

"I cannot accept this," he said softly.

The Aghori didn't withdraw. He tilted his head, eyes narrowing, and nudged the chillum closer. Raavan stepped back—but the old man seized his wrist with a grip like stone. Raavan pulled, but the grip didn't break.

Smoke drifted between them. Raavan breathed it in. His head swam. The scent—he knew it. It was the scent of confinement. The same one that filled the tank Ahindra had built. The same one that haunted his earliest visions. It crawled through his mind like a thousand spiders.

He staggered. Visions surged: frozen fish, shattered mountains, the dying breath of a mother he had never seen. And the scream. Always the scream.

Then sound. Real sound.

Temple drums. Conch shells. A rising tide of devotion. The morning aarti had begun at the Vishwanath temple.

The Aghori turned, as if summoned by the very pulse of the divine. Without a word, he released Raavan's wrist and vanished into the crowd—a ripple folding into the Ganga's current.

Raavan stumbled to a nearby mandap, collapsed onto its cool stone steps and surrendered to unconsciousness.

✦

It was nearly dusk, and the ghats of Varanasi buzzed with life as people gathered for the Ganga Aarti. The sound of conch shells rang out across the water, echoing through the alleys and temple domes, jolting Raavan awake. He sat up on the stone steps of the mandap, drenched in sweat, breath shallow and confused. Blinking away the haze, he slowly pieced together what had happened. The Aghori. The chillum. The scent—thick and strange—still clung to the edges of his memory.

Still shaken, he rose to his feet and made his way back to the house. The streets of Kāsi blurred past him—a flurry of bells, chants, footsteps, and incense—but his mind reeled with one thought: that smoke. It hadn't smelled like anything known, yet something about it was painfully familiar. He tried to name it. Lotus and honey? That was the closest he could come.

When he entered the library, his limbs still felt heavy, but his mind yearned for grounding. He sat at the table and picked up the book he had left unfinished the night before. The familiar texture of the pages calmed him. The ancient words steadied his breath. Slowly, he fell back into the rhythm of reading—the wisdom of Ayurveda washing over his confusion like cool balm. He finished the book. Then another. He wandered between shelves, eager to find more.

That was when it returned.

The scent.

Subtle, sweet like honey dripping onto lotus petals. He froze. His pupils widened. He inhaled again. The same scent. It was here.

Books still clutched in his arms, he turned his head, sniffed his sleeves—nothing. It wasn't on him. It was in the air. He dropped the books and began to follow it, led only by instinct. He moved slowly, adjusting his path with each inhale, bumping into shelves, stepping over fallen scrolls. The trail pulsed and faded, like a rhythm that only his senses could detect.

And then, he stopped.

He stood in front of a shelf he hadn't explored before. The scent was strongest here. His eyes scanned the spines until one book stood out. It looked ancient, but untouched—not worn like the others. Almost as if it had been waiting.

He lifted it.

Brought it to his nose.

The scent bloomed—unmistakable now. Lotus. Honey. Memory.

He opened the book and began to read.

It wasn't a medical text. Not Ayurveda. Not Jeeva Shastra. Not even a treatise.

It was a story.

It began with the fall of Dashanan in battle against Lord Ram. The aftermath. The coronation of Vibhishan. The secret theft of Dashanan's body by Pashupati, Kanaka, and Veerabaahu.

But the voice wasn't Pashupati's.

The writer described guards scouring Lanka in desperation. He spoke of Mandodari collapsed in grief in the very chamber that once held her husband's body. He described Vibhishan as furious and shattered. The language was precise, vivid, filled with the weight of foresight.

Then came a line that stole the breath from Raavan's lungs:

"The three stole my Guru's body, and I know where they are. I saw them as they fled, in a cart near the mountains. I can also see what they intend to do next. I must stop them. If they proceed as they are, they will fail to bring him back. They need me. I must see further. But to do that, I must give up what I have, to gain what I need."

Raavan's heart pounded.

Dharmapaala.

The fourth disciple who helped revive Dashanan.

The seer who mastered Drishti.

✦

The one whose name was never spoken, yet whose presence had always been felt—like a shadow at the edge of the story.

This was his vision. His warning. His vow.

Raavan clutched the book tighter. His breath quickened. Somehow, the dream, the scream, the scent, the Aghori, and now this manuscript—they weren't separate events. They were all threads of the same loom.

And now, for the first time, the shape of the truth began to emerge.

Raavan kept reading.

Though Dharmapaala had opposed the theft of Dashanan's body, his longing for his Guru's return was no less fierce than that of Pashupati, Kanaka, or Veerabaahu. From his distant ashram, he had watched over the trio using Drishti—guarding them from afar, ensuring Vibhishan's men never caught them. He peered into the threads of time, desperate to find signs of Dashanan's revival.

He looked one year ahead—Dashanan remained dead. Two years—still lifeless. Ten years—no change. A hundred—Pashupati and Kanaka were gone, and still, Dashanan had not returned. One year more—Veerabaahu vanished from the timelines as well.

That was as far as Drishti could reach.

Dharmapaala wailed.

His vision had reached its limit—bound by the fundamental rule of Drishti: it could only trace the lifelines of the living. Dashanan, being dead, lay beyond its reach. Dharmapaala had watched his brothers pour their entire lives into a resurrection that would never come. They would all die—faithful, brilliant, devoted—yet ultimately unsuccessful.

The burden was his now.

If anyone could bring their Guru back, it had to be him. But how?

His hands trembled. His eyes closed. Tears streamed down his face as memories of his Guru and fellow disciples flooded his mind. Then, like a whisper from the void, an ancient phrase surfaced—a lesson once spoken, long buried:

Tyaagam Veera Lakshanam – Sacrifice is the sign of the brave.

He opened his eyes. They burned red—not from pain, but from clarity.

Without hesitation, he stepped out of his ashram and walked towards a large stone near the river—the very same rock Shantinatha would one day use for meditation. Dharmapaala had made his decision. He would perform a ritual to gain Ananta Drishti—an ancient extension of his skill.

To use it, the seer must sacrifice his physical sight. In exchange, his astral self would gain freedom to travel through time—into the future, the past, and the invisible folds between.

He would see the end of time.

But first, he had to give up his eyes.

He sat cross-legged on the rock. The mantra formed in his mind, clear and unwavering. He began to chant.

At first, everything was still.

Then, it responded.

The river swelled, rising into a frothing torrent that battered its own banks. Trees cracked and toppled, torn from the soil by water's fury. The wind shrieked, spinning into dust devils that encircled him. Animals fled in terror. A storm gathered above—not a storm of rain, but of shadow.

Still, he chanted.

Thunder cracked across the sky. Lightning flashed—and then struck the earth beside him. The bolt hurled him from the rock, his body flung through the air and hit the ground hard, skidding through dust and gravel. The mantra ceased.

Silence followed.

The winds stilled. The river receded. The storm dissolved.

Dharmapaala lay on his side, blood trickling down his face. He coughed, choked, and crawled towards the river. Dust clogged his throat. He splashed water on his eyes, tried to blink it away, but saw only darkness.

He tried again.

Still nothing.

It wasn't the dust. It wasn't the blood.

He had gone blind.

His sacrifice was complete.

For a moment, his heart faltered. A single tear slipped from his ruined eye. He wiped it away, clenched his jaw, and stood. He returned to the rock. Sat. Straightened his spine.

He had known the cost.

He was Dashanan's wisest student. And now, even without sight, he could see.

He closed his physical eyes. Entered stillness. Slipped into the breath between worlds.

And then, with a whisper on his lips and the threads of time trembling at his touch—

He activated Ananta Drishti.

✦

Dharmapaala detached from his mortal shell. His astral form surged forward in time—a century, then a millennium. He crossed the thresholds of yugas, passing through Dvapara into the final, fading days of Kali Yuga. Yet Dashanan remained absent. Still dead. Unrisen.

Within hours, he had witnessed the unfolding of ages—from the moment of Dashanan's death to the silent end of time itself. And in all that span, his Guru did not return.

Dharmapaala returned to his body, shattered. He stood in stillness for a long while, then began walking back to his ashram. Each step felt heavier than the last. What use were divine gifts if they could not fulfil the one vow that had defined his life?

Through Ananta Drishti, he had seen his brothers' futures. Pashupati and Kanaka wandered through foreign lands, chasing remnants of forbidden knowledge. After their deaths, Veerabaahu carried the torch alone. But ultimately, all three would perish—their lives consumed by the resurrection they could never achieve. Dashanan's body and his Jeeva Tatva would remain sealed in the mountain cave until the very end of Kali Yuga, when a tectonic collapse would crush both vessel and crystal into dust.

Inside the ashram, Dharmapaala collapsed beside the ancient Shiva Lingam—the one he and Dashanan had once worshipped together. His tears merged with the sacred water at the deity's base. He mourned not just his Guru, but the futility of all they had sacrificed.

He had seen too much. Too clearly. The three disciples would endure suffering, hunger, and exile—yet remain unwavering in their loyalty. They would die broken, but faithful.

As he sat in grief, a small black ant caught his eye. It marched towards the offering at the base of the Lingam. Almost absently, Dharmapaala placed a mango leaf in its path, as the offering was made for Mahadev. The ant paused, then changed direction. He placed another leaf. Again, the ant adjusted. Leaf after leaf, obstacle after obstacle—and still, the ant persisted. Finally, Dharmapaala poured a thin circle of water around the offering.

The ant approached the water, paused—then turned back.

He smiled and drifted into thoughts of his failure to bring his Guru back.

But then, the ant returned.

This time, the ant climbed the wall, crossed the ceiling, and dropped onto the food from above.

Dharmapaala's breath caught.

In that tiny, defiant creature, he saw something divine: determination. The same fire his Guru had once instilled in them. And in that moment, two revelations struck like lightning.

First, he must not give up. Like the ant, he must find another path. No matter the obstacle, there was always another way.

Second, time does not flow. Everything flows *in* time. It is not linear. It is a current that can be redirected. Just as the ant had created new paths when the old ones were blocked, perhaps the future could be rewritten—if the present was shifted just enough.

He didn't yet grasp the full implications. But he had something now that he had lacked for centuries.

Hope.

He returned to the rock outside the ashram—the same one where he had sacrificed his sight. He sat for hours, deep in stillness. He searched the futures of Pashupati and the others, tracing their footsteps, their limitations, their blind spots. He noted what they would lack—and what their descendants might one day rediscover. He studied the lines of fate until they frayed at the edge of comprehension.

Then, he crafted a plan.

It was far from perfect. It would take generations. But if everything unfolded precisely, Dashanan would return—not in the distant end of time, but early in Kali Yuga. His wisdom could be reborn. The flame could be rekindled.

The first step was urgent: reach Pashupati.

Vibhishan's guards were closing in. Through Drishti, Dharmapaala saw that the trio would soon leave Lanka. If he missed this window, it might never return.

He walked to the riverbank and shouted, "Suparna!"

His voice echoed through the valley. Moments later, a shrill cry split the sky. A majestic eagle descended in spirals and landed upon his arm. Suparna—his old companion. The bird rubbed its head against Dharmapaala's chest, purring with recognition.

Back inside, he wrote two messages on thin strips of cloth. He tied one to Suparna's leg and the other beneath its wing.

Then he stepped outside, whispered "Pashupati," and let the eagle fly.

Suparna soared northward, slicing through clouds—the first ripple in Dharmapaala's new current of time.

But he was not the only one watching.

From across the river, hidden behind an outcrop of black stone, another figure watched the eagle's ascent with quiet intensity.

Another student of Dashanan.

✦

Dharmapaala turned away, unaware, and returned to the ashram stables. He saddled his horse, tightened the reins, and mounted. He knew where Pashupati would go—the northern shore. That was where he must follow.

But one final challenge awaited him.

Though they were both disciples of Dashanan, Pashupati had always doubted him. He respected Dharmapaala's knowledge, but considered Drishti a delusion. That scepticism had festered into quiet animosity.

And now, Dharmapaala would need his trust.

He urged the horse forward, wind against his blind face, as the mountain trail opened before him.

The path was uncertain.

But he had chosen it.

There would be no turning back.

After a long and gruelling ride, Dharmapaala finally reached the northern port. He stayed hidden on a hill overlooking the shoreline, waiting for Veerabaahu and Kanaka's ships to vanish into the horizon. Only after the sails had disappeared did he descend towards the coast, where Pashupati was preparing to depart.

Though the waves crashed and dockworkers shouted, Pashupati heard the hoofbeats. A knot of dread twisted in his chest. He turned quickly, expecting to see Vibhishan's soldiers.

Instead, it was Dharmapaala.

Dread twisted into fury.

Pashupati clenched his fists but said nothing. He turned his back and continued packing the last of his supplies.

As Dharmapaala approached, Pashupati snarled, "I don't know why you're here—and I don't care. Just let me leave Lanka in peace. Vibhishan's men are hunting me, and if they catch me, they'll kill me. But don't mistake me for a coward. I would gladly die, but only to bring back our Guru. But if I die… I know you won't be the one to revive him."

Dharmapaala smiled. Not out of pride—but something gentler. Hope. That only enraged Pashupati more.

He spun around, storming up to Dharmapaala. His eyes blazed. "I thought you respected our Guru. I thought you would stand by us. But I was wrong. Maybe you're a coward. Or maybe... maybe you always wanted the Guru's place for yourself. Maybe you wanted him dead all along."

That shattered something in Dharmapaala.

With a cry of fury, he shoved Pashupati. The healer stumbled backwards, tripping over a coiled rope, landing hard on his back. Before he could recover, Dharmapaala was on him—fists flying, voice trembling with rage and grief.

"How could you say that?! He took me in when I was a child. He raised me. He taught me. He loved me! Everything I am—everything—is because of him! And you—you always thought you were above the rest of us. That the Guru favoured you. Let me tell you something—he did. But not because you were better. He felt guilty. Guilty for what he did to your family!"

Pashupati didn't fight back. He just stared in stunned silence as the blows landed.

"I didn't join you because I didn't care! I didn't join because we weren't ready! I was the one who sent the message. I told you to extract the Jeeva Tatva. I—" Dharmapaala's voice cracked. "I was the one… who gave up his sight."

Pashupati blinked.

And saw the truth.

Dharmapaala wasn't looking at him. He was staring into the sun—unblinking, unmoved. His pupils were blown wide.

Blind.

He wasn't lying.

Pashupati caught his hand mid-strike. "Why... why would you do that to yourself?"

Dharmapaala didn't answer. He pulled away, stood, and walked towards the sea.

Blood trickled from his knuckles—some his, some Pashupati's.

He looked like a shadow against the fire-red sky. Slender, white-robed, shikha tied, a philosopher among warriors. Unlike the others, who bore Rakshasa blood, Dharmapaala was fully human. Pashupati, though nearly six feet tall, had diluted Rakshasa ancestry. Veerabaahu too. Kanaka, a half-Rakshasa, towered over them all at ten feet—brute strength incarnate, intellect rare among his kind. Most Rakshasas were primal: powerful, but estranged from knowledge, cursed with clouded minds. Dharmapaala stood beneath them in height, but never in clarity.

As he passed, Pashupati placed a hand on his shoulder. "Why?" he asked again, voice softer.

Dharmapaala gently removed the hand and kept walking.

A second later, the sky went dark.

Arrows. Dozens—then hundreds—rained from the hills.

Dharmapaala had seen this coming. He moved his hands with grace and agility in a circular motion. In a split second, rocks, branches, twigs and roots from the ground shot up and made a wall in front of the brothers, shielding them from the arrows. The arrows struck the wall with deafening thuds. Another volley followed. The wall kept the two brothers safe. But the arrows kept coming. Before the arrows broke their defence, Dharmapaala snapped his fingers. The wall groaned, cracked—and then, the wall burst outward, lashing back towards the archers. The stones, roots and branches shot with deadly speed.

Screams erupted from the cliffs. Bodies fell. The earth stilled. Silence.

Pashupati turned back. Dharmapaala stood amidst the ruin. Several arrows pierced his chest. He looked at Pashupati and smiled. Then, he collapsed.

Pashupati ran to him. Dropped to his knees. Cradled his head in his lap. Blood soaked through white robes. He tapped Dharmapaala's face. "Wake up. Please. Wake up."

✦

Dharmapaala stirred in sleep.

Through Drishti, he saw the hut he lay in—a modest shelter of woven branches and green leaves. Outside, the sun was setting, casting long golden fingers through the trees. A gentle wind rustled the foliage. Pain throbbed through his chest and abdomen as he shifted slightly.

Outside, Pashupati heard the faint grunt. He turned from the sword he had been sharpening, dropped it, and rushed into the hut. It was too small for his tall frame; he had to hunch awkwardly to enter. He knelt beside Dharmapaala, took his hand gently, and said, "Thank you... for saving me."

Dharmapaala smiled faintly and squeezed his hand. "I have the plan," he whispered. "A way to bring our Guru back..."

Pashupati's eyes widened.

He leaned in, breath catching. "Tell me. I'll brew any potion. I will make Amrit if I have to. Just tell me what—"

Dharmapaala smiled again and beckoned him closer. When Pashupati leaned in, Dharmapaala pressed his thumb to his forehead.

A golden glow pulsed from the touch.

Pashupati's eyes rolled back.

He collapsed.

The entire plan—the knowledge, the rituals, the timelines, the people—flowed from Dharmapaala's mind into his.

Pashupati awoke minutes later, gasping for air.

As he sat up in shock, the fragile hut collapsed around them—branches falling with a loud crash. Dharmapaala lay buried beside him.

Still dazed, Pashupati sat up amid the wreckage. His thoughts raced—overwhelmed by the vision he had just received, the weight of what it implied. Then, from under the debris, he heard a muffled voice:

"I'm getting crushed here."

Pashupati laughed—a rare, startled sound—and quickly cleared the branches. He lifted Dharmapaala gently and carried him outside to a grassy patch beneath a tree. He set him down carefully and lit a fire nearby.

"How did you know about the arrows?" he asked. "Why would you give up your sight?"

Dharmapaala looked towards the darkening sky. "Because I saw you fail."

Pashupati fell silent.

"I watched through Drishti as you and the others tried. You crossed oceans, sought forbidden knowledge. You gave your entire lives. Even after a hundred years… even after your deaths… Dashanan never returned. So, I did the only thing left to do. I sacrificed my eyes. To gain Ananta Drishti. And with that… I saw beyond your lifetimes."

He took a shallow breath, wincing from the pain.

"And when I began to act—to change things—I saw something shift. A flicker of possibility. A timeline where Dashanan could return. If we follow every step. Precisely. Down to the last breath."

He smiled. "I'd say that's a fair deal for my eyes."

Pashupati chuckled softly. "You haven't changed."

But then his voice darkened. "The attack. The arrows. Who were they?"

Dharmapaala's expression shifted.

"That… was Jalajakshamukhi."

Pashupati stiffened. The name was a blade in his chest.

Jalajakshamukhi—another student of Dashanan. Brilliant. Unpredictable. Dangerous.

"She followed me," Dharmapaala whispered. "She knows that we have Dashanan's body."

✦

Pashupati stared into the fire, his thoughts spiralling. "So... what now?"

Dharmapaala didn't respond immediately. His face became still, eyes closed. Slowly, visions began to flood back into his mind. The entire plan—all of it—replayed before him.

And he collapsed to his knees.

Tears streamed silently down his cheeks.

Pashupati knelt beside him. “What did you see?”

Dharmapaala didn’t answer.

He remained motionless, overwhelmed by the scope of it. Then, voice trembling, he whispered:

“So many sacrifices... across so many yugas. Just to bring him back. So much blood... so many lives...”

His voice cracked.

Pashupati moved closer, placing a steady hand on his shoulder.

Dharmapaala looked up slowly. His face was wet with tears.

“Most of them are your descendants,” he said. “Children who will never know why they suffer. One of them was a boy named Ahindra Pashupati, just ten years old. He’s the one. He’s our best chance. By then, the Rakshasa Tatva will be gone completely. His body will be pure. He’ll be the vessel to bring our Guru back.”

Pashupati’s breath caught.

Ahindra.

The name echoed inside him like a drum.

A child. His own descendant. Bearing his name.

But then, a deeper dread stabbed into him—cold and sharp.

For the plan to succeed, someone would have to protect Dashanan when he returned. The forces of Kali in the age of Kali Yuga would be brutally strong—and they would try to claim him as their own. Pull him into their shadow. Corrupt his purpose before it could take root.

Someone would need to guide Ahindra. Speak through time. Walk through fire. Lead the boy when he became more than human.

And to do that…

Dharmapaala would have to sacrifice everything.

Even his life.

Pashupati stood in silence, eyes locked with Dharmapaala's milky, unseeing gaze. "There has to be another way," he said softly. "You shouldn't die for my failures."

Dharmapaala rested a trembling hand on his shoulder. "This is the only way, my friend."

And for the first time in his life, Pashupati believed him without question. He had once mocked Dharmapaala's detachment, dismissed Drishti as illusions—but the last few days had shattered every doubt. If there were another way, Dharmapaala would have found it.

With heavy breath, Pashupati said, "At least let me make something—a potion, to ease the pain."

Dharmapaala hesitated. His skin paled. In all his calculations, he had forgotten one detail—the pain. His hands trembled faintly. "The mantras must be perfect. I can't risk slurring them. Not even if I'm numbed."

"Then I'll make something that doesn't cloud your mind—only dulls the agony," Pashupati said, already turning.

Dharmapaala nodded, softly relieved. "I'll need sandalroot, shoolantika, and black serpent's milk for the ritual."

"I'll bring them by sunrise," Pashupati promised.

With misted eyes, he vanished into the forest.

✦

Pashupati had returned, as promised, carrying herbs, roots, and a potion—one that dulled pain but kept the mind clear. Dharmapaala had prepared the fire altar—its base crafted from sacred sandalwood, its corners aligned to ancient sutras. A silver blade rested beside it.

Though blind, Dharmapaala's gaze was steady.

As Pashupati approached, he asked one last time, "Are you sure?"

Dharmapaala said nothing. He simply drank from the leaf-bowl and offered a wan smile. "Stand back. Blood tends to spill."

He took a long breath and began.

He chanted softly, crushing herbs, roots and powdered minerals into a thick black paste. With each strike of the pestle, sparks danced upward—green and sharp. The air thickened with energy. Pashupati felt it vibrating on his skin, whispering against his bones.

As the paste began to hiss and glow red, Dharmapaala lifted the mortar high.

And poured its searing contents across his face.

Pashupati gasped.

The liquid coated Dharmapaala's skin like molten iron. Flames burst from the earth where it dripped. Blisters rose. Skin blackened, curled. Smoke wreathed his face. But Dharmapaala did not falter. His chanting grew louder, stronger—a cry rising from the pit of pain.

He sat before the altar, took up the silver knife, and did what no man could ever do.

Pashupati turned away.

Behind him, Dharmapaala peeled the scorched skin from his face. The sound was sickening—wet, scraping, animal. Blood poured freely. His chants continued, ragged but intact.

Once the skin was scraped into the mortar, he raised the blade again.

And slit his own throat.

The blood flowed into the vessel. He held the mortar until his last breath, and before he collapsed, he placed the mortar in the centre of the altar.

Pashupati wept—not from sorrow alone, but from reverence. He knew the procedure. He remembered every step from the vision. Only one thing remained—the final sequence.

"Grind the mixture," a voice whispered in his ears. "Chant the last mantra. Three times."

The forest held its breath.

No wind stirred. No birds called. Time itself seemed to bow in reverence.

Pashupati quickly turned around, looked for the mortar, and picked it up. He closed his eyes and began to grind the mixture slowly. Once. Twice. Thrice.

Then silence.

Pashupati opened his eyes.

What he saw would haunt him for the rest of his life.

Dharmapaala's body was burning in the altar's sacred flame—his white robe already ashes. The mortar, now filled with the remnants of a man who had given everything.

Charred skin. Sacred blood. Essence.

Pashupati stepped forward, numb.

He sealed the mortar with a sacred leaf, tied with a prayer thread.

And without a word, turned and ran.

Towards the cave.

Towards Dashanan.

Towards the impossible future that Dharmapaala had seen.

Above him, the sky turned crimson. The wind howled with sacred purpose.

And Pashupati disappeared into the mountain—carrying the vessel that would reshape the world.

By early evening, Pashupati stood at the mouth of the mountain cave. The weight of the day of loss, of revelation, pressed heavily upon him. He knew what he had to do.

He left his horse behind and stepped into the stone maw of the mountain.

Every footfall echoed with memory. The walls bore faint carvings, and the floor showed grooves left by wheels and carts. The smell—a fusion of ash, herbs, and cold metal—lingered like the ghost of past labours. Here, he and his brothers had once tried to defy death. Here, they had carved hope into silence. His heart ached for them now—Veerabaahu, Kanaka, and Dharmapaala.

He reached the chamber where Dashanan's Jeeva Tatva had been hidden. The glowing crystal, still faintly luminous, rested deep within its stone cradle.

Pashupati opened his satchel and withdrew the mortar.

Inside, it was Dharmapaala's sacrifice—a red, pulsing paste made from blood, herbs, skin, and mantra. It shimmered faintly in the cave's dim light, an unnatural gleam born of pain and power. This was no ordinary substance. It could shift its form, disguise its host, and—when the time came—pass on the mind of its maker.

He gently placed the crystal carrying Dashanan's Jeeva Tatva into the mortar.

At once, the substance reacted. It slithered upward, encasing the crystal, then hardened—mimicking its shape and glow with uncanny precision. The disguise was perfect. The essence sealed.

He returned the vessel to its hiding place.

Then, walking deeper into the cavern, he approached the wagon that bore Dashanan's preserved body. He stood for a long moment, silent. Then, as Dharmapaala had shown him, he turned to the nearest stone wall.

And began to chisel.

When he finished, the wall bore no spell, no prayer, no threat.

Just a single line:

To repair something, it must be broken first.

✦

Back in the present, Raavan stood frozen.

The manuscript trembled in his hands. The words swam on the page, blurred by the force of something he couldn't name—not fear, not awe, but something between.

A shiver ran down his spine. His breath came slowly, shallow. He closed the book, fingers trembling.

Everything made sense now.

He had not suffered alone. He was not a mistake. He was a culmination—the living answer to the question Dharmapaala had once screamed into the void. His agony had never been meaningless.

Others had suffered too.

The only difference was: they chose it.

He hadn't.

Until now.

A memory flickered. Something his father had once scribbled in an old notebook—a line about carvings on the cave wall. He had dismissed it back then as a delusion. Nonsense. But now, he knew.

His father had told the truth.

Though cold. Though broken. Though cruel…

He had not lied.

For the first time in years, Raavan smiled at the thought of his father.

But the smile did not last.

A deeper question stirred.

Dharmapaala had chosen Ahindra Pashupati as the vessel. But Raavan now saw the truth—the fate had changed. The flow of time had shifted. Somewhere, somehow, fate had bent.

He was no longer following prophecy.

He was rewriting it.

And that raised a burning question.

"If I am Dashanan," he whispered, "what must I do to gain everything he once knew?"

He didn't have the answer.

But he knew someone who might.

He walked to the phone.

Dialled a number he knew by heart.

Lalit answered.

Raavan told him the plan.

Then, without another word, he lay down to sleep.

Eyes open.

Heart pounding.

Mind awakened.

Raavan opened his eyes; someone stood before him, lighting a candle.

Lalit.

"Are you ready to return to the ashram in Sri Lanka?" he asked, smiling.

✦

Two days passed—by car, by train, by boat, and on foot.

At last, Raavan and Lalit stood at the gates of the ashram.

Memories surged like floodwaters. The courtyard where he and Devadatta once played. The banyan that whispered childhood secrets. The gate—where Shantinatha had expelled him. His eyes welled with tears.

"My leg is killing me," Lalit muttered. "Can we go in and sit?"

Raavan wiped his face and stepped inside.

The ashram was quiet. Sparse. Fewer students than he remembered. Many were packing, preparing to leave. Something had changed.

He approached a young student. "Where is your Guru?"

The boy pointed to the sacred tree.

Raavan followed the path.

There, beneath the great tree, stood Divyateja, staring across the river into the forest.

"I was expecting you, Raavan," he said, without turning.

Raavan moved to bow, but Divyateja lifted him and embraced him.

"There's much to discuss," he said. "But first, go bathe in the river. One last time."

Raavan obeyed and walked to the river. As he stepped into the cool current, a familiar scent surrounded him—calming. It soothed his limbs, quietened his thoughts.

The same aroma had once filled the sacred hill where Shantinatha trained him.

He looked towards that hill. Its peak loomed in shadow.

Then he returned to Divyateja.

In the Guru's chamber, Divyateja was speaking with Lalit. When Raavan entered, he smiled. "Lalit tells me you've started reading everything Pashupati ever wrote. Looks like you've found your path."

Raavan nodded.

Divyateja's gaze sharpened. "By now, I'm sure you understand why the Anveshi was formed. And who orchestrated it all?"

Raavan nodded again.

Without waiting for questions, Divyateja answered, "According to Dharmapaala's plan, Ahindra was the chosen vessel. At ten, he was injected with Dashanan's Jeeva Tatva. But it failed. His body rejected the energy. He bled from his eyes, ears, and pores, and Jeeva Tatva came out of his body. He was unconscious for days. Everyone thought he would die."

Divyateja continued. "When he awoke, he remembered nothing. But something had changed. The Tatva had sharpened his mind—gave him clarity, brilliance. That was the key."

He looked Raavan in the eyes. "Not all the Anveshi seek knowledge. Some seek power. Dominion. But what you've received… is not a gift. It's a burden. A sacred one."

His voice dropped. "And don't worry about retrieving Dashanan's wisdom. It will come—when the time is right."

Students entered then, breaking the moment. They came to receive blessings—the last disciples of the ashram. Divyateja gave each a gold coin and sent them off.

Raavan looked around, puzzled. The ashram was emptying.

Divyateja answered the unspoken question. "This ashram was founded by Dharmapaala and his disciples—to protect the forest and the sacred hill. But our work is done. We harvested the plants. Burned them. Mixed their ashes into the river."

Raavan's face fell. "You destroyed the forest Shantinatha protected?"

Divyateja's eyes did not flinch. "We did not destroy the plants. Shantinatha preserved them so we could burn them now. A war is coming, and these ashes might give us a chance to win it."

Raavan's fists clenched. "I would've fought your war. You shouldn't have burned the forest."

Divyateja smiled. "This isn't your war, Raavan. Your war is coming. And it's closer than you think."

He stepped closer, his voice low. "I know about your dream. But you don't have the strength to complete it. You need peace and absolute clarity of mind to see it through."

More students arrived, ready for pilgrimage.

Divyateja embraced Raavan one last time. "I must leave now. You two can stay here tonight. Return to Varanasi in the morning. We will meet again soon. And when we do, tell me everything you saw in your dream. Until then—may Mahadev protect you."

Raavan and Lalit walked to the edge of the forest and watched him disappear among the trees.

They returned inside.

The silence of the ashram stretched through every hall.

Raavan ate fruit from the garden.

Then he lay down in the same room where he had once slept beside Devadatta—once a boy, once a student, once a soul in search of answers.

Now, he was no longer searching.

He was becoming.

✦

Raavan had returned to Varanasi. Lalit had gone back to Ayodhya.

Days passed in a rhythm that felt familiar but hollow. Raavan buried himself in the library—reading, brewing, experimenting with herbs and minerals to create potions and tinctures that he learned from the ancestral texts. On the surface, everything seemed calm.

But the dream persisted.

Ever since leaving the ashram nearly three weeks ago, the same vision returned each night. Always incomplete. Always ending too soon. It wasn't the dream itself that broke him—it was the waking. Each time he opened his eyes, he felt drained, agitated, haunted by the absence of closure.

He tried everything. Potions to deepen sleep. Oils. Mantras. Ritual chants.

Nothing worked.

Then he remembered Divyateja's parting words: Peace and clarity of mind.

In desperation, Raavan made a vow.

He would not sleep until he found the answer.

He crafted potions to keep himself awake—sharp, bitter tinctures that heightened the senses and stilled the need for rest. For the first few days, it worked. He read endlessly, chasing symbols and following every trail the texts could offer.

But the body has limits.

His hands began to tremble. His thoughts grew jagged. He grew irritable, but never violent. He kept his suffering private.

What truly unnerved him… was the Aghori.

Every morning, the man stood beside the Ganga. Every evening, he followed Raavan back to the library. Always silent. Always offering the chillum. And every day, the smoke smelled different—honey, camphor, fruits, burning hair.

Raavan ignored him.

Until he couldn't.

The potions lost their power. The words in books turned into inkblots. Even his thoughts began to fragment.

One evening, his body gave in. He collapsed onto his bed, not in surrender, but in desperation.

The dream returned.

Frozen wasteland. Howl. Mountains. Lake.

He woke again too soon.

In rage, he slammed his fists into the wall and stormed out of the library. The sky outside was streaked with bruised violet and orange. He didn't know where he was going—only that he had to move.

That's when he heard footsteps.

The Aghori.

They walked together, without speaking, through alleyways, across courtyards, along the moonlit banks of the Ganga. They reached a ledge on the opposite shore where the Ganga Aarti was underway. Lamps danced across the water. The chanting rose like thunder wrapped in devotion.

Raavan sat on a stone, staring into the flames. His eyelids fluttered. His body begged for sleep, but he fought it.

The Aghori approached.

This time, he did not offer the chillum; he inhaled deeply from the chillum, then exhaled—a thick cloud of smoke—directly into Raavan's face.

The world dissolved.

Raavan coughed violently. The smoke forced itself into his nostrils, his lungs. It was dense. Oily. Alive. His vision doubled, then spiralled. He tried to stand, but his legs failed him.

The smoke clung to him. Every breath pulled him deeper into dizziness. Into the dark.

He stumbled towards the river, desperate to wash his face.

He slipped.

And fell into the shallows.

All went still.

He did not resist. Did not flail. The river enveloped him like a womb—warm, eternal, mother-like.

His back settled on the riverbed. His head rested on a smooth stone.

And for the first time in weeks...

Raavan slept. He was finally at peace.

✦

Raavan opened his eyes.

He lay in a frozen wasteland, the wind howling like a curse. All around him stretched a world of endless white. A blizzard roared across the plains. He stood, trembling, and began to walk—drawn, as always, towards the frozen lake.

Beneath the surface, something moved.

He chased it, running against the wind that clawed at his skin. But the shadow vanished.

Then he stopped.

The terrain had changed.

The mountains he had once seen were now distant—tiny specks on the horizon. Everything shimmered unnaturally.

The dream was brighter than ever. That's when he saw the lake again. It was as vast as the ocean itself.

The realisation chilled him deeper than the ice ever could.

He turned back, searching for the shoreline. As he moved, he noticed something beneath the ice—just a few feet below. He knelt, began kicking, punching, clawing. After several brutal blows, the sheet cracked.

He scraped the shards aside.

And froze.

A torso lay beneath the ice.

Short. Bloody. Familiar.

His own.

Same clothes. Same frame. Lifeless.

He stumbled back, panic surging. Crawled away, breath ragged. Never had a dream cut so deep.

He turned, fled across the ice.

But more bodies of him appeared—scattered beneath the surface. Dozens. Hundreds. Heads. Arms. Legs. All his.

A graveyard of Raavans.

He ran, each step more frantic than the last.

And then the sound.

It started low. A vibration. A tremor in the bones.

The sound grew.

From the mountains came a howl—ancient and monstrous.

He looked up.

Two glowing red eyes burned in the distant peaks.

Then he saw it.

What he thought was a mountain… moved.

It wasn't a mountain.

It was a wolf.

Colossal. Red-eyed. Thundering across the ice like a god of death.

Raavan screamed, summoned lightning. A bolt struck the beast's head—but it didn't slow.

The wolf grew angrier. Faster.

Its breath was like fireless smoke. Its feet shattered the ice.

Raavan ran, but the beast was gaining.

Then the ground cracked beneath him.

From the depths… something stirred.

Something worse.

A shadow, vast and black, slithered under the ice.

Then the eruption.

The surface exploded, hurling Raavan into the air, spinning amidst shards of ice and freezing mist.

He looked back.

The wolf leapt, jaws wide.

He looked down.

A serpent. Ancient. Titanic. Its head alone dwarfed the wolf. It rose from the lake, mouth open.

Time slowed.

Both monsters lunged.

The snake struck first.

Its jaws closed around Raavan's legs. He screamed. Lightning tore through the sky. The serpent did not flinch.

It shook its head.

And his body was torn apart.

His torso crashed onto the ice—bleeding, broken, still conscious.

The wolf landed beside him. It sniffed the body. Then it walked away.

The snake swallowed his legs.

And slithered back into the lake.

Raavan's torso lay on the ice.

His eyes are still seeing.

His heart still beating.

The pain was real.

The agony was unbearable.

But he smiled.

He had finally completed his **Swapna**.

CHAPTER 01

He remembered the scream before the tear—the flash of lightning, the wolf's breath, the serpent's jaws. The ice had shattered. His legs were swallowed. His torso bled on a white void of death. And yet he smiled. That smile had carried him through the agony, through the graveyard of his own bodies. His dream was over, but the truth it revealed would haunt every step he took.

Raavan woke choking, lungs rebelling as he spewed a ribbon of cold river water. Trembling and soaked to the bone, he lay on the muddy banks of the Ganga. Harsh light needled his eyes; dream-ashes still smeared his vision—if it had been a dream at all. Shadows crowded in, murmurs fluttering like restless wind. One face stilled him: Divyateja. Calm and observant, he stepped forward, parted the onlookers, and knelt with unexpected gentleness. He helped Raavan upright onto a rock, dismissed the crowd with a small gesture, and waited while Raavan found his breath.

Raavan's thoughts were a tangle. He scanned the bank, searching for the Aghori—but the man was gone, as if he had never existed. Before Raavan could speak, Divyateja's mouth tilted with a smirk. "Feels like you finished the dream," he said. Raavan stared, still reeling. "I was just sitting on the rock," he answered slowly. "An Aghori blew strange smoke into my face. I blacked out… fell into the river." Divyateja chuckled and leaned in, folding Raavan into a brief, grounding embrace that carried warmth beyond the physical. "Well," he murmured, "looks like something divine is helping you."

The story continues in

Dashanan: Vidhi

A wormhole at Silathoranam, Tirumala, India

www.ingramcontent.com/pod-product-compliance
Lightning Source LLC
LaVergne TN
LVHW090304210926
848480LV00001B/122